Healing Skye

A Coastal Hearts Novel

Janet W. Ferguson

Publisher's Note: This book is a work of fiction. Names, characters, any resemblance to persons, living or dead, or events is purely coincidental. The characters and incidents are the product of the author's imagination and used fictitiously. Locales and public names are sometimes used for atmospheric purposes.

Dauphin Island, Alabama, and locations mentioned in Alabama are real places, but other than the name, the events in the location are fictional. None of the events are based on actual people. The charming locations made the perfect backdrops for my novel.

Southern Sun Press, LLC

ISBN-13: 978-1-957138-00-8

Acknowledgments

This novel took so much research! I never studied much science in business college, so all mistakes on the marine biology portion, are my own, and I apologize. My thanks go out to so many who helped me along the way.

Thank you to:

The Lord, who is the healer of our hearts and souls. Any good I do, to God be the glory!

My husband, Bruce, for supporting me while I write for hours or drag him along on research trips. He also puts up with my traveling in the name of research.

Elizabeth Thompson, who gave me the idea for a story involving the Dauphin Island Sea Lab and manatee research after she spent her summer there as an intern.

Neddie Joye Tolleson, who drove me down to Dauphin Island for research and took me to pretty much every store, art gallery, park, and restaurant. And of course, the beach! Her mother, Jean Cockrell, cooked us a wonderful dinner in her home, bought us lunch at the Lighthouse Bakery, took us to the Art Gala, and more. Such a wonderful trip!

Elizabeth Heib, who leads the Manatee Sighting Network at the Dauphin Island Sea Lab. She answered countless questions about what they do, about the lab, about marine science, and so much more. I hope I didn't mess this up too much!

Crystal Hightower, Senior Researcher from the Fisheries Ecology Lab, who answered questions about the Alabama Deep Sea Fishing Rodeo, the scientific research conducted during the event, and more.

Other researchers and educators at Dauphin Island Sea Lab and Estuarium also answered questions, led interesting excursions, and made educational videos that I watched online.

My college roommate Angie Renner, who hosted me in Florida and accompanied me on my quest to see a manatee, even donning scuba gear to swim near them on a tour at Florida's Crystal River. We always have fun!

Captain King Marchand, Trey Graham, and Iris Thierry with Captain Mike's Fishing Charter, and also Captain Ronnie Daniels from the Mississippi coast, for answering my sometimes dumb questions about fishing. Special apologies to Trey for being a slow learner and tangling my fishing line more than once.

Clara McKinnon for hanging out with me on the island and exploring more.

Hailey Johnson for helping me with ideas early in my marine biology research.

Maria Tafra who shared about growing up on the island and running a business there.

For those who shared about the difficulties of growing up as a PK, also known as preacher's kids.

For those who shared private stories of your pain from abuse. I'm so sorry that you went through something so wrong. I pray for God's healing.

My amazing ACFW critique partners, beta readers, volunteer proofreaders (you know who you are!), and my street team.

Editor Robin Patchen, mentor author Misty Beller, photographer Melanie Thortis, models Carol and Isaac Parker, and cover artist Carpe Librum Book Design.

I am making a way in the wilderness and streams in the wasteland.

Dear Reader

Abuse is a subject I didn't want to delve into, but unfortunately it happens all too often, and I felt called to write about its aftermath in a young woman's life. If it's been part of your story, I pray you find healing. That kind of break in trust can shatter a person's heart. It's good to get counseling and help to overcome the sorrow and trauma that comes with such a betrayal. We have a God who cares about your pain. We have a God who loves purely—a Savior who heals.

Blessings in Him,

Janet W. Ferguson

Chapter 1

Almost to the Gulf. Almost to the part of the world she'd left behind nearly a decade ago. Skye Youngblood had loved these warm waters, the golden marsh grass bowing in the southerly breeze, the hungry herons peering out at the surf, the dolphins crowning in the golden light, the rhythm of the tides. Nature's dependable laws had a way of soothing rattled emotions inside a cracked human soul. During her chaotic childhood, the humid salt air loosened the relentless feelings of hopelessness that had squeezed around Skye, allowing her to breathe. Days wading in the Gulf's warm waters with her sister had chased out some of the darkness that haunted her.

Beneath the shining surface of the deep, the glory expanded and multiplied. The bays, marshes, and sea clamored with hidden life. Hidden death too. All shrouded below the frothy waters, where few took the time to observe.

She lived that hidden life, too, out of sight as much as possible, hoping her past wouldn't catch up to her.

Because some horrors should stay buried.

Even on this small island, almost an hour south of Mobile, Alabama, danger lurked too close. She couldn't let her guard down. Couldn't allow herself to forget the risks of coming here.

A heavy gust whipped through the van window, lashing strands of Skye's hair against her face, rousing her senses, driving home her purpose. She needed to be here for Miss Lydia. For Sparrow.

Though Miss Lydia had tried to downplay her medical condition, the pain and fatigue in her voice had uprooted Skye from her research in Florida and sent her scrambling to come up with a plan to temporarily move to Alabama. The grant she'd received to study manatee migration should allow her to be here long enough to make sure Miss Lydia and Sparrow were okay. Then she could go back home where she felt safe. Or as safe as she could feel, knowing there were men like Denny Beasley in the world.

Enough about that monster. She focused on mindful breathing and centered herself on the present.

The bridge across the Intercoastal Waterway to Dauphin Island, Alabama, stretched out like a gateway to paradise. The Mobile Bay and the Gulf of Mexico met here to form a home for a myriad of aquatic life forms. In this little pocket of the world, she'd concentrate on her work while keeping tabs on Miss Lydia and Sparrow over in Mobile.

She swung a quick glance in the rearview mirror to her faithful crew in the back seat. Poor things. "We're almost there, babies. I know you're ready to get out."

Returning her gaze to the road, Skye gasped. A truck crossed the middle line into her lane. Concrete barred both sides of the bridge, and water flowed below. Pulse thrashing, she slammed on her brakes and swerved right, as close as she could to the edge of the wall.

"Oh, no!"

The screech of tires and the crash of metal colliding roared in her ears.

Impact threw her forward and then jerked her back. An airbag exploded into her face, but she held tight to the steering wheel. She couldn't allow her helpless charges to careen over the bridge to a watery grave.

At last, her vehicle stilled, and a whistle of steam hissed. The acrid scent of airbag sulfur and engine smoke filled her nostrils.

Stunned, Skye looked down at her body, then the floor. No sea water. Had they made it?

Another pungent odor overpowered everything else. Gasoline.

She ripped off her seatbelt, yanked at the door handle. Stuck.

Open. Please, open.

Thick black smoke poured from the truck that seemed to be attached to her van's left fender.

Despite a bone-deep ache in her back and left shoulder, she scrambled over the middle console to the passenger seat and pushed at the door. It opened only an inch before it hit the concrete barrier.

Maybe the back door behind the driver's seat would open. "It's going to be okay, guys," she crooned as she climbed onto the console. "Just give me a second."

"Hey, mister, back here!" a male voice yelled.

A dark-haired man opened the rear cargo door and climbed inside the van between her suitcases. He held out his hand. "Hurry, one of the vehicles might blow any minute."

"I have to get—"

"Your stuff can be replaced. Come on." The urgency in his voice sent a spike to Skye's adrenaline.

She had to move faster, but her thoughts clouded. "I'll hand them to you, but do not let them go. Put them in your vehicle one at a time." She unlatched the first harness. Thank goodness she'd purchased the special seatbelts for this trip or they'd have been thrown around the van.

"What are you talking about?"

"Come on, it's okay." She lifted the ever-steady pug and then handed the small dog through the bucket seats to the stranger. "This is Sam."

Frowning, the man stared at the dog then took him into his arms. "What else?"

"Take him and come back."

She unlatched Frodo's harness. He quivered, ducked his head, and tucked his short tail. She'd have to be the one to carry the poor thing. Fear already had him immobilized.

The man sprinted back from wherever he'd gone and held out his arms. "This is dangerous. That smoke coming from the engine is no joke. I mean, animals aren't worth your life."

Wrong. "Here. Take Rocky. I got it after that." She held out the cat's crate, glad she'd kept him locked in.

"Come on, I'm risking my life, too, you know." Sharp blue eyes squinted at her, but he took the handle. "I have a daughter depending on me."

A daughter. Her mind raced. "I'm coming." Her ears rang almost as loudly as her heart thudded, and she battled that old impulse to freeze. Her babies needed her.

A blaze of flames caught the corner of her eye, and intense heat warmed her back.

Move, Skye!

Hefting the seventy-pound Pudelpointer, she maneuvered between the captain's chairs, over the laid-flat third-row seat, then around the plastic tubs that held her belongings.

She scrambled out, and the man draped an arm around her waist. She flinched at his touch.

"I'm trying to help you." His tone was gentle, despite his obvious exasperation. Or was that fear?

"I've got it." Glancing over her shoulder, the red blaze surrounding the other vehicle grew to an inferno and popped like an automatic weapon. It might spread to her van any second.

Frodo squealed and tucked his big head under her arm.

She looked up at the stranger beside her. "What about the other driver?"

"Someone helped him out." The man led her to a four-door black pickup parked about thirty yards behind her van. Traffic snarled to a standstill on the bridge. Other drivers stood outside their cars, gaping at the wreckage.

He pointed at her nose, almost touching, but then stopped himself. "You're bleeding. Where else are you hurt? Let me take that…enormous animal so we can look you over." Sirens wailed in the distance. "You need to go to the hospital. What's your name?"

So many questions. Did she need a hospital? Did her pets? The weight of the dog tugged at Skye's arms. Her whole spine felt as though it had been thrown in the dryer with a fifty-pound dumbbell. But she'd gotten through worse.

"I just need to sit. Maybe a ride to my rental house once the police do an accident report." More than likely, she could treat any wounds she or her pets may have. She'd managed in the past. If only her supplies made it out.

"Here, lay the dog in the back seat of the truck. Maybe you should get in and sit down too." He held open the door.

Frodo fought being let go, but at last she settled him beside steady Sam. Then she climbed in with them and shut the door.

The man slid behind the wheel and turned to face her. "You could have sat up front."

"They need me." She and the animals needed each other, really. And now—with the van burning in front of them—it seemed like she'd be starting over with nothing.

Again.

~~~

He was going to be late.

Pete Thompson shot a quick text to Hope to ask for her help. He hated depending on her so much. He'd already missed the meeting about this year's fishing rodeo, and now Mom's renter would be stuck without a key for a while.

He glanced at the clock on the dash, then back at the girl—the girl he'd thought was a young man at first, dressed in jeans, a tee, and a baseball cap. But as soon as he'd taken in the arc of her cheeks, the fullness of her lips, the smoothness of her skin, he'd realized his mistake. No matter that she wore not one stitch of makeup, she was totally feminine.

Long strands of obviously dyed-black hair escaped her cap. Her light brown eyes caressed her pets as she ran petite fingers over their bones and paws, checking each for injuries. New injuries, anyway.

Now that he'd gotten a good look, he noticed the scraggly pug had only three legs, and the ugly black cat was missing an eye.

"Are they okay?" If they were, maybe she'd let him come around and look her over. Or a paramedic could, if one ever made it around the traffic jam.

"I think so." She dabbed at the blood on her face with the corner of her T-shirt.

"I have tissues over there." He pointed on the floor in front of Olivia's booster seat.

"I see." The girl bent over, eliciting a soft moan.

"You're clearly hurt. We need help." He hopped out and rounded the truck. Where was a paramedic? Since the plumbing on the *Sea of Grace* was being repaired—again—Caleb should be around. He scanned the road for flashing lights and spotted a reflection. At least they were getting closer.
~~~

As the captain of a charter boat, he knew first aid, but spinal injuries…

She cracked the power window. "I'm just stiff and need to rest."

Frustration boiled, though he respected the way she cared for her haphazard trio. "You won't be any good to your pets if you're injured. You have to take care of yourself."

Caramel-colored eyes met his and stayed there, evaluating him, piercing into his soul, it seemed.

She's the one.

The words came clearly into his mind, sending a fresh burst of adrenaline.

What? No. I'm not ready. Probably never will be.

The stress of the situation had to have triggered the disturbing thought.

The door opened, and the girl slipped out. She stood before him. Not a girl, but a woman. He reached for her face, but she jerked back.

A scared wisp of a woman. There was nothing he could do if she wouldn't let him near her.

She glanced down at herself, felt along her arms and legs like she'd done with the animals. Gave a stiff stretch. Groaned. "I'll be sore for a week or so. That's all. Does my nose look broken?"

The pert nose appeared straight. A little red with only a tad of swelling. "I don't think so. What's your name?"

Her lips pressed together before she spoke. Was that a sign she was about to lie, or was it fear? Maybe she'd forgotten with the knock to the head.

"Syd Smith," she answered at last.

No way. It couldn't be.

"You rented a house? On the island?"

Eyes darting, she gave a single dip of her chin. Okay, she didn't trust him, but she didn't understand.

"You're the Sydney Smith who rented a house from Dorothy Thompson?"

He couldn't believe this twist of coincidence.

Lips parted, her gaze locked onto him now. "How would you know that?"

"I'm Pete Thompson, Dorothy's son. I was on my way to give you the key." And pick up his daughter from school.

She's the one.

Pete pressed his palm to his forehead. Kenzie had made him promise to listen for this…this still small Voice that would guide him when it was time. As much as he'd fought her, she'd made him promise he'd try at love again.

But this peculiar woman?

No. She can't be the one.

Chapter 2

"Pete, what happened? Were you in the accident? Are you hurt?"

Spinning around, Pete found his best friend and business partner, Caleb Donnelly, running toward him. Finally. Between all the ruckus of sirens, not to mention concern for the woman standing by his truck, he'd not noticed his buddy's approach.

As part of the volunteer fire department, Caleb wore his protective gear. Another firefighter sprinted around vehicles and worked to contain the fire.

"I'm only a bystander. This young lady was the driver of the van." He motioned toward the woman—Syd. At least that's what she'd claimed, though the name didn't suit her. It even sounded stilted coming from her lips, as if her mouth wasn't familiar with forming the words.

Had Mom rented to a scammer?

Or someone in a witness protection program? The girl's gaze flitted about like a frightened deer that would take off running any second, if not for her pets.

As Caleb neared Syd, she stepped backward, bumping into the truck.

"Are you experiencing any pain?" he asked.

She stared at the ground. "I don't need medical attention. You can check the other driver."

Her chin trembled with the words.

"Someone's helping him." Worry furrowing his brow, Caleb's gaze traveled to her mangled and burning van.

"I could feel down your spine, palpate from cervical to thoracic to check—"

"No." Cringing, she held up her palm. "I'm okay."

She needs you, something shouted within Pete. Fingers of sympathy wrapped around his chest and squeezed. He could at least try to help her, since she'd apparently rented his grandparents' former home.

He breathed a long sigh, resigning himself to this new obligation.

Part of it, anyway. "She's renting Nana and Pop's place. Olivia and I will watch out for her when we get there. Hope will probably want to help too."

Caleb's face fell that way it always did when someone mentioned Hope. He crossed his arms, facing Pete. "No one can make her get medical attention, but from the look of that collision, she had to have taken a pretty hard blow." He shook his head. "No symptoms of concussion or brain injury?"

Pete scrubbed a hand over his unshaven jaw. He'd seen the wreck. Stopped in plenty of time to avoid adding to it—thank the good Lord—then jumped out. Syd had been aware of what happened and had vainly attempted to get out the front doors of the van, but that was a normal reaction. Then she'd obsessed over her pets. Fairly reasonable, for an animal lover.

"She's been alert," he said finally. Between running the charter business, caring for Olivia, and now dealing with the aftermath of his mother's stroke, he had too much on his plate already. He didn't need to be responsible for his family's rental house and the renter.

Yet… He glanced at her, took in her narrow shoulders, the slant of light that illuminated her soft brown eyes—timid doe eyes. Perhaps she did need him.

Temporarily.

"I'll watch over her." No need to mention Hope again, though he prayed she'd volunteer to take on most of the tending to this girl. Hope loved taking care of people. Too much so, at times.

The girl's eyes whipped toward him as if he'd threatened to kill her. Maybe that did sound kind of stalkerish. "My daughter would love to feed your animals. She'll be excited." He thumbed toward his truck. "Unless they don't like kids."

"The dogs enjoy children." The tension in her face loosened. "How old is she?"

"Almost seven now." And the joy of his life. Often, since losing Kenzie, the only joy.

~~~

After what seemed like days, the police finished their report. Her demolished van was towed away, and now Skye sat in the front seat of the man's truck.

What a coincidence that her landlord's son would be directly behind her during the accident.

Of course, Miss Lydia would tell her that there were no coincidences. And once she found out about the wreck, the kind woman would have wheels on the ground out of Mobile and heading this way. Skye hated causing worry, but at some point, she would have to tell her. Not yet, though.

She peeked back at the boys. They seemed to have finally settled down. Sam allowed Frodo to rest his big head across him. Rocky gave the two dogs his usual hard, one-eyed, don't-mess-with-me stare from his cat carrier.

"Here we go. Finally," Pete mumbled, maybe to himself, once a policeman waved them forward.

Other than the ferry from Fort Morgan, the only way onto or off Dauphin Island, located forty-five minutes south of Mobile, Alabama, was this three-mile bridge. People on both
~~~

sides were probably as frustrated as she was at the delay. The fourteen-mile-long island had only a handful of shops and restaurants. Everything else pretty much came across this road.

She turned to study her rescuer. Pete Thompson.

He looked well-groomed, other than needing a shave, and his almost-black hair had been neatly trimmed. The color of his eyes was unique—deep blue swirled with lighter hues, like ocean and sky caught up in a whirlpool. A few stress grooves were carved into his forehead, contradicting with the smile lines gracing his temples. Deep pain and deep joy?

Sunglasses hung around his neck. Tanned skin, so he probably spent a lot of time outdoors. Construction work or fisherman? Maybe a landscaper? His truck held no clues. It was much neater than her own vehicle.

He wore a crisp blue button-down short-sleeve shirt, allowing a view of chiseled biceps.

A shiver crawled up her aching spine. The man possessed too much strength to be trusted.

She jerked her attention out the window. Toward the end of the bridge, the marina came into view. Back on solid land, they passed one of the few gas stations on the island and the general store. Then palms, pines, and live oaks lined the divided highway. Her nerves needled and ramped her pulse as they neared the turn for her new neighborhood. How long would this guy hang around?

I'll watch her, he'd said.

The last thing she wanted was any man watching her. Or anywhere near her. She'd dismiss him and bolt the doors when they arrived at the rental. But as the landlord, he'd have a key.

The thought sent skitters of fear along her skin.

She could block the doors with heavy furniture at night. Except for the fact that her back was killing her.

Frodo whined, interrupting the racing thoughts. As if he wanted to remind her that they needed food. And soon. The big pig.

She couldn't stop a groan.

"What's wrong?" Pete looked her way. "Should I get you to a doctor?"

"No." She hadn't meant to attract his attention. "The boys will be hungry, and everything I own was in the van."

"Maybe Hope can bring some food. I can ask when I pick up my daughter."

Interesting. "Is Hope your wife?"

At the stop sign, he shook his head. "A lifelong friend."

"Where is your daughter's mother?"

The question was probably too forward. If only she could limit her communications to animals.

The truck turned onto the neighborhood street. "She's gone," Pete said.

Skye's chest locked up as she recoiled. A little girl being raised alone by a man?

"What do you mean gone?" None of her business, but he was the one who'd brought up his daughter and the Hope woman.

He pulled into the driveway, but she barely spared a look at the house she'd only seen on the Internet. He put the truck in park and inhaled deeply. Blew it out. He seemed to be gathering strength to answer. "Passed away. Gone." He spit the words as if he despised them and their meaning.

Skye couldn't tear her gaze away.

She didn't interact with many males of her species, other than at work—for good reason. But this one appeared to be devastated over the loss of his mate.

Could he be a decent man?

For the little girl's sake, she hoped so. But she didn't plan on being around them or anyone else enough to know their personal business.

Because she surely didn't want anyone nosing around in hers.

Chapter 3

Skye took a cautious step out of Pete's truck onto the driveway. Her tennis shoes crunched on the cracked concrete mixed with sand and shells. Every muscle coiled into stiff knots. Despite the pain and stress of the accident, her anxiety eased at finally arriving at her new place. Plus, she was happy to be out of this stranger's truck. Would he leave once he gave her the key? The sooner, the better as far as she was concerned.

Before attempting to go farther, she took in the view. Wind swayed the tops of the pines and rustled the oak leaves, the sun glinting off the foliage that waved like shining flags, welcoming her. They seemed to whisper stories she couldn't quite make out.

The house was older with exterior walls forming an octagon. Pale yellow siding lined the frame, accented with a soft white trim. Wide windows overlooked the landscape. The place was more adorable than the pictures she'd seen online. A deck served as the front porch with two wrought iron lawn chairs, one just waiting for her to settle into.

"Are you okay?" Pete's voice beside her earned a flinch. He stood so close. How had she not heard his deck shoes on the driveway? Maybe her head had taken a worse whack than she'd realized.

"I'm soaking in the atmosphere." She nodded and instantly regretted the movement of her stiff neck.

Pete inched closer to her side, carrying Frodo in his arms like a seventy-pound infant.

The dog licked Pete's chin in appreciation.

Strange, because Frodo disdained men, often snarling at them between quiet whimpers. The rescued hunting dog had his mental issues. Of course, many creatures did.

She had a few maladies of her own.

"Syd, I need to tell you that Mom was in the middle of cleaning out Nana and Pop's house when she had a stroke—last weekend." His lips tightened with the words.

"I'm sorry." And she meant it. If something like that happened to Miss Lydia… Skye hated that thought, although the possibility of an illness was the reason she'd dared move back to this corner of the world.

"I'll get Sam and Rocky." At least they were light. She walked around the front of the truck, retrieved the other two animals, and stopped a step behind Pete. "Lead the way."

He turned to look her in the eyes, causing all manner of unforeseen turmoil inside her.

"The thing is," he said, "I know you rented this house furnished, but Mom didn't finish emptying the closets. There are still old clothes and personal items in there. And the fence is broken. My dad hadn't gotten to it."

Her stomach plunged practically to the driveway. "Do you not want me to move in? Finding another rental on the island this late in the spring—"

"I didn't mean that. Only, Nana and Pop's stuff might be in your way. The dogs won't be able to stay in the yard. Nothing's cleaned yet."

She blew out a sigh. "Everything I owned was in the van. Nothing will be in my way. I'm not picky." Never had the luxury.

"Those were *all* of your possessions?" His angled jaw dropped.

"Pretty much." Except a few items at Miss Lydia's. "I gave up a furnished rental in Florida." And she'd never had the need for sentimental knickknacks or decor.

A shining black SUV pulled up the drive, interrupting the pity party she was tempted to indulge in. After parking, a woman emerged and smoothed her hair. Dark hair with lighter highlights that framed her perfectly sculptured face. Perfect cosmetics as well. A short red jacket fit over a white shirt that tucked into navy ankle jeans. She wore a chunky red necklace and earrings to match.

Moistening her lips, the woman's almost ebony eyes honed in on Pete. "Are you okay? I was worried to pieces when I got your text, then heard the sirens."

"Nothing happened to me." He motioned with his head at Skye. "Syd wasn't so lucky. Someone hit her van while she was on her way to move in."

"Syd? Oh, hello. I'm Hope Martinez." Finally, the woman's keen gaze landed on Skye, swept her up and down. "Bless your heart. I'm sorry you had such a bad experience. I'll get Olivia out of the car and then help you get settled however I can."

And perhaps hurry Pete back out the door.

Skye flattened her lips.

Humans had their body language that spoke as loudly as any other species' nonverbal communication. This female's expression and mannerisms said volumes. They virtually shouted that this was her man. Whether he knew it or not.

Pete pivoted and headed toward the house. "Hope helps out with my daughter Olivia."

"I see." Skye measured her tone as she followed.

She'd had years of practice with veiling her emotions, so schooling her features around these two would be a breeze.

They reached the door, and Pete somehow managed to get a key from his pocket and unlock the deadbolt while still holding Frodo.

"After you." He stepped aside, and when the dog gave him another sloppy kiss, his mouth tilted in a smile. His blue eyes crinkled when he chuckled, and they held a light she hadn't noticed before.

"You're quite the multitasker, Pete Thompson," Skye said.

"Single parents have to be."

"Yes." Memories of her mother rushed in, darkening the grimy corners of her mind. *If only Momma had remained single.*

Inside, the décor, full of light blues and pastels, oozed a combination of nineties beachy and country chic. A few Bible verses painted on artsy wooden plaques adorned the walls. Miss Lydia would love that part. The place felt light and airy with aromas reminiscent of books and cinnamon, two things she adored.

Well-worn armchairs stood beside an old plush brown couch. Perfect. She didn't have to worry about the animals messing up new furniture.

"What can I do?" Helpful Hope hightailed it toward them—hightailed as much as she could, considering the tall pumps. An adorable child clung in her arms.

"I can walk, Miss Hope. I'm almost seven." The girl's butterscotch brown hair hung down her back with soft curls near the ends. The longest natural lashes Skye had ever seen lifted and lowered as Olivia blinked, taking in the dogs. "Are those your pets?"

Skye's heart leapt at the adorable voice, which reminded her of Sparrow's. "They are. You're welcome to pet them. Except for Rocky."

Skye held up the cat carrier. "He has a bit of an ego, plus, he'll have to do an investigation of the premises."

"This place needs a good cleaning." Heels clicked on the hardwood floors as Hope shut the door and let Olivia down.

The girl ran to Pete and squeezed his legs. "Daddy! Can I hold the puppy next?"

"Hey, princess." A deep laugh rumbled in his chest, jolting Skye with its tenderness. No hint of a maniacal undertone that caused fear, but a gentle sound that spread warmth through her.

"Take a step back, little minnow, and I'll set him on his feet," Pete said. "The poor fellow is shaking like an out-of-balance propeller." He cast a wary look Skye's way. "They don't bite, do they?"

"Both dogs are gentle." She smiled at the girl and set Sam on the floor. "Rocky—the cat—shouldn't be picked up. He has trust issues." Waiting until everyone left to release the testy fellow might be best, so she set the carrier down but didn't open its door.

"Yes, ma'am." After giving her father more space, Olivia tugged at the hem of her flowered shirt and waited while Pete set Frodo on the floor.

Such a polite child. Was something being done to her to achieve this perfect behavior? A memory crushed dirty fingers around Skye's throat. Polo cologne, the stench of stale cigarettes, welts and deep purple bruises. But more heinous than that—

Leave me alone! You don't control me anymore.

Skye sucked in a deep breath, held it, and then released the air.

"About the cleaning," Hope began again, her comments directed at Pete. She pulled a phone from a designer bag on her shoulder. "I can schedule it right away."

"No!" Skye held up a shaky palm. "I don't want strangers in here."

~~~

Pete took in the woman in front of him. Syd was shivering, despite the eighty-something temperature outside and the equally stifling air inside Nana's house. What would cause her to be so afraid? A bad experience with cleaning crews? Or was she injured more than she'd let on and going into shock?

Eyes rounding, Hope had fallen speechless.

"I can help with the cleaning," he volunteered. Although, he had no idea when he could squeeze one more thing into his schedule.

With Olivia still petting the large dog, he needed to stay by his daughter to make sure the animal showed no aggression, but he also felt a pull to move closer to Syd in case she was about to keel over. At least Syd had claimed the dog would be okay around children.

"Olivia, how about you sit with Syd on the couch and pet both of her dogs?" He pointed across the room. "We don't want to leave one out, and Syd might need to rest a minute."

"Yes, sir." Wasting no time, she skipped to Syd and took her hand. "Nana and Pop's couch is so soft. One time I slept on it all night, so if you're tired, the cushions will feel really good."

Pete's heart squeezed watching his baby girl lead the distraught woman across the room. Kenzie would be so proud of their daughter.

If only his wife had made it even a few years after giving birth. That familiar bottomless pit threatened to swallow him whole again. What he wouldn't give to see Kenzie and Olivia hand-in-hand like that.

Syd's face brightened as she sat beside Olivia with the dogs
~~~

at their knees, the animals' wet noses pressing against them, vying for petting. Then her gaze lifted, and she caught him staring like a stalker.

Face burning, he shoved his hands in his pockets. "You have a knack for putting children and animals at ease."

"I've heard that before." Her mouth formed an almost smile. Then she aimed her focus on Olivia. "Someone has a knack for putting people who've been in an auto accident at ease."

"I can't take any credit for Olivia." Pete shook his head. "She was born kind." And it was true. Though God hadn't answered his prayers for Kenzie the way Pete would have liked, the Lord had blessed him with a wonderfully sweet child.

A second later, Hope was at his side, her arm encircling his waist. She stared up at him. "That's not true. You're a perfect daddy. Any little girl's dream."

His face scalded. He didn't need coddling. She was trying to be nice, but it made him feel worse. He glanced at Syd and found her brows lifted, gaze flitting between him and Hope. She probably had the wrong idea already. Like his partner, Caleb. The man would never believe Hope was only a friend.

Pete sidestepped the one-armed hug and clapped his hands. "How about we pick up dinner for Syd?"

His new renter shook her head. "You don't need—"

"Nope." Hope caught his forearm. "I whipped up a batch of gumbo this afternoon that could feed a fleet of shrimpers. I'll run pick it up. I can be back in fifteen minutes." She turned on her heels, then grinned over her shoulder. "Mama's recipe. Your favorite."

Once Hope cleared the door, Pete made his way to the couch and sat by Olivia. "I hope you like gumbo. Looks like that's what we're having."

A quiet chuckle rose from the woman. "Looks like. What version is *your favorite*?" Awkward emphasis noted.

"A mixture of shrimp, crab, oysters, and Hope's mother's secret seasonings."

"No sausage?" She slid a glance his way.

"Is that a deal breaker?"

The corners of her mouth tugged downward. "I normally avoid eating animals with eyelashes whenever possible. But since I have no wallet, cell, or anything else, it won't be a deal breaker."

Oh, man. That bit of information slapped him in the face harder than a flying Asian carp. With no money, phone, or car, Syd was basically stranded here in his grandparents' old house.

Help her.

Yep, he was going crazy. His brain was talking to itself.

Pete let his eyes shut a long moment.

Fine, he said to the bizarre requests nudging inside him. *I'll get her settled.*

That was all he'd commit to. But how long would that take? Because he wasn't looking for another woman, and it didn't appear Syd was looking for a man.

Chapter 4

"I'm back." Hope's sing-song voice bounced through the door.

The sound rattled Skye's nerves, and her head whipped up, launching another muscle spasm in her neck. Helpful Hope must have broken a few traffic laws and sprinted up the drive to return so soon with the enormous pot of gumbo in her arms. Olivia and Pete had barely settled onto the couch to help calm Sam and Frodo. Of course, the island wasn't big. Maybe Hope lived a few blocks away.

"Hey, Pete…" Hope made herself at home in the open kitchen area connected to the living room. "There's a package on the deck for a Skye Smith. Want me to return it when I leave?"

"No." Skye's voice came out grumpier than she'd intended, but this woman acted as if she were the one moving in. "That's for me."

"I'll grab it." Pete slipped through the door and retrieved the mail. "Who is Skye?" Pete's brows rose above wary blue eyes as he laid the box beside the couch.

Skye blinked hard. Nothing about this move was going the way she'd planned. But when had anything in her life ever gone like she'd wanted?

At least her last name had been legally changed from Youngblood to Smith. "Skye's my middle name," she managed to spit out.

Pete studied her, as if waiting for more.

Her cheeks heated at his scrutiny. "A few people from my past still use… My first name is Sydney, so in my professional life…" She couldn't seem to finish a sentence.

"Sydney Skye?" Hope set bowls and spoons on the nearby farmhouse table. "That's beautiful. Oh, and your initials are SSS. What an interesting monogram."

As if Skye had ever owned anything monogrammed. And if she had, growing up, her initials wouldn't have been SSS since her last name had been Youngblood.

"We used to call that one Petey when we were little." Hope thumbed Pete's way, and he let out an embarrassed huff, but the woman kept talking. "Did your parents like to visit Australia or something? May I call you Skye?"

This conversation had Skye's mind bouncing like the tennis balls she threw for Frodo. She'd hoped to go by Syd here since Denny was nearing the end of his prison sentence. Changing her last name to the most common surname she could think of might throw him off her trail, but she couldn't be too careful with that psychopath.

Olivia's petite hand took Skye's. "May I call you Skye? It's a really pretty name." The adorable girl's lips squeezed together for a second as she studied Skye's face. "You don't look like a Syd."

How could she say no to that? "My friends can call me Skye." She smiled down at the child.

"I'm your new friend, right?" Olivia looked as hopeful as a rescue puppy.

And as precious as Sparrow. Pain and longing crushed Skye's chest at the thought. "I hope so."

"The table's ready," Hope called, waving a ladle. "You can fill your bowl, then come take a seat." She turned her attention to Skye. "I can bring it to you if you feel too bad to move."

Did she? Skye glanced down at her blood-spattered shirt, then touched her sore nose. She probably looked a wreck.

"I should wash up." She scooted off the couch and pushed to her feet, ignoring the achiness flogging her.

Pete stood, too, his blue eyes scanning her up and down, causing a shiver to scurry along her skin. Creases lined his forehead at whatever he observed about her. "Let me show you down the hall to the bathroom—"

"No." Skye's palm popped up. She couldn't be alone with him. Couldn't breathe at the thought. She couldn't trust any man. Even with other people in the house.

~~~

Be gentle. She's fragile.

Exceedingly fragile, Pete whined to the persistent Voice.

Good grief. What had happened to Skye? He stared at the woman who stood shivering before him. Her arms hugged around her waist, and the blood had drained from her face. You'd think someone held a loaded gun to her head.

Gentle. The thought came again.

Got it. Gentle.

Had he finally gone crazy? After six years of dealing with torturous grief, he'd believed he could hold his sanity together for Olivia's sake.

Throwing off the temptation to be annoyed with the continued instructions, he held out his hands and lowered his voice to barely above a whisper. "I meant only to show you where there might be soap and a towel. Maybe a clean shirt of Nana's, though it would probably swallow you."

Wide-eyed, the woman stared, until Olivia slid to her feet and took Skye's hand. "I'll go with you."

His precious daughter. Pete's eyes burned as Skye responded with a slow nod and followed Olivia down the hall.
~~~

The big dog—Frodo—whimpered and shook, watching them leave.

"They'll be right back." Pete bent to rub the dog's head. *Am I responsible for the woman's weird pets too?* He looked up at the ceiling as if the Voice might answer but heard nothing.

Sweet perfume met his nose as Hope sidled up to him. "Are you sure Skye doesn't have a head injury? She's…well, acting peculiar. I don't know if she's always that way or if it's from the accident. Maybe we should ask Caleb to dinner. He can observe her—check her pupils or something."

Not a terrible idea. Caleb might make more sense of the woman. Growing up as a foster child, Caleb had learned to read people. He had insight about them.

Pete pulled out his phone. "I'll text him."

He didn't want an unstable person getting too close to Olivia.

A minute after he'd sent a long message, explaining the predicament, Olivia reappeared with Skye in tow.

"We found something that fit Skye, Daddy."

Pete's mouth went dry, and his blood pulsed in his ears. Not that. She couldn't wear that. It wasn't right. How had that dress been left here?

Yet, Skye looked…so very beautiful.

The pale blue sleeveless dress fit her form perfectly. A nice form. Though he should not be noticing her. Didn't want to notice any woman. Didn't want to ever endure another loss.

He and Olivia were fine on their own.

Still, his eyes rose to take in Skye's dyed-dark hair, which had been freed from the baseball cap to lay down around her bare arms. Red marks from the collision and the airbag marred her skin, gutting him.

Maybe she could wear Kenzie's clothing for tonight. But not forever. Skye could never fill anything of his precious wife's. And she could never fill the gaping hole in his heart. No matter what the Voice said.

Chapter 5

"What's wrong?" Skye already felt awkward wearing the dress Olivia had found in an old armoire. Pete's peculiar stare as she entered the kitchen made it all the worse. Not that he was ogling her exactly. The twist of his mouth and the furrow of his brows above glassy blue eyes indicated more pain than lust.

"That color looks amazing on you, Skye." Leaving the stove, Hope made a beeline their way. Her gaze dropped to the whip marks the wreck had left across Skye's upper body. "You took a beating today, poor baby."

Then, observing no personal-space boundaries, Hope fiddled with strands of Skye's hair. "I could bring you back closer to your natural color. A golden brown, I bet, right? Besides working at our family's boutique on the island, I help Mom coordinate weddings. I'm licensed to do hair and makeup for the bridal parties if needed. In fact, we could buy a few outfits from our shop, if you want, before I leave for Mobile tonight."

Boutique? Skye scanned Hope's high-dollar designer clothes. Even if her credit cards had survived the car wreck, Skye wouldn't be shopping at the boutique. Fancy clothes weren't in her budget, plus she had no need for them in her job as a marine biologist or anywhere else.

Her hair, though? Maybe she had gotten the dye a bit dark this time, but she'd been alternating colors for years, hoping to throw off Denny if he ever came looking. Even with him in prison, his sadistic parents were prowling free somewhere.

"Give Skye a minute." Pete had regained his composure. "Let her eat before you start planning one of your makeovers."

A knock on the door turned their attention away from her. Thank goodness. But who was here now?

When she'd envisioned her first evening on Dauphin Island, she'd imagined a walk on the beach watching the sunset, breathing the briny air and then relaxing here alone. Well, alone other than Frodo, Sam, and Rocky.

"That'll be Caleb." Pete must have noticed the question on her face. "I invited him to eat with us."

Invited him? Who'd decided she should be hosting a dinner party? Skye didn't do dinner parties. Or any other form of societal gatherings if she could help it.

"I'll get it." Hope's heels clattered across the hardwood floor.

Pete thumbed over his shoulder. "I thought he might have news about your belongings—if they were able to salvage anything. I hope you don't mind."

At least that made a little sense, but they could have just called the guy.

Skye shrugged. "I hope he found something." Her gaze flicked to the food bubbling on the stove. The sooner they ate, the sooner they could all leave.

The man, Caleb, entered, his focus mostly on the floor, his expression as uncomfortable as her own likely was. Was he embarrassed about something? Socially awkward? At the accident earlier, he'd exuded confidence.

Curious.

While Hope chattered to the guy, Skye examined him further. Freshly showered and clean shaven, his short light brown hair appeared damp. He wore a long-sleeved T-shirt, despite the warm temps.

When he turned to speak to Pete, she spotted redness on the right side of his neck. Patches of muddled skin.

Scars. And she knew scars well. She and her sister, Star, had enough of them hidden beneath their clothing.

These marks on Caleb were burns, and bad ones from the looks of it, perhaps extending down that side of his torso.

Her throat closed as a buried memory hurtled into the present. She and Star wore pink matching dresses that Momma had found at a garage sale. They were so proud of the frills and lace. Until they got home.

Then Momma's husband—she'd never call that man stepfather—lurched at them in the doorway. Accused Momma of unspeakable things. That look of rage, the kicks, shoves, and fists pushing them down the hall of the trailer. No AC. The summer heat drenching them with sweat. The crack of a slap to the head. Dizziness. Then the scorch of a cigarette on thin bare skin—

Dense darkness descended—that crippling helplessness weighing her down. The room grew hazy, and paralysis immobilized her lungs. Staggering forward, she reached for something—anything—to hold onto. Why again? Why now? After she'd worked so hard to get better.

Who was she kidding? She'd probably never truly heal.

The urge to just give up tugged at her.

Was this how her mother had felt?

~~~

Pete reached for Skye as she stumbled forward. He scooped her up and stared at her fluttering lashes.

Had she fainted? Was it a head injury? Or did she just need to eat?

"Get her to the couch," Caleb snapped. "I'll grab my bag from the truck." He dashed out the door.
~~~

Pete eased Skye onto the cushions and propped her head on a throw pillow.

Her eyes fluttered open.

Seconds later, Caleb sprinted back in. "We should have taken her to the hospital in Mobile." He produced a small light and shone it in Skye's eyes, one at a time.

"No hospital," Skye mumbled and attempted to sit up. "I'm okay. I saw your burns, and I…"

"What?" Caleb stiffened, his jaw slack as if she'd slapped him.

Pete held his breath. There could hardly be a person more insecure about his scars, no matter how many times Pete had tried to tell Caleb they didn't matter. Didn't make him less of a man.

After blinking a few times, Skye's eyes widened. "Sorry. That came out inappropriately. It's just that I…I know someone who was burned, and it brought back a disturbing memory. After the trauma of the accident today, I wasn't able to ground myself and reorient to the present."

With a slow nod, Caleb stood upright and took a step back. "I understand." His voice was quiet. "You've had a rough one." He picked up his bag and threw it over his shoulder, his expression softening. "No nausea, vomiting, or headache?"

"None." Skye sat up, then rattled off the date, the name of the president, and a few other facts in an attempt to prove she was coherent. "Let's eat, and you'll see that I'm okay other than a few abrasions and stiffness. I'll sit with everyone at the table for observation."

"I'll fill everyone's bowls." Hope grabbed her ladle and began serving up the gumbo. "Y'all just take a seat."

"Are you sure you're okay?" Olivia asked, coming closer. "Caleb is a good doctor."

Bittersweet pride rippled through Pete.

Olivia was as compassionate as Kenzie. So much like her mother that it sometimes ripped him in two.

Face reddening, Caleb shrugged. "I'm not a doctor, only emergency medical training."

"Did you hear how the other driver is?" Skye asked as she scooted to the edge of the cushion.

"Banged up, but he'll be okay."

Pete offered a hand to Skye. "Let me help you up and over to your chair."

Hesitantly, she accepted. Her soft fingers clasped his, and she stood. Fire zapped up his arm, and he stifled a gasp at the intensity.

Don't let her go.

Like a ship cut from its moorings, set adrift in choppy waters, his heart undulated with warring emotions.

The pleasant sensations her touch evoked, her obvious vulnerability, the hard tug in his chest, and this Voice in his head he kept hearing…

God help me. What in creation is going on?

Pete blinked in a vain effort to clear his head, and then led Skye to a seat at the table. He pulled out a chair, waited until she'd sat, then helped Olivia do the same before taking his own place between them.

Still reeling, he took a deep breath and attempted to regain his composure.

"Someone should stay with her tonight." Caleb's voice broke through the mist that was blurring Pete's thinking. "To make sure she doesn't have any other symptoms of a concussion." He turned his focus on Skye. "Do you have a relative or a friend who could come?"

Please let her have someone.

For a long moment, Skye's gaze studied the steaming bowl of gumbo Hope set in front of her. "I'll be fine." Her voice barely rose above a whisper.

"I would if I could." Hope settled on the other side of Olivia with her own serving of food. "But I'm helping Mom set up for a huge engagement party in Mobile."

All eyes—other than Skye's—landed on Pete, twisting his insides, threatening his last bit of sanity. There was no way Caleb would stay here alone with a single woman. His friend had way too many hang-ups. If only Mom hadn't had a stroke, she would have loved to take care of Skye. If Nana were still here and healthy…or if Kenzie—

"Me and Daddy can stay with her." Olivia's little voice chimed in.

"You don't have to." Skye shook her head. "I can call if…" She bit her bottom lip. "Is there a working landline here?"

Oh, right. She had no phone, no vehicle, and no access to money.

She needs you.

"Olivia and I can stay." The words slipped out of Pete's mouth, stunning him. "I'll sleep on the couch."

What else could he do, though, other than be the kind of man his parents had raised him to be? Because apparently, Skye did need him. For now.

Chapter 6

When would these people leave?

Skye breathed a quiet sigh. She didn't know how much more she could take. As an introvert, she'd already expended an enormous amount of energy with this unexpected social assembly of strangers.

Snoring loudly, Frodo lay his big head across her lap, and Sam curled against him. Both dogs would need to go outside again soon. She'd released Rocky into the back bedroom with a bowl of water. No telling what sort of mess she'd have to clean up, but the cranky old feline needed to be able to walk around. The sooner she was alone to tend to her babies, the better.

Except, she wouldn't be.

Olivia had settled onto the cushion next to her, looking at—or perhaps reading—a little book with multicolored unicorns adorning the pages. The child was charming, but it would be uncomfortable having her and Pete spend the night. Mainly Pete.

"Thank you for everything." Skye gave an awkward wave to Caleb and Hope from her perch on the couch. Maybe they'd take the hint.

Hope flashed a smile Skye's way. "Happy to. We can work on your wardrobe as soon as I finish in Mobile." Her gaze drifted to Pete. "Are you sure I can't help clean up?"

"I've got it." Hovering nearby, Pete had insisted Skye rest, then kept assuring the others they could leave to attend to their various duties elsewhere. He'd handle the dishes. And her care, of course.

Which she did not need.

At least there would be two fewer people to deal with soon.

Once the others left, Skye could convince Pete and Olivia to go home as well.

Hope strutted over to Olivia and planted a kiss on her head. "Be good for Daddy. Love you."

"Yes, ma'am. Love you." Olivia's concentration remained on the story's pages.

Then Hope trained her gaze on Pete and smoothed her hair. "Good night." She gave him a tender look. "I'm only a phone call away if you need me."

With her soft tone, dilating pupils, and the preening, clearly Hope was infatuated with the man.

"We'll be fine." Pete nodded, his expression neutral.

Skye had spent years studying nonverbal communication of both animals and people. If Pete felt the same for Hope, he did a good job of concealing his emotions.

These two humans were an interesting enigma.

Near the door and shuffling his feet, Caleb swiped a hand over his scarred neck. "I forgot. I brought a leash, pet food, and some litter. It's in the truck. And we were able to salvage one thing from the fire." He dug into his pocket, plucked out a plastic bag, and brought the item to Skye.

It couldn't be. Her hands shook as she took it. The silver chain. With the pendant attached. She'd thought she'd lost her mother's necklace months ago. If going through the wreck today brought this back to her, it was almost worth losing everything else. "Thank you," she breathed.

"What's that?" Olivia's attention snapped to Skye. "Can I hold it?"

"Not right now, Olivia." Pete's tone was firm but gentle. Yet, the child's lips turned down.

"It's okay." Still trembling, Skye pulled the silver chain free of the bag. The attached blue sapphire and the silver star glittered even in the room's low light. "Hold out your hands."

Complying, Olivia's eyes widened. "It's so pretty. Where did you get that?"

Unwanted and painful images flooded in. The ones that had split open her soul and emptied her until she'd become a vacant cavern. Momma's pretty face—distorted and void of life. Those feelings of abandonment and betrayal and panic clutched her throat.

"Skye?" The cushions shifted as Pete sat on the other side of her. "Are you dizzy again?"

This is only a memory. It's in the past—over. I've moved on. I'm safe.

Swallowing back the currents of anguish strangling her, Skye shook her head. "It was my mother's. I thought it was gone forever, lost at work offshore."

Standing a few feet away and studying her, Caleb's forehead creased. "Offshore, like on a rig?"

As if she'd live trapped on a platform with that many men. Although, she had completed underwater observation of the sea life that made their habitat beneath the monstrosities. "I participated in a two-week-long excursion on a research vessel to do a migration study. I'm a marine biologist."

"What's that?" Olivia handed the necklace back, and Skye clipped it around her neck for safekeeping.

"I study sea life. Particularly sea mammals, like manatees and dolphins."

"I love manatees. Daddy and I saw one when we were on his charter boat."

Skye's head swiveled toward Pete. "A fishing charter?"

"Captain Thompson Charters." He nodded. "Originally started by my grandfather."

Her insides churned at the declaration. The recent incident of a fellow scientist being slashed by a drunken charter fisherman's propeller in Florida still angered her. The careless man had struck and killed a manatee too.

She'd keep her mouth shut about that issue for now. "May I use your phone to make a quick call?" Skye summoned the strength to keep her voice somewhat pleasant.

"Sure." Pete unlocked and handed over his cell, and Skye took it to the bedroom.

She'd call Miss Lydia, let her know she'd made it, and try to downplay the accident. Somehow, they'd have to come up with the documents and IDs needed to replace almost everything she owned. But she couldn't handle the stress of having Miss Lydia and Sparrow here right now. Being back in Alabama was hard enough.

~~~

After bringing in the pet supplies from Caleb's truck, Pete shut the door and turned toward the kitchen, fatigue weighing him down. This had been a long day. Once he'd dropped Olivia at school, he'd taken his mother to her doctor's appointment in Mobile while Dad spoke at a previously scheduled meeting. The stroke had caused bewildering changes in Mom's personality—so much anger. The respectable woman who'd raised him would be appalled.

When Dad had remembered Mom had rented this house, Pete was slapped with another unexpected situation.

Soon, he'd need to get Olivia ready for bed, but right now she chattered to Skye about pretending she owned a unicorn named Princess Peaches.
~~~

He could only guess the silly title came from her love of the fuzzy fruit doused in whipped cream.

Skye, on the other hand, had clammed up as soon as he'd mentioned his fishing business, looking as if he'd grown two horns and a tail. Most of the commercial fishermen had good relations with the biologists here, often working shoulder to shoulder to make sure the fish population remained strong and healthy. If she hung around long enough to get to know him, she'd find out the environment was important to him too.

Not that he cared if she hung around, or even cared what she thought. Much.

He made his way to the dishes in the sink, rinsing and tucking them into the dishwasher the way Kenzie had taught him. A sad smile played on his lips, remembering one of their arguments over the placement of the bowls. He used to stick them any which way, and it drove her crazy. She'd insisted on placing them on the top rack in the center. One of their tiffs had led to her squirting him with the spray nozzle, and that had led to a tickle fight, which then… Pleasure coursed through him at the memory. Not a bad night, in the end. Possibly one that had led to Olivia.

If only their daughter's birth hadn't contributed to Kenzie losing her battle with cancer. He blinked away the wetness blurring his vision. Even after six years, he missed his wife's touch, the sound of her laugh, the feel of her silky hair slipping through his fingers. That lotion she wore with the scent of vanilla and roses.

A hollow place in his core ached. He'd never love anyone the way he loved Kenzie, no matter what games his mind had been playing with him today.

The insanity had to be the result of watching that accident unfold after dealing with Mom. The adrenaline of helping Skye escape a vehicle about to burn had been a jolt to his system. That had to be it. Shock.

He barely had time for his current missions in life. Serving God, being a good father, being a good son, making an honest living running Pop's charter, and honoring his grandfather's memory this year at the fishing rodeo.

None of those involved this woman.

Okay, serving God meant helping others. Sharing about God's love. He could do that much. Maybe that was all Skye needed from him.

"You know," Skye said, "I'm okay. Y'all could go home and sleep in your own beds."

"No!" Olivia raised her voice in a frantic tone Pete had never heard the child use. "You need us."

Skye's wide eyes and gaping mouth probably mirrored his own.

"We'll stay." Pete directed his comments toward Olivia. "But you'll have to go to sleep, so we can get up early."

His daughter's head bobbed. "I promise. Do we have church tomorrow or work?" She turned to Skye. "My daddy's a preacher." The pride in Olivia's voice made his heart squeeze even though he'd never call himself by that term.

"I thought you were a charter fisherman?" Skye's mouth took a hard downward twist.

"Not a preacher, only a man sharing the Good News with a few friends on the beach on Sunday mornings. Tomorrow's Saturday, so we'll be on the boat."

Skye gawked at him, her forehead creasing in sharp angles.

Maybe he should explain better.

"The charter is a family business, but it skipped a generation. My father decided to be a pastor instead, but I love running my grandfather's fishing operation. After living in the glass house growing up as a preacher's kid, I left a large congregation and started a small, casual gathering on the island. Just a group of people who love Jesus."

"So, you're a *preacher's son*?"

She practically spat the question. Skye didn't like fishermen or ministers?

"I am a *PK*. A preacher's kid."

"I'll sleep out here on the couch with the dogs," she snipped. "You two can take the bedrooms."

Her chilly words were an obvious dismissal, and he could take a hint. In fact, he couldn't wait until morning so they could get out of there and away from this peculiar woman.

"Let's give Skye her space." He bent to gather Olivia, but she twisted from his reach.

"Good night, Skye." She wrapped her arms around the woman and kissed her cheek. "Good night, Frodo. Good night, Sam." She hugged each dog, kissing them too. "Love you. Sleepy good, and say your prayers."

The same phrase he spoke each night coming from his daughter's mouth melted his annoyance. Children loved and trusted so easily. They didn't know the danger and the pain that could come from that trust.

Skye knows. Look at her.

What did that mean? He didn't want to look at her—didn't want to know why he had this weirdness going on in his head—but he couldn't seem to stop himself.

He focused on Skye's face, really focused. Her frightened doe eyes shone with tears as she watched Olivia still hugging the dogs. There was sadness that pressed on the corners of her pretty mouth, a weariness that went deeper than a car accident. What had happened to Skye?

Did he even want to know?

"Good night, Olivia." Skye's lips quivered as she spoke, then her fragile gaze rose to meet Pete's, stirring up protective instincts and muddling his mind. "Thank you for your help today."

"Happy to… Let me know…let us know if you…" Where was he going with this? "See you in the morning. I hope you sleepy good. I mean—good night."

Ears scorching, Pete clamped his jaw tight.

God, please let Skye be fine tomorrow and get her things replaced. Let life go back to normal.

Because normal without Kenzie might not be great, but he'd gotten used to his world being about just him and Olivia. They sure didn't need complications. He'd had enough of those to last a lifetime.

Chapter 7

The creak of a floorboard popped open Skye's eyes and stole her breath. Every muscle locked and nailed her to the couch. A shadowy vision flashed through her mind—Denny slinking in, eyes dark, his breath against her face. *No!*

Her heart battered her ribcage. How had he found her?

"Skye, are you okay?" a little voice asked.

"Shh. She's sleeping," a man whispered.

"Her eyes are awake, but they're crying, Daddy."

Daddy?

Yesterday's accident rushed in. Skye forced herself to inhale.

It was just the little girl…Olivia. And Pete. The fisherman.

The preacher's son.

Of all the people in the world, she had to rent a house from him. Denny had been the son of a preacher too. The spawn of a violent and abusive pair of people who pretended to be Christians. And Denny had worked a string of odd jobs on the docks along the Gulf, getting fired and moving on to the next one as often as some folks went through a gallon of milk.

In the hazy early morning light, the father and daughter duo stood at the edge of the hall that led to the bedrooms, peering at her.

"Are you hurting, Skye? Do you need to go to the hospital?" Pete flipped on the overhead light and strode to the couch in three long steps.

He hovered over her, his dark hair poking up in the back.

"I can call Caleb. He could send for an ambulance, or I could drive you to the ER," he said.

"I was having a bad dream." A nightmare she'd lived for years. Though her pulse still whipped through her frigid body, she managed a ragged inhale and exhale. This was a false alarm. She needed to be logical.

Neither Denny nor his demented parents knew her location or what name she went by now. She'd studied enough biology and been to enough counseling sessions to know the auto accident had simply triggered a release of cortisol and other stress hormones into her system. So, along with aching muscles and joints, she'd need a few days to recover her sanity. Except, she only had until Monday, when she'd start work with the Sea Lab.

"Are you sure?" Pete's blue eyes studied her.

"I need to take these guys out and check on Rocky. Y'all can go about your normal routine." She pushed away the sleep jumbling her brain and slid her legs from under Frodo and Sam's weight so she could sit up. She stifled a groan. No need for Pete to know how sore she actually felt.

Lightning flashed outside the window. Then thunder boomed, rattling the roof.

Frodo yelped and ducked his big head. Now it would be near impossible convincing the huge baby to do his business in the yard.

"Daddy, I don't think we can fish this morning." Olivia ambled to Pete's side and shook her head, her mouth in a tight line. "No fishing, no dollars."

Pete smiled down at his little girl and mussed her hair. "You're probably right about not going out today, but don't you worry yourself over dollars. I bet I can come up with one or two for your allowance."

She put a dainty finger to her chin. "Still better check the weather app and call Caleb. See if he told the passengers that we can't go."

An amused chuckle spilled from Pete. "You'll be captain by the time you're eighteen at this rate."

Skye waved him off. "I'm fine if you need to go take care of your boat." Or anything other than her.

"What happened to your pet?" Olivia gazed at the dogs beside Skye on the couch, her green eyes glistening, tugging at Skye's scarred heart.

"Sam was hit by a car, and the vet had to amputate his leg. His owners didn't want to pay for the operation and never came back for him. So, I took him in and paid off his debt."

"Almost like what Jesus did for us. Right, Daddy?"

"That's right, sweet girl." Pete's face practically glowed.

Heat pricked Skye's eyes. If only she could believe the whole account of those ancient stories that described a Loving Healer. Obviously, Olivia had been raised in church. If Miss Lydia ever met this child, she would love her. But it would be best for everyone if they never crossed paths.

"What about the other one?" Olivia cocked her head.

"Rocky the cat?" Skye thumbed toward the hall. "He was another cast-off because he had cancer in one of his eyes. It's a high probability the disease will spread to his other eye. People aren't always willing or able to care for pets with illnesses."

"But you can?" Olivia asked.

"I worked part-time at a veterinary clinic while I was in college, and I loved animals, so I often traded extra work to pay for their treatments or surgeries. I wanted to save as many as I could." And she was heartbroken for those she couldn't.

"My mommy died of cancer. I wish someone like you

could have saved her."

Pete's eyes misted, and sadness clutched Skye. The child had lost her mother so young.

"I'm sorry that happened. There's not always a cure for our diseases." Inadequate, but what else could she say?

Her own father had died when she was a toddler, and Momma's depression had never healed. The disease had stolen her mother. Or the atrocious second husband had.

Guilt slapped Skye across the face. More likely, she'd been the last straw for her mother. Despite what counselors assured her, she'd contributed to her mother's death.

"Your mom loved you more than…" Pete's voice cracked. "More than life itself, baby girl."

Skye's stomach twisted. Something in the way he spoke the words felt more tragic than terminal cancer. As if that weren't bad enough.

"I know, Daddy. I wish I could remember her."

Pete bent and lifted her into his arms. "Me too."

The girl turned her attention back to Skye. "Why is Frodo so afraid, even though he has all his legs and eyes?"

Goodness, the child was perceptive.

"Sometimes, the cruelty of others doesn't show up on the outside. It creates damage that can't be seen." A fact she knew well, and the reason she'd been drawn to this particular rescue animal.

"Poor Frodo." Olivia sighed.

Skye glanced up, and Pete's steady examination seared her face, so she pushed to her feet. She straightened the borrowed dress she'd put on the night before. It didn't seem like a fabric she'd want to get drenched in.

Far too thin.

"If you don't mind, I'll find something to change into so I

can walk the dogs and see about Rocky. He's been closed off in that bedroom for too long."

Pete nodded. "Help yourself to whatever you need."

A loud blast of air emitted from the back end of Frodo's body.

Giggles burst from Olivia, and she scrunched her nose. "Uh-oh. Someone tootled."

Pete's lips pinched, obviously trying to hold in his own laugh. "You don't have to announce it, little minnow." He pressed a kiss on his daughter's cheek.

Olivia laughed harder. "Your scratchy beard tickles."

Skye shook her head. Now her face had to be all kinds of red. "That was Frodo. I better hurry and change." Without waiting for an answer, she trudged down the hall, the ache in her joints worsening with each step.

Her mind boggled at how Olivia appeared so comfortable in Pete's arms, with his closeness. Would that change as Olivia grew older? It was hard to imagine a wholesome relationship like that.

Because of the raw stains on her own psyche, Skye had never felt comfortable with physical touch. It had taken years for her not to stiffen when even Miss Lydia hugged her.

And intimacy with a man—that would never be a reality for her. She was much too broken for that.

~~~

Pete swallowed against the tightness in his throat and waited for Skye's return. No matter how many times she claimed she was fine, he could see that the accident had left her more injured than she let on. There was pain in her eyes—those pretty swirls of brown.

He'd also spotted shadows of something darker than just the car wreck. So fearful—like when they'd woken her.
~~~

Not that it was any of his business.

"Can I pet the dogs?" Olivia asked.

"Sure." He released her. His emotions rocked more than a ship in a squall, between the enigma of Skye and the fact that he'd never heard Olivia share about the loss of her mother the way she had—and with someone they'd just met. He had no idea she'd given so much thought to Kenzie's death, especially since she'd been a baby when her mother passed away. He needed to be more careful about what was said in front of those alert little ears. And careful about who Olivia spent time with. Like this woman Skye.

She needs you.

That again? He'd thought his head would clear once he'd had a good night's sleep. Not that he'd slept well in the twin bed across from Olivia, his feet hanging off the mattress half the night. The comforter held a good bit of dust that had his throat itching. Since the charter would be canceled until at least after lunch, he could clean up around this place.

"Okay, Sam, Frodo, let's go potty." Skye appeared from the hall, his grandmother's favorite purple sweat suit swallowing her.

"Oh, my. Looks like the Purple People Eater got you." He couldn't stop a laugh.

Glancing down at herself, she tugged the pants higher. "I didn't see a raincoat, and these were…" Her mouth twitched into a slight smile. "They'll be fine for a few minutes."

"I can walk them for—"

She held up a palm. "You've done enough, and I only have the one leash. Sam responds to my commands, but Frodo, not so much."

In no time, she'd coaxed the dogs outside and then returned, all of them dripping on the kitchen floor.

Man, the sky was pouring out there. "Olivia and I will fetch towels."

Ahead of him, Olivia scuttled to the bathroom and opened the cabinet beneath the sink. "Come on. We have to hurry, Daddy."

"I'm right behind you. What's the rush?"

"I don't want Skye to be scared without us."

Scared? What was Olivia sensing?

A hard knock on the door, followed by a shriek, spun him around. Both dogs barked an alert. What was going on?

"Stay right here, Olivia."

"But, Daddy—"

"Promise me."

Eyes wide, she nodded, and he sprinted back down the hall.

Skye stood frozen in place, staring at the door.

"Are you expecting someone?" Pete asked.

Dumb question, considering her state. "I'll answer it."

What in the world was she afraid of?

Chapter 8

Why did her body betray her this way?

Kneeling beside the dogs to hold them near, Skye tried to force air into her lungs. She'd taken self-defense classes, gone to counseling, and studied mindfulness, but, in certain situations, she still lost control—still found no peace inside.

The knob rattled and turned as Pete opened the door to see who had knocked. "Can I help you?"

"Who are you?" a woman's voice asked. A familiar voice.

"Pete Thompson. Who are you?" His tone came out polite enough.

"Lydia Sharp. I'm looking for my daughter. She's supposed to be renting at this address."

"Miss Lydia?" Skye's muscles unlocked, and she made her way around Pete. The dogs followed at her heels, wagging their tails. Being this close to the correctional facility where Denny had been incarcerated had her riled, plus the stress of the wreck. Her anxiety would lessen.

Eventually. She hoped. But she hadn't meant for Sparrow and Miss Lydia to come.

She took in the dear woman standing under the dripping eaves, water splattering her short curly hair and the shoulders of her navy jacket. "What are you doing here?"

Miss Lydia stepped inside and took both of Skye's hands. "I had to see you, precious one, and make sure you're really okay."

"I'm stiff and sore. That's all."

And slightly crazy, but nothing new there. Skye studied Miss Lydia. Though her dark skin still appeared smooth and flawless, especially for a woman over sixty, the tone was off, and circles shadowed her eyes. Was that a yellow hue muddling them? Jaundice?

"But you're sick, aren't you? And where's Sparrow?" Heart thumping, Skye craned her neck to look outside.

"Baby girl is in the car." She peered over at Pete. "Why is he…?"

"Pete and his daughter insisted on staying here. Their friend thought I might have a concussion."

"My friend, the paramedic," Pete interjected. "Plus, Skye had no money, vehicle, or phone to use to call for help if she did take a bad turn. We couldn't leave her alone."

Gaze bouncing between the two of them, Miss Lydia mumbled to herself in her eccentric way. The practice had freaked out many a student at the high school where she'd taught—the school where they'd first met.

Then Miss Lydia focused on Pete. "Peter. The rock. You must be the one. I've been praying for you."

Fire scalded from Skye's neck to her scalp, and she took a step back, pulling her hands free. "Miss Lydia. Don't. That's not...appropriate." She tolerated the woman's faith and continuous pronouncements about it, but this…

Pete's chin neared his collar, his mouth had fallen so far open.

How embarrassing.

Unperturbed, Miss Lydia patted his shoulder. "We'll talk later. I need to get my other daughter out of the car." With that, she turned on her heel and headed toward the deck stairs.

Steam receding, Skye followed. "Let me. You don't need to get drenched." And sicker.

Whatever ailed Miss Lydia, getting rained on couldn't help.

"Are you up to it, dear one?" The usual compassionate grin lifted Miss Lydia's cheeks.

"I am. I promise."

"I packed suitcases in the trunk."

"Suitcases?" They shouldn't stay here.

"We can stay as long as you need us."

"You didn't have to. I—"

"The Lord prepared us for your accident." Her gaze nailed Pete. "He's in control. You'll see."

Rain rolling down her cheeks, Skye stared as Miss Lydia slipped into the house. She needed to get a move on. No telling what would come out of Miss Lydia's mouth next.

At the car with the dogs rubbing against her legs, Skye knocked on the window before opening the door to the back seat. "Hello. I heard there might be a pretty birdie in here."

"Skye! I've missed you." A smile lit the child's whole face and sent a spike to pierce Skye's heart.

"I've missed you too." Night and day.

The dogs whimpered happy squeals. "The boys are happy to see you."

Sparrow latched her arms around Skye. "I'm happy too." The precious girl planted a kiss on Skye's cheek and held her there a moment, that little girl smell of pancakes and outdoors filling her senses. If only circumstances hadn't been so cruel… She shook off the pointless train of thought. "We better go inside. I heard you brought luggage. Are y'all staying?"

"I hope so." Sparrow held open her mouth to catch raindrops, reminding Skye of her sister, Star. So alive and full of life.

Wouldn't she love for Sparrow and Miss Lydia to live here through the summer?

Fear and gloom dried Skye's mouth—snaked around her throat. The risk could prove too dangerous.

~~~

Miss Lydia's brown eyes regarded Pete, as if she could see straight into his soul.

"Pete the rock Thompson, tell me what you do to make a living," the eccentric woman asked.

"I'm a charter fisherman."

A huge grin lifted her full lips. "Peter the fisherman? Do you have a brother named Andrew?"

"Oddly, I do. Got ragged about it plenty growing up." He shrugged. "Dad's a minister."

"And you?" Head tilted, her gaze bore into him. "Do you ever think about catching men's souls rather than fish?"

"I try to do both when I can."

"You are *the one* then." Her head bobbed, and she mumbled something toward the ceiling.

The haunting words from the Voice jarred Pete, this time from a person standing right in front of him. The air in his lungs froze. "What did you—?"

"I can feel it's you." She wagged a finger at him. "My girl, Skye, is fragile. She needs you. Don't let her go, you hear?"

The words poked around in his heart, pricked goosebumps on his arms. What did all this mean?

His head swam with questions.

Lord, help me understand.

"Daddy, can I come out now?" Olivia hollered from the place he'd left her in the back of the house.

He snapped from his stupor. "Yes. Sorry, princess."

He'd been so distracted by this unexpected visitor that he'd forgotten.

Olivia ran in, grabbed his legs, and stared up at the stranger
~~~

standing there.

"Well, hello." The woman extended her hand. "I'm Miss Lydia Sharp, but you can call me Miss Lydia. Who might you be?"

"Olivia." His daughter offered a shy smile and accepted the handshake. "Are you Skye's friend?"

"I'm her mother."

Forehead crinkling, Olivia scanned her. "People say I look like my momma, but Skye doesn't look much like you."

"Olivia. That's not polite."

Although the differences between Skye and Miss Lydia's skin color were obvious, warmth rushed to Pete's cheeks. Kids could be blunt.

Lydia struggled to kneel to look at Olivia eye-to-eye. "Sometimes when your first mother goes away, another mother steps in to love children in her place."

"I'd like one of those." Olivia cocked her head. "How do I get another momma?"

Pete's throat tightened. Had he been selfish to keep Olivia to himself all these years?

Maybe. But not every woman would love someone else's child as her own. And that would be worse than not having a mother at all.

Chapter 9

How long did Miss Lydia plan to stay? Rolling one of the larger suitcases, Skye ambled behind Sparrow toward the door. Thank goodness, the rain had lessened to a sprinkle for the moment, or she'd be even more drenched. Sparrow's straight blond hair had grown longer, and her tanned arms proved she still loved to play outdoors. How hard was that on Miss Lydia if she'd not been feeling well? Taller and thinner, Sparrow had turned nine already. Time passed so quickly, it seemed. A hollowness cloaked Skye's every molecule. How many milestones had she missed living so far away?

It couldn't be helped, though. They were together for now.

Inside, Skye took one look at Pete and halted. Why had his expression become so mangled?

"What's going on?" Skye directed the question to Miss Lydia. What in the world had the woman said? Though awkward, usually Miss Lydia's ruminations didn't cause sadness. Yet, the corners of Pete's lips tugged low.

Struggling to push to her feet in front of Pete's daughter, Miss Lydia smiled. "Olivia and I were discussing how adoption works."

Razors of anxiety sliced into Skye's already aching muscles. "Why?"

"This smart girl noticed how different we look for a mother and daughter." She pointed to Sparrow. "And surely she'll notice the same with Sparrow. My other adopted daughter." She directed that last part to Olivia and Pete.

"Adoption's no biggie." Sparrow puffed air through her teeth. "Lots of people are adopted these days. Even from different countries." Her nose crinkled as she looked Skye up and down. "What on God's green earth are you wearing?"

"Sparrow." Miss Lydia's tone scolded while Skye held in a chuckle. "She's made an older friend in the homeschool group who's a little mouthy."

"Sorry," Sparrow huffed, then pushed a fist to her hip. "But that outfit looks ridiculous."

Skye glanced down at the rather large, dripping purple velour jogging suit. The fabric somehow both clung to her and hung from her like the skin of an old elephant that had lost weight. She couldn't argue with Sparrow's assessment. "My clothes didn't survive the accident, so I borrowed this."

"It was Nana's." Olivia giggled.

"A purple manatee got her." Sparrow snorted.

Skye rolled her eyes but smiled. It might be a little funny. Other than the reason for her limited choices. "I'll change later."

"I can get their other suitcases." Even Pete snickered, and laugh lines lifted the dark scruff on his jaw. "Nana might have a matching green one of those you can exchange for in the back."

"Thanks a lot," Skye deadpanned. She'd let him carry their bags while she changed again. "You'll need the keys. I locked it." As she handed them to him, the door opened.

"Do I hear someone giggling in here?" Hope burst through as if she lived in this house, wearing a bright turquoise rain jacket and matching shiny clogs. She held a large white paper bag and a covered ceramic mug. "Oh." Her head rotated as she took in everyone. "I'm Hope." A cautious smile lifted her rouged and powdered cheeks.

In fact, all her makeup had been perfectly applied—like yesterday—and none had been smeared by the weather.

How did she do that?

Miss Lydia held out her hand. "I'm—"

A knock rattled the door hinges.

Skye's eyes widened as Hope turned to answer it. Again, as if she lived here. This place might as well have a revolving door. Except, she definitely didn't want anyone else coming and going. Already the full room threatened to suffocate her.

Caleb stood, dripping, in a light green Columbia weather jacket, also holding a white paper bag.

"Hey." Hope laughed. "Looks like we had the same idea." She shook her sack in front of him. "I stopped at the bakery too."

"Oh, well…I…" He scuffled his work boots. "I can go…" He focused on Skye. "How are you feeling today?"

"Are you the paramedic?" Miss Lydia waved. "Come in and check out my girl. Please. I'm sure we will devour your pastries, kind sir."

Perfect. Skye held in a groan. Now they all stared at her and the weird dripping outfit. "Let me change out of the Purple People Eater before we have any more examinations."

Both girls burst into giggles, and the adults might have, too, but Skye bounded down the hall without looking back.

Being around all these people went against her natural inclinations. The inclination to be alone. She was used to alone, other than the necessary interactions with fellow marine biologists. She preferred alone, even better if she was alone enjoying nature. When outdoors, she sensed a Presence that led her to new treasures, often guiding her to injured animals needing help.

Probably a creation of her imagination, and of course,

she'd never tell anyone that tidbit, especially Miss Lydia. That would start a sermon series for sure.

In the back of the house, Skye thumbed through clothes designed and sized for a woman much older and larger than herself. Indeed, there were plenty of colorful house dresses, sweatsuits, and knit tops with matching elastic-waist pants. Finally, she chose a red striped short-sleeve top and blue paisley lounge pants that had a drawstring she could pull tight enough to stay up.

After stripping off the wet velour, she stretched muscles which burned with each movement. Her head joined the aching, and a bit of nausea made her stomach quiver. She'd keep that to herself because it was probably stress and not a concussion. As quickly as she could manage, she dressed and prepared mentally to go back to the living room.

This would be a long day. At least Miss Lydia could help with reordering as much as possible of Skye's life before work on Monday.

~~~

The bakery never disappointed. At the kitchen table, sitting with an extraordinarily quiet Caleb, Pete sank his teeth into the cream cheese Danish. His favorite, though everything the specialty restaurant sold tasted like love in a crust.

A little guilt niggled since Hope had purchased him a hot coffee but hadn't gotten one for Skye, claiming she didn't know if Skye drank the dark nectar they brewed.

But Hope had placed an extra single-serve pot and pods in her SUV in case Skye did. Now, Miss Lydia sat on the couch, drinking a cup and chatting with Hope about purchasing cleaning supplies.

They'd already formed a plan of attack for the job, which seemed to involve all the people currently in the house—
~~~

himself, Caleb, and Olivia included until the next charter. Maybe the rain would pass, and he could pick up a few passengers after lunch. Then they could make a little money.

The girls giggled from their perch at the table, both their mouths circled with pastry sugar. Too bad no one had bought any protein. The sweets would have them bouncing off the wall. Pete turned to see what had them tickled again. Hopefully not more of the big dog passing gas. That obscenity had burnt his nostrils too many times today already.

He choked on his coffee when Skye walked farther into the room, her cheeks pinking almost to the color of the red on the large shirt of Nana's. This outfit hung more loosely than the other, maybe looked more ridiculous. But in a cute way on this bashful woman.

"Child." Miss Lydia took Skye in. "Pete brought in the other suitcases, and the gray soft-sided one has two outfits I bought for you last week at a clearance sale. Praise the Good Lord for His tender care. Let me roll it back so you can dress like the beautiful woman you are." Miss Lydia lifted herself from the sofa with a moan.

"I've got it." Skye and Pete spoke in unison, her face crimson now and his heating at the new nickname the woman had chosen for him.

He stood and made his way to the luggage. "You look like you're feeling stiff."

More giggles from the girls.

"Not stiff, just silly," the one they called Sparrow quipped. Was that her real name or a nickname? She seemed more of a firecracker than a tiny bird.

"Young lady." Miss Lydia raised one brow and eyed the girl. "Be nice to your…Skye."

Your Skye? Adoption must make the connection awkward.

"Yes, ma'am," Sparrow said, seemingly repentant.

"I can manage." Skye grasped the handle of the bag and disappeared again.

Pete couldn't blame her. He'd like to do the same. Thunder cracked outside and rattled the house. More rain echoed on the metal roof. No excuse to leave any time soon.

Once they'd eaten their fill and Hope had made the supply run, the cleaning began. Pete bent over the tub with a scrub brush and cleanser while Caleb wiped down the bathroom counters and mirrors. Seemed they'd received the dirty jobs, but both were well accustomed to cleaning up after customers on the charter. Too often they ended up with men who missed their target. Then there were the ones who found out too late that boating made them seasick. This housework felt like a ship on glassy seas comparatively.

In no time, they had the lavatories in shape and headed toward the living room to check in for more orders from Hope.

They passed Skye, who was cleaning in one of the bedrooms. In the living room, the girls played on the floor with two small toy unicorns and the dogs. They jabbered away as if they'd known each other their entire lives. Hopefully, the sassy talk wouldn't rub off on Olivia in one day.

That was all he and Olivia would be there, right? Now that help had arrived, and the place was on its way to habitable.

In fact, the kitchen gleamed and smelled of pine. The dishwasher churned. Though the bedroom closets and dressers still needed to be cleaned out, this area had been transformed to almost like when Nana and Pops still lived here.

That was before age, Alzheimer's, and diabetes had landed them in an assisted living facility. Then a virus had taken them both home only a month apart. The same facility where his own mother now recuperated from her stroke. Her health issues arrived much too soon for her age.

Please, don't let us lose Mom yet. Please heal her.

"Oh!" Miss Lydia gripped the back of a kitchen chair, wobbling its legs.

In an instant, Caleb rushed to her side, supported her, and guided her to the couch. "Are you dizzy?"

She placed her elbows on her knees, her head in her hands. "Just a sinking spell."

"Momma? Are you sick again?" Sparrow scrambled up from the floor and climbed to sit beside the woman. "Do you need a wet cloth or some ice chips?"

"It'll pass, dear one."

Worry twisted Caleb's forehead.

"Does this happen often?" he asked.

"Not much." Miss Lydia's voice became a whisper.

"It does too." Tears coated Sparrow's eyes, and her lip quivered. "She went to the doctor last week and won't tell me why."

The child was obviously terrified. He knew that feeling—had seen that expression in the mirror when Kenzie had grown weaker each day.

"What's going on in here?" Skye poked her head in, then took one look at Miss Lydia and darted to her other side. "I knew it. You are sick. What did the tests say?"

"No results yet." The barely audible answer ushered in a thick silence and pimpled Pete's skin with goosebumps.

They need you. They need a rock.

The words blazed through his mind, and he let his stinging eyes shut. He couldn't battle the truth of the facts before him. Skye and her unusual family did need someone. A rock.

Something inside him screamed that Miss Lydia was

gravely unwell. As ill-equipped as he was to be their *someone*, he could no longer deny this calling.

But it didn't mean he'd ever have feelings beyond Christian charity for any of them. It didn't mean they had to be anything more than a temporary project.

Chapter 10

"I'm much better now." Miss Lydia sat up straight and tidied her shirt.

"Take it slowly." Skye studied the woman who had rescued her when she'd needed it most, the woman who had held her together in those dark days after Momma's death and beyond. The skin on Miss Lydia's face sagged as if she'd lost weight, but her abdomen appeared inordinately distended. Was she accumulating fluid there? If so, that, plus the possible jaundice Skye had noticed earlier, meant Miss Lydia's condition could be serious.

Though Skye's studies involved illnesses of marine mammals rather than humans, she fumbled through possible diseases that came to mind. The best scenario might be gallstones. Even that would require surgery. And someone to look after Sparrow, plus Miss Lydia.

A pit of dread wormed through Skye. How could that care be coordinated with her work schedule?

"You've had your blood sugar checked recently, and you're not diabetic?" Caleb still sat beside Miss Lydia, even after he'd checked her vitals and fully questioned her. The shy man seemed caring and thorough. Or zealous about his volunteer paramedic-fireman position. Qualities to be admired, either way.

Hope gathered her designer purse, moved close to Pete, and took his elbow.

"Why don't you and I go to the store and buy a few groceries? Pops was diabetic, so you'll know what to pick up, just in case." Hope stared at Pete with puppy eyes.

Really? The woman was aggressive in her pursuit. They'd already ruled out diabetes. Meanwhile, Caleb's expression wilted.

What a murky unrequited love triangle these three humans had created.

"I can take Miss Lydia's car to buy food." Skye shooed away Hope's suggestion. "Y'all have lives to get on with. We've monopolized too much of your time." Though the cleaning had already taxed her achy muscles. Surely, the soreness would work out soon. Monday, she'd probably only be doing a tour of the lab and computer work, but her job as a marine biologist would require physical strength when she eventually went into the field. She needed to be full speed soon.

"Can I go?" Sparrow jumped up and down. "I want to pick out snacks."

"Me too!" Olivia spoke louder than she had since Skye had met the child. The two girls sure had become fast friends.

"That would allow Miss Lydia a bit of quiet to rest. I'll have to borrow a credit card until I have replacements."

As much as she'd wanted everyone to leave, telling the little girls no proved impossible for her. The thought of being recognized with Sparrow in tow knotted the muscles in Skye's neck. She could throw on her cap just in case and buy a new pair of sunglasses while they were out.

"My pocketbook is on the counter, dear one." Miss Lydia pointed. "What's mine is yours." She focused on Sparrow. "Obey Skye, follow our rules, and remember, you're allowed only one selection of junky food, so choose well, okay?"

"Yes, ma'am."

"Can I go, too, Daddy? Please." Olivia stood at Sparrow's side, hope widening her big green eyes.

"Skye already has a lot to deal with today, princess. She doesn't need an extra person to watch."

"Awww." Both girls dragged out the grimace, but Olivia added, "Pretty please, with sugar on top?"

The corners of Pete's lips lifted, and he shook his head before kneeling next to her. "You know you're Daddy's girl, right?"

"Yes, sir."

"You can go *if* I come along, too, but we'll need to head home soon after. That's the deal, squeal."

He wanted to come? Why? Maybe he just couldn't say no to his daughter. Or he was scared to let Olivia go with a virtual stranger. Yet, that meant spending more time with him. She'd already been around him more than any man outside of work in like…ever.

Lips twisting, Olivia considered the compromise a minute, then sighed. "O-kay."

"I'll go to the boutique if I'm not needed." Long lashes batting, Hope popped on a strained smile and made her exit while Caleb's sad eyes tracked her all the way out the door.

"Sweetheart, how about you stay here?" Miss Lydia patted Caleb's hand. "While you keep an eye on me, we can talk about what's got your lip dragging the ground and how to heal you too."

The man's jaw dropped as he stared at Miss Lydia, but then the small tilt in his chin offered an agreement.

Oh, Miss Lydia.

The precious lady never pulled any punches or avoided the truth. Caleb better hang on tight.

Pete's blue gaze bounced to Skye, but all she had to offer was a shrug.

"Are we riding together or taking separate vehicles?" The sooner they left, the sooner they could get back and rescue Caleb.

"I'll drive," Pete offered. "Let me get an umbrella. I don't want you sopping wet again and having to come up with another outfit."

She couldn't stop a smirk. But he was correct. She'd hate to see what else she'd have to change into, even if Miss Lydia had bought her a few new clothes. The outfits might fit better, but the older woman definitely had a different sense of style. None of the selections would be the practical work clothes Skye would choose, the kinds that didn't call attention to her.

The less anyone noticed her, the better.

~~~

The wipers thrashed as Pete checked the weather on his phone and read messages from customers before he started the truck. The rest of the day, storms would rock the Gulf. No outings this afternoon, but maybe tomorrow after early church.

"Daddy, are we leaving soon?"

He glanced at Olivia in his rearview. "Just checking on things before I start driving." Turning to Skye, he offered an apologetic look. "Sorry."

"Not necessary." Her caramel eyes met his. "You have a business to run. The weather's not cooperating, I assume."

"Not at all. Passengers don't fare well in choppy seas or deep swells like they're predicting today." He cranked the truck and backed out of the drive. "I guess you've ridden out a few of those on your research trips."

"More than I can count. The seas have a mind of their own."
~~~

"How do they have a mind, Skye?" Sparrow had good ears.

"It's a figure of speech. The seas don't literally have a brain." Skye twisted to face the girl. "I meant that storms blow up unexpectedly on the Gulf or the Atlantic. Sometimes we get caught in rough water when I'm at work."

"But you're safe?" The girl's voice cracked.

"I'm as safe as we are riding in the car or crossing the street."

"You had a wreck, though," Olivia said. "Are we safe now?"

Pete held in a groan. Skye needed help in the art of talking to young children, that much was obvious. "God's in control of all of creation. Jesus calmed the seas and the wind with His words, *Peace, be still.* So, we don't need to worry here or out on a boat or anywhere. He has us in His hands."

Quiet permeated in the back seat, but probably not for long. Thankfully, on this small island, the store was close. He pulled into the lot and parked. Maybe they could change the subject once they went in. When he opened Olivia's door, he made eye contact with both girls. "If we're ever afraid, we can talk to God. He'll be with us."

Sparrow gave a dramatic nod as Skye opened the back door to help her out before rain drenched them all. "Momma talks to God *all the time.*"

Pete smiled at her. "Miss Lydia seems like a really good mother. Let's go in." He unbuckled his daughter's straps.

"But she's sick." The girl's words came out barely above a whisper.

"My momma died." Olivia wasn't helping matters. When had she become so obsessed with Kenzie's death? Maybe something had happened at school?

Once he'd helped her out, he took her hand and rounded

the car to run under the awning.

Skye had done the same. Rain splattered them, but not too badly.

"Will Momma die too, Skye?" Sparrow asked.

Fear hollowed out Skye's expression, paled her skin, and appeared to swallow her whole being.

"Will she?" Sparrow pressed.

Blinking, Skye regained her focus. "All life ends at some point, but I'll talk to her doctors. We'll find out her condition and how to best treat it. She'll live longer that way."

A cloud of doom descended. Why would Skye give such a depressing answer to a child? Pete scrambled to come up with a wise and hope-filled comeback. Nothing came to dispute the truth of what Skye said.

Anything, God?

"Do you girls like beach toys?" He heard the words come from his mouth, but hadn't known he'd speak them. "If y'all are good, we can buy one to play with when the sun comes out."

"Yay!" they answered in unison, and the heavy dread wisped back to wherever it had descended from.

Inside the store, the girls chattered and skipped down the aisles, looking at the peculiar array of wares. From hardware to groceries, boating needs to souvenirs, this store provided a little bit of everything. Being the only grocer on the island, it had to.

At the meat counter, Pete took in Skye's profile beneath the baseball cap she'd donned and pulled low before they left. She'd tucked her hair back up too. For a pretty woman, she sure tried to hide herself. The situation with her, Sparrow, and Miss Lydia piqued his curiosity. He'd love to ask how they all ended up together, but it was none of his business.

"What is it?" Skye's shy gaze lifted to meet his. "Am I taking too long?"

"No hurry." He shouldn't be staring. "It's not easy finding meat that came from something with no eyelashes, I suppose."

Her lips parted with a small laugh, which gave him an inordinate amount of pleasure. "Miss Lydia and Sparrow aren't as picky. And like I said, it's preferred but not required."

"I'm sure there's a story there."

"Dissections. Biology. Anatomy. Any of those classes." She lifted one shoulder. "Crazy, but I sometimes picture the animals with eyelashes staring up at me when I eat."

"But you stuck with it."

"Yes, and I loved the idea of veterinary medicine, but I landed an enticing scholarship in marine biology. Plus, vets often have to deal with the public, depending on their position. Not my preference. I love being out on the water. In nature."

Pete bobbed his head. "I get everything you just said."

"You do?" Her eyes widened.

"Growing up as a preacher's kid, I learned some people could be…cruel. I'd already fallen in love with going out with Pops on the charter anyway."

Her expression soured at the mention of his career. Or was it the preacher kid thing? Or both?

She made a few selections, threw them in the basket, and turned, her head swiveling up and down the row behind them. "Where are Sparrow and Olivia?"

Panic swept over Pete. How had he allowed himself to become so distracted? "I'll go right, you go left." They had to find them. If something happened to his little girl, he'd never forgive himself.

Chapter 11

The pulse of Skye's heart flailed like a fish on a line. How had she lost Sparrow already?

"We'll find them." Pete's gentle nudge to her elbow set her in motion down the store aisles, searching one by one.

Dauphin Island hosted plenty of tourists in the spring, and any sort of monster might be lurking. A multitude of horrific scenarios unleashed a deluge of panic. Because Skye knew full well how cruel people could be.

Her chest locked tight as she searched, finding no sign of the girls, only one greasy-haired man studying types of beer. His gaze slid her way, and her brain stuttered, but her steps sped up.

The aisle brimming with sugared cereals hid no small girls looking for treats, nor did she find them digging through the cookie packages the next row over. After another pass of the canned foods row, ribbons of fear sliced through Skye's gut. She rounded another aisle of goods, and Pete's fearful eyes slammed into hers.

He hadn't found them either. "This way, I bet." He turned toward the front of the store. "There's a little nook near the checkout counter with souvenirs."

Breathe, Skye. In through the nose, out through the mouth.

The last thing she needed to do was pass out from holding her breath.

"Stranger danger!" Sparrow's voice rang out and clamped down Skye's ability to exhale.

In front of her, Pete sprinted toward the sound. "Olivia?"

She raced behind him, his form hazy from her lack of oxygen.

They neared the glass entrance doors, and a man in khaki shorts, blue polo, and sunglasses quickly shuffled out of the store.

When they reached the area filled with beach supplies, T-shirts, and toys, Sparrow was pointing a finger at Olivia. "We aren't supposed to talk to strangers. Momma says bad people use treats and tricks to steal children."

Relief flooded Skye. They were still here. Still safe.

"Olivia, you can't leave me like that." Pete knelt beside the girls, his voice tight with strain. "What happened?"

Olivia's face crumpled, and her bewildered eyes filled with tears. "I wanted to show Sparrow the beach toys."

"I told her we were supposed to stay with an adult." Sparrow lifted one hand with an expression that read exasperation. "Then that man talked to her, so I yelled like Momma told me."

Pride swelled within Skye. Miss Lydia had taught Sparrow well. While Skye hated for Sparrow to live in fear, a healthy dose of caution was necessary. No matter the age.

"I'm sorry, Daddy." Olivia's lip quivered.

He wrapped his arms around her and held her close. "I'm just glad you're okay. You have to stay where Daddy can see you. Some people aren't nice, and we may not know it by looking at them."

Truer words had never been spoken. Like Denny's parents. "You did well, Sparrow." Skye smiled at her, and Sparrow launched over to take Skye's hand.

"Can we still pick out a toy for the beach?"

Could they?

Or would Pete not want to reward the behavior? She slid a questioning glance his way.

Easing back, he cradled Olivia's cheeks in his hands. "Promise you won't leave Daddy again?" Lines crinkled his cheeks when he gave her a tender look. "At least until you're twenty-one. Or maybe thirty would be better."

"I promise." She gave a solemn nod.

"It looks like I have some wisdom to impart later today." He directed that comment to Skye, then stood and pointed at the toys. "You girls can each pick out one thing. My treat."

"Yay!" The girls clapped and began running their fingers over the various choices, chattering like nothing scary had ever happened.

How quickly they moved on, while Skye's insides still roiled. She turned to the man. "That lesson is really important for young girls, Pete. It's vital they know who to trust and how to ask for help." Skye kept her voice low. "It's a dangerous world." She shuddered as unwanted images crashed over her.

"You're right." Peering at her as if he could see her tainted past, his Adam's apple rose and fell with a hard swallow. "I hate even the thought of the evil some men do. Maybe I'll call my buddy at the police department, just in case that guy was a creep, and give him a heads up."

"The store might have a camera or something."

He considered her idea. "The man could have been trying to be friendly, but I'll ask before we leave."

Friendly? Doubtful. Pete must be extremely naïve.

"You don't have to buy anything for Sparrow. I have Miss Lydia's—"

"Groceries and everything on me today." His blue gaze locked on Skye. "As a welcome to the island and an I-hope-things-go-better-from-now-on treat."

Even accidental eye contact with men normally set off warning flares inside her. *Don't let them see you. Don't let them get close.* But somehow, in this moment, the kindness glowing in Pete's aquamarine eyes soothed her. If he wanted to buy a basket of groceries and an overpriced sandcastle kit, so be it.

As long as he didn't think she owed him something for all he'd done.

As if he'd read her mind, he added, "I'll feel better knowing you have all you need before I leave this afternoon. If my mother were well enough to be here, I know she'd do the same. Probably more. She's a lot like your Miss Lydia."

Maybe he'd been raised right then. She supposed it was possible some men had been. "If you insist."

"I do." His whole face lit up when he smiled, and Skye struggled to pull her focus back to the girls.

"It's so hard to choose just one." Sparrow blew out her cheeks.

"Am I big enough to play this with you, Daddy?" Olivia held a paddle ball set.

"We can try it." He nodded and then teased, "I bet you'll eventually beat me, but I might win a lot at first."

Once Sparrow finally snagged a turtle-shaped sand sculpting kit, Pete paid for everything. They stepped outside to find the rain had slackened, and a milky fog blanketed the island. The murkiness veiled the bridge that had almost become her grave, making both it and the water below disappear into the mist. At least they wouldn't be drenched getting back in the truck.

On the short drive to the house, the girls continued their easy conversation, while Skye and Pete rode in silence.

His jaw worked. Was he thinking about how to explain to his daughter about the predators she might face?

Olivia was still such a sweet child, while Sparrow seemed to have grown up so much over the past year. Even since Christmas, when Miss Lydia had come to Florida for their holiday visit, the child had become spunkier. Maybe that was a good thing. Sparrow would be strong like Star instead of the soiled, scared doormat Skye had been.

It's not your fault, child. None of it.

Miss Lydia's constant assurance echoed. Over and over, the dear woman had reminded Skye that nothing Denny did, nor the final choice her mother had made, were caused by anything but their own sicknesses.

But the guilt still gnawed at Skye's very marrow.

"I'll unload the groceries then get out of your hair." Pete's voice broke into her self-destructive thoughts. "I'll give y'all my number in case you need anything."

She'd rather he didn't, but he *was* her landlord since his mother had become ill.

Having his number would be necessary.

Parked, he climbed out, helped Olivia unbuckle, and then grabbed the atrocious plastic bags grocery stores used. Those things were bad for the environment, but her reusable ones had gone up in smoke. Skye forced herself to move and pick up some too.

Inside the house, Miss Lydia turned from where she and Caleb stood wiping down the refrigerator. "Hey, precious ones. I feel much better now, and we've got this baby ready to hold the goodies you bought."

Caleb smiled brightly at them. Miss Lydia had a special way of cheering even the saddest people up.

Arms held out to take the bags, she headed their way. "Let's see what you bought. Caleb tells me church starts at sunrise, so we'll need to be up early tomorrow. He gave me directions, and it sounds wonderful. I'll go ahead and plan our breakfast."

Church? Here? Couldn't Miss Lydia take one day off? Skye handed a bag over but kept the others to unload herself. "You haven't been feeling well. Maybe you should take tomorrow to rest."

"Praising the Lord is both restful and energizing for these old bones. And I bet Sparrow will love their church out on the beach."

"Can I take my new toy Mr. Pete bought me?" Sparrow held up the sand kit.

"How nice of him." A thoughtful, yet serious expression lifted Miss Lydia's brows. "I guess as long as you can pay attention to the service, you can bring it."

"I can. I promise."

"No need to promise. Let your yes be a true yes and your no be honest too."

Sparrow shook her head in a way that said she'd heard these words many times. "I remember."

"We'll see you at sunrise then." Pete placed the rest of the groceries on the counter.

"Seems so." Skye held in a sigh. It would just be one Sunday. She'd do this for Miss Lydia.

~~~

A chill clung to the salty morning air, but the sun's fiery orange rays already burned magenta strands across the eastern waves of the Gulf's waters. In his canvas lounge chair, Pete read over his lesson notes once more as fishermen and other friends settled onto towels or beach chairs on the cool sand.

Sleepy-eyed, Olivia sat on a towel, holding her favorite blanket and doll close. Caleb read his Bible beside them. A nearby scrappy palm rustled in a light gust of wind, and Pete's
~~~

fingers thrummed an anxious beat on his thigh. A rare case of nerves over teaching today had sprouted as soon as he'd left Nana and Pop's house yesterday afternoon.

He'd chosen his topics for the year back in January and had begun preparing his talk well in advance, so being apprehensive made no sense. The presence of Skye and her family shouldn't change anything. Visitors often joined their small motley crew. Why should these three be any different?

Maybe it was the displeased press of Skye's mouth when she'd agreed to come.

What did she have against church? Or was it God? And how could he reach her, if that was what God was calling him to do?

He'd been through some church-hurt himself—the gossip as he'd grown up under the microscope. People criticized his father or his sermons, how Pete and his brother behaved in Sunday school, and even the casual clothes his mother wore to Wednesday night Bible study.

It had felt like church-goers thought everything about a minister's life—and their family's lives—fair game for examination. They had to be perfect. And honestly, Dad was about as perfect as a person could be in Pete's eyes. Mom too. But Pete had made his share of mistakes, particularly in his junior and senior years of high school.

If not for God leading him to Kenzie that first day of college in Birmingham, his story might have ended up very differently. Which might have been better for Kenzie in the long run.

No. Don't you ever think that way. Kenzie's admonishment from her hospital bed returned to him.

Trust God's plans, she'd said again and again. *He has a grander purpose and a longer timeline.*

His gaze fell to his beautiful Olivia, her angelic face and soft curls falling down her back. *Their* beautiful Olivia. Though his heart had splintered into a million pieces over Kenzie's choice to forgo treatment during her pregnancy to make certain nothing damaged their baby, now he could put himself in Kenzie's place. He'd easily give up his life for his little girl.

"Hello, Peter the rock. We're here to worship." Miss Lydia's distinct voice came from behind him, and he turned.

Still a few yards away, she trudged slowly in the damp sand. Skye and Sparrow followed, holding hands. Both had their hair pulled back, but Skye had tucked hers under her baseball cap as usual. They looked cute together like that, similar sloped noses, the curve of their chins…

Skye spotted him, and her brows arched.

Shoot. What was wrong with him? He needed to quit gawking and get started. He motioned toward empty beach chairs. "Welcome. I put a couple of extra seats on the other side of Caleb, and I'm sure Olivia can make room for Sparrow."

Releasing Skye's hand, the girl ran over and plopped down. "I like your doll. What's her name?"

Caleb stood and showed the ladies to their chairs while the girls chattered.

Pete spoke loudly, so that everyone gathered could hear. "We have a few guests here today. Introduce yourselves when we finish if you have time." Pete scanned the small group for any other newbies. Not seeing any, he glanced at Skye. The way she'd folded into herself at his announcement pinched his heart.

Should he not have said anything?

But beside her, Miss Lydia grinned and waved at the circle of people, as if they were the best of friends.

"I've got our song for the day," one of the younger guys said and then began an easy-to-follow worship tune.

Thank goodness, someone had given him time to collect his wits.

Help me speak Your word, Lord, the words they need to hear.

The song finished, and he cleared his throat. "We're pretty casual here, so chime in if you feel led. We've been going through the fruits of the Spirit, and we've come to self-control. That's a loaded one." He puffed out a breath. "There's so much to control—our thoughts, our words, our desires, our bodies. It's like trying to pick up an armload of water."

"Not easy," one of the men said with a chuckle.

"Right. You may get a few drops, but much more escapes. It's simply impossible—but for God."

Pete pointed toward the sunrise radiating a blast of colors beneath a swath of wispy clouds. "In the beginning, the world God started was more perfect than we can imagine. The relationship between man, woman, and God was perfect too. But, like all of us, those people made bad choices. The relationship broke, and the weed was planted. Like a biological weapon, evil entered and wreaked havoc on all creation, causing pain."

"Help us, Lord," a woman whispered.

"People allow their appetites and addictions and lusts to hurt each other—to hurt themselves. Our bodies fail." His voice cracked, thinking of Kenzie, Nana, Pops, and now Mom. "We lose people. But this is not our eternal home."

"Amen," Miss Lydia said, and Pete couldn't help checking Skye's expression.

Her eyes shone in the expanding light.

Were those tears, or was he simply seeing the reflection of the glowing sky?

"Yesterday, I had a situation that reminded me that there may be evil close by. In fact, it scared me."

Her gaze slid to meet his.

"We have to be on guard for the evil on the outside. But we also must watch out for the evil battles within. As Christians, we're to be different from those who allow themselves to be led by their own emotions. Only by seeking God daily and walking with Him can we develop that spiritual muscle of self-control."

Pete forced himself to break from the hold of her gaze to check the expressions of the rest of the group.

After expounding a few more minutes on the subject, he ended. Shorter than he'd intended—he must have forgotten half of it—but many of these guys went to work on the water every morning, even on Sunday. "Chime in with your thoughts, then Caleb will lead our prayer."

Once they'd finished, Caleb scooted out to finish readying the boat for their passengers, who would arrive soon.

Miss Lydia stood and gave Pete a pointed look. "Your fellowship is worthy, but I believe you could share your special gift of preaching on a bigger scale. But you know that, don't you?"

His stomach tightened. He'd heard that bit of advice before, but he had no desire to go back to living in that glass house. "Fishing brings me peace of mind."

She gave a sad nod, then busied herself meeting the people that lingered. Skye, on the other hand, stayed seated, her elbows on her knees, staring at the sand.

What should he do?

All of creation groans. Romans eight.

What did that chapter have to do with the situation? Was he supposed to bring it up to Skye?

After taking a deep breath, he stood and took the few steps over to her chair with heavy feet and slicking palms. He eased into the chair Miss Lydia had vacated. "So, this may not be your thing, but I was thinking of a scripture in Romans."

Looking around, she seemed to be making sure he was talking to her, then she stared at him, eyes wide. "Okay."

"In Chapter eight of Romans, the writer talks about how all of creation is groaning, waiting to be freed from its bondage of decay."

Lips parting, her forehead knotted.

Probably because he sounded nuts.

"Um…" he sputtered. "Maybe read it, and if I see you again, we could talk about it?"

Like that would happen. He doubted she'd look it up, but he'd tried. Hadn't he?

Chapter 12

When one loses their wallet plus almost all their possessions, there are way too many calls to make and details to remember. So many passwords.

Sitting at the kitchen table with Miss Lydia, Skye checked her to-do list again and fought to keep a positive outlook. It would be too easy to let dark thoughts bring on a bout of depression if she didn't. That was the last thing any of them needed.

While she had Miss Lydia's phone, Skye needed to get as much completed as possible. If only she had her laptop, but that had been lost too. At least she'd stored most everything in the cloud. She could replace the computer as soon as she had access to her accounts. A newer model would be nice, and insurance should cover most of the cost. Eventually.

Tapping her head with the pen, she sighed. "I've gotten in touch with my credit card company, the bank, and the pharmacy. I sent a list to the insurance company, and I requested a new driver's license. But since my permanent address is in Florida, the replacements will go east first and then get forwarded. I can't rent a car without my license, but the island is small. I can rent or buy a bike to go to work until it comes. If you can loan me the money, of course."

"You know I will, but are you sure you don't want to keep my car? I could rent one for a week or so." Miss Lydia took a sip from a glass of water, then added, "Or I can stay here until you get things settled."

In the living room, Sparrow sat on the floor, coaxing Rocky out from under the couch with a kitty treat. Despite his salty personality, the one-eyed cat had never bitten or scratched Sparrow. They seemed to have an understanding, and maybe Sparrow had a way with animals too. Beside her, the dogs patiently watched, salivating and wagging their tails. As if they hadn't already had four treats in the past few hours.

Dampness misted Skye's view of them, and sadness weighted her body like an anchor. As much as she'd love for both Miss Lydia and Sparrow to stay here with her—forever—it was safer if they went back to their normal lives without her. Unless Miss Lydia needed help.

"Do you need to stay here?" She studied her dear friend's gaunt face. "For me to help you?"

"Precious, don't worry yourself over me." She patted Skye's hand. "I bet that doctor will call tomorrow with a prescription to fix my problems. Plus, you know my sister is close by. Gertie bought a cute little house over in Spanish Fort."

"Yeah, but with Sparrow and homeschooling…" For a woman Lydia's age—even a strong woman—raising an active youngster like Sparrow could be a challenge. "Your sister has her own grandkids who drop in. She doesn't need to worry about Sparrow."

"Tell you what, if anything happens that causes concern, I'll call you. Or Gertie will."

Skye let her head dip. "I really need to get a phone. That's one item I haven't figured out yet, since I'd have to go off the island to get one. Maybe I can order a replacement online with my provider somehow."

"Take mine, and I'll add another line." She shrugged one shoulder. "Then we can trade back if you want. Or you can cancel your service. I don't mind covering it."

"I'd hate for you to have to sign a contract."

"Aw, pshaw." Miss Lydia waved her off. "Those people won't rope me into anything. You know I can wrangle a fair price."

That brought a chuckle. The woman could wheel and deal with the best of them. "I remember when you went with me to buy my van. That salesman didn't know what happened to him."

"Wise as a serpent, gentle as a dove." Grinning, she spread her fingers and wiggled them as if they were in flight. "One of my favorite verses."

"I'll agree to the phone but not the car, *if* we can get you another cell today." Skye shook her head. "I don't want y'all driving around without one in case there's an emergency."

"I bet if I call them, they'll have one ready and waiting. Let me see that thing." She took the cell back, then searched a location. "There's a store near Tillman's Corner. I'll get in touch with them and pick it up. I'll be even faster if Sparrow waits here with you."

It'd be nice to have a little time alone with Sparrow. They didn't get that chance often. "That works. Maybe we can rent bikes before you leave and take a ride while you're gone."

"Bikes! Yes!" Sparrow perked up. "I love riding."

"I believe we have a plan." Skye smiled at Sparrow.

Once the rental bikes had been paid for and dropped off, Skye pocketed a small map of the island and set out with Sparrow. The child's tanned legs pumped hard on the pedals, but she had no trouble keeping up, since stiffness still troubled Skye. The sun shone warm on their shoulders as they rode down the path between the main road and the alternating dense vegetation and yards along the side.

The spring breeze against Skye's cheeks cooled her face. Dozens of birds twittered in the trees, flitting among the branches, an array of bright colors and patterns.

"A lot of people come here to bird-watch this time of year, so we need to be aware of people and cars darting out," Skye called to Sparrow ahead of her. Other visitors came to fish, boat, and walk the beaches too. Traffic could get congested, reminding Skye that she really needed to keep a low profile.

"Look at that yellow one." Sparrow pointed to a bird on a bush ahead of them and slowed to a halt.

"It's beautiful." Skye gasped as the bird stilled, watching them with a cocked head. Stopped next to Sparrow, Skye lowered her voice to a whisper. "It's a species of warbler. We could get an identification book. The island's a resting spot for thousands of migrating birds."

"Aww. They're so cute." Sparrow's eyes widened. "I wish I could see them all. I love birds."

"That's good, since you're named after one." Skye couldn't help but reach out and caress Sparrow's cheek.

"Momma says I'm named for a Bible verse and a song." The adorable child's big blue eyes gazed up at her.

"I know what she says about God not forgetting the birds." And Skye wished she could believe the truth of Miss Lydia's optimistic notions, but that wasn't how the evidence had presented itself in Skye's life, nor her mother's and sister's lives.

No one had rescued them when they needed it. But she wouldn't discourage Sparrow from being hopeful.

"God cares for all creatures great and small." Sparrow parroted one of Miss Lydia's favorite phrases. "He cares for the sparrow, and He cares for me."

Emotion swelled within Skye. How many times had the woman said those exact sentences after Momma's death, those strong arms holding Skye as she wept? So many of those black days, when death curled its dark fingers around her heart, Skye had longed to join her mother in the grave.

All of creation groans.

Why had Pete said that strange phrase?

"Can we keep going?" Sparrow asked.

Forcing herself back to the present, Skye looked around, noting the progress they'd made on the ride. "You know, I think we're almost to the Sea Lab. If someone's there, we could stop in and see where I'm going to work."

"Yay! Can I see a manatee?"

"Those are out in the water, but I hear there's a public aquarium across the street with fish, rays, and maybe turtles." If someone would let her in without her credentials and only her word, they'd visit. "I don't have my wallet, but we'll for sure go sometime."

"I wanna go now."

The pout of Sparrow's lip tugged at Skye's heart. "I'll do whatever I can, but no promises." The last thing she wanted to do was cause the child disappointment.

Chapter 13

All of creation groans…

In the bedroom she'd chosen to make her own, Skye folded and put away the clothes Miss Lydia had bought her. Pete's strange statement at church had rattled through her thoughts during the tour of the aquarium with Sparrow.

As soon as they'd parked their bikes by the Sea Lab, they'd run into one of the marine educators. The blond blue-eyed surfer-looking guy, Michael, led them through the facilities and the aquarium. Unfortunately, Sparrow had called her Skye, so her plan to go by Syd was failing miserably already.

At least Sparrow shared a love for science. The child had been enthralled with every single exhibit and even the lab.

Like always, Skye's heart sank seeing the creatures confined to such small spaces, though she understood the educational value. Then Pete's verse—or whatever it was—had popped into her mind, and she couldn't shake it. What did it mean about creation? Didn't matter. Probably some religious fluff.

"Skye." Sparrow's voice echoed down the hall. "That lady, Hope, is back."

Was she kidding? Did living on this little island mean people felt comfortable dropping in whenever they wanted? If so, Skye should have taken a position over in Ocean Springs. That would have been close enough to check on Miss Lydia.

"I'll be right there." Sighing, she set the rest of the shirts on the oak dresser and made her way to the living room.

Standing beside Miss Lydia, Hope set a large crockpot on

the kitchen cabinet, plugged it in, then turned and smiled. "Homemade chicken soup. I couldn't stop thinking about Miss Lydia not feeling well. This is good for what ails the body and soul." She flashed a huge smile, her lipstick still perfect. And never on her teeth.

"Aren't you a blessing, dear one." Miss Lydia folded Hope into a hug.

"I also brought my beauty kit." Hope's sculpted brows raised above her almost-ebony eyes. "I can get your hair back to a beautiful light brown for your first day at work."

Was that an offer or an edict?

Skye stared at the pretty woman, dressed in black jeans, designer tennis shoes, and a yellow short-sleeved shirt tucked partially in the front of her pants. How did Hope make casual look so dressy?

Skye's fingers traveled to the nape of her neck. Her hair was an odd color that probably drew more attention than her natural one, and she couldn't wear a hat every day to work. "Okay."

"Wonderful!" Hope's face lit as if Skye had given her a birthday present. The girl must really love doing hair. "I can give you a makeover too. I have everything we'll need."

Makeover? Oh, mercy. Maybe she should have passed on the hair. She kept it dyed for a reason, and this sounded like an ordeal.

"I want a makeover." Sparrow bounced on her toes. "Can I, please, please?"

"That's up to your mom," Hope said.

The center of Miss Lydia's forehead creased in a deep notch. "You're too young for makeup."

"I just want to play dress-up." Sparrow's bottom lip poked out. "There's nothing to do."

Skye regarded the exchange, thankful she didn't have to make these decisions.

No doubt she'd make a disaster of parenting choices.

"Okay, young lady. If Hope really doesn't mind." Miss Lydia held up one finger. "But no wearing makeup without permission and never out of the house until you're in high school."

Sparrow grinned. "Yes, ma'am!"

"Let's get going then, girls." Hope gathered a large pink plastic case and motioned for them to follow her to the bathroom. "Oh, by the way. I asked Caleb to stop in and have a bowl of soup so he could check on Lydia."

What? Hope not only felt at liberty to drop in, dye hair, and do makeup, but she also thought she could invite people over? This was turning into a nightmare.

"He's such a nice guy," Hope said over her shoulder. "You should get to know him. I think you two would hit it off. He loves the water. You must love the water if you're working at the Sea Lab." At the bathroom door, she turned and smiled. "Right?"

Wait. Skye's feet halted. Hope was trying to fix her up with Caleb? This was too much. "My post-doctoral work will occupy most of my time for the few months that I'll be here."

"Oh." Hope's smile faded. "You're only temporary?"

"I'll go back to Florida when I complete my manatee migration study at the end of July." So, no fixups.

Sparrow took Skye's fingers in her smaller ones. "Please don't go back. I miss you."

The usual cannonball of guilt and pain barreled through Skye's chest, but their situation couldn't be helped.

"I miss you, too, but we always have visits on holidays and in the summer."

The child's lips folded into a frown that said Skye's answer didn't help at all.

"Let's enjoy ourselves now and worry about the rest later." Pressing on the best smile she could conjure, Skye squeezed Sparrow's hand. "Like with the makeover, right?"

Skye dreaded someone touching and fawning over her hair and face, but she could fake it.

"Okay." Though Sparrow acquiesced, her spirits seemed dampened.

Wasn't she happy with Miss Lydia?

Hope reached over and fiddled with a strand of Skye's hair. "Let's start with your color, and while it develops, I'll work on this darling girl."

An hour and a half later, both Skye and Sparrow had been primped and fussed over enough to last the rest of Skye's stay. Sparrow ran out to show Miss Lydia, but Skye hadn't been released yet.

Chewing her bottom lip, Hope stood in front of Skye and surveyed her work. "Let's tie one side of this shirt at your hip, and we'll be finished."

"Why would I tie it?"

"So we can see your trim waist and feminine curves."

Exactly what she did *not* want anyone looking at. "That's okay. I'm not going anywhere." Already, she felt awkward enough. As soon as Hope left, Skye would comb out the waves from the curling iron and find something to use to remove all the cosmetics.

"Humor me." Hope helped herself to the corner of Skye's shirt and twisted it into a knot.

"There now. Hmm, if only you had some shoes like mine. I have these in several colors. What size do you wear?" The doorbell rang—thank goodness—and interrupted Hope.

"That'll be Caleb. Good timing. We can all eat together."

Skye's pulse skittered. Caleb would see her with this hair and all the makeup? The last thing she wanted was for anyone to see her like this. Especially not a man.

But Hope locked Skye's arm in hers and led her down the hall. "Let's go show them how beautiful you are."

Now it was all making sense. Hope was setting Skye up for a date that was happening *right now.*

Definitely should have chosen to do her post-doctoral work in Ocean Springs.

~~~

"Are you sure Skye knows we're coming?" Holding Olivia's hand in his, Pete shuffled his feet under the glare of the porchlight at Nana and Pop's house. Or rather, Skye's house for now.

Caleb shrugged. "Hope said she wanted me to check in on Miss Lydia when we finished for the day, and I'd rather not come alone. I didn't know Hope would still be here."

The least Pete could do was go along. The situation would be out of Caleb's comfort zone, and Pete was the one who'd gotten them involved with these people in the first place.

The door flew open, and Hope stood there, dressed slightly more casually than her norm. But only slightly. "Oh, Pete. I didn't know you…" Her lips pinched together, then she waved them forward. "Come in. Y'all are just in time for supper. There's plenty of chicken soup."

Supper? No one had mentioned a meal, though he was hungry. "We don't mean to impose." Pete stepped in.

"Come on, Pete the rock, and fellowship with us," Miss Lydia said from her perch at the kitchen table.

"I'm hungry, Daddy." Olivia turned and gave him puppy-dog eyes.
~~~

As if he could say no to that. "Okay, but we can't stay long. It's already getting late."

A woman with light brown hair stood looking in the refrigerator with Sparrow. Had Hope brought someone else too? Surely not. Skye didn't seem to want many people around.

Once she'd grabbed a juice box, Sparrow spotted Olivia and squealed. "You're back! Maybe Hope can give you a makeover too." The child looked way too mature with mascara and pink lipstick on. There was no way his girl—

The woman in the kitchen turned, and her caramel eyes met his, throttling up his pulse. "Skye? Your hair and your face…" He snapped his gaping mouth shut.

Her lashes fluttered, and her gaze dropped to the floor. "Hope got me too."

A chuckle slipped from his lips. Obviously, Skye had been moved out of her comfort zone. "You look very…pretty. But you did before this. I mean…you look good either way." *Lord, shut my mouth.*

"Please, Daddy. Can Hope do my hair and makeup?"

"Let's eat first." Anything to stop him from blathering.

Memories of family dinners washed over Pete as they all took seats around Nana's old oak table. He'd loved spending summers here, learning to fish with Pop. He sure did miss those dear people.

Hope placed steaming bowls in front of everyone, along with iced sweet tea.

His lifelong friend sure loved to serve.

"So, Caleb." She passed saltines to Lydia. "I was telling Skye how much you love being on the water. What are your favorite things when you're out on the waves?"

Caleb's eyes grew three sizes. Talk about a deer-in-the-headlight look.

Weird, Hope putting Caleb on the spot that way.

"Guess what!" Sparrow spoke between bites. "Me and Skye got to tour the Sea Lab and see the aquarium. We rode bikes, and Skye knows everything about animals and fish."

"Not everything." Skye's face took on a pretty pink blush.

"My daddy knows a lot too," Olivia piped up.

"Maybe we can go again together. Can we take them, Skye?" It was Sparrow's turn to give the pleading look.

Lifting one shoulder, Skye nodded. "One day when you're on the island, before I move back to Florida."

A dejected slump lowered Sparrow's shoulders. "What about tomorrow?"

"It's a workday, and I thought y'all decided to leave in the morning." Skye pointed a look Miss Lydia's way.

"We can stay as long or as little as you need. Your call."

Hope stood and took her bowl to the sink. "My shop's closed on Mondays. I could go. What about you, Pete?"

Oh, Hope. Why can't you let things lie? Pete held in a groan. "Olivia has school. Maybe late in the afternoon, but I can't promise anything."

Skye's eyes closed for a moment, then she got up and retrieved a phone from the kitchen counter. "Add your number, and I'll text when it's a good time for a tour."

Pete couldn't help but feel sorry for Skye. Looked like they'd all be invading her space. Again.

Chapter 14

"Good morning. I'm so glad you're here." In the atrium of the building that housed the Sea Lab, a very pregnant brunette shook Skye's hand. "I'm Lisa."

Skye gave the obligatory smile and eye contact. "I'm looking forward to collaborating with the lab and learning about the procedures for the Manatee Sighting Network."

"Let's get started then." She motioned for Skye to follow as she waddled across the open room beneath soaring ceilings and through another doorway. "I'd like to cover as much as possible before I take off."

Though here for her own manatee migration study through a research grant, Skye had agreed to man the network while Lisa left for three months of maternity leave. Based on the swelling of the woman's belly, her time off could begin at any moment. Taking on the network responsibilities would give Skye the opportunity to see or track as many manatees as possible. The only issue would be dealing with the public—their phone calls and all.

"How was your trip over from Florida?" Lisa asked as they entered the pale gray halls of the research area.

"Fine until someone crashed into me on the bridge."

Mouth gaping, Lisa stopped and turned to stare. "That was you? Oh, my goodness. I heard about the terrible accident with vehicles catching on fire. Are you okay?"

"Still sore, but it could have been much worse. I made it out with my pets, but everything else went up in flames, including my computer and my phone. I'll have replacements soon, but if there's an extra PC or laptop here, I would love to borrow one."

"I'll see what I can find, and if you need anything else, we'll do our best to help. That had to be scary."

Tears gathered in the corners of Lisa's eyes, probably due to the pregnancy hormones.

It had been a close call, but Skye would rather not dwell on it. She had enough trauma haunting her already. No need to add one more to her list. "Tell me more about the facility."

"We have a seminar auditorium, conference room, faculty research labs—including a clean lab and a necropsy lab—plus faculty, post-doc, and graduate administrative offices."

Skye pointed toward one of the doors several feet away that read *Necropsy Laboratory*. It also said *Restricted* and *No Photography*. "May I? I'm excited to see your workspace."

"By all means." Lisa opened the door for them to enter. "We have a well-equipped lab."

Skye surveyed the large room and noted the gear. As sad as it was for an animal to be found dead, the postmortem necropsy provided vital information about the animals' diets and travels. Though one could be performed on a beach in some circumstances, much more complete data could be collected in a lab like this one.

"We maintain research vessels and other watercraft you can use if you get a call about a sighting or a stranding." Her lips turned down. "Or if you need to bring in a carcass."

"How often does that occur with manatees?"

"Fortunately, not too often."

"You don't have many boat strikes with your manatees?"

"Only four or five with manatees in the last decade that we've been alerted to, but we've had cold stress rescues during cooler months and an issue with red tide a few years ago."

Just because they'd been alerted to so few strikes didn't mean there hadn't been more. She'd seen too many in Florida. "What day will you leave?"

"I'm due at the end of next week." Chuckling, Lisa patted her large abdomen. "But I feel like I'm about to pop."

That didn't leave much time for the woman to bring Skye up to speed—if Lisa even made it through the day.

"How does the network operate?" The more information Skye could ascertain, the better.

"One of the main ways to collect data is using citizen science, meaning we ask the public to call us when they spot a manatee. We have numerous signs posted near the water with our number, and we also maintain social networks online for reporting as well. This approach has allowed us to accumulate almost a decade's worth of data. We partner with our sister network to respond to mammal strandings, not only to manatees, but for dolphins as well. We even had a stranded sperm whale, which is rare for this area. Sadly, it had to be euthanized."

"I read about that." Skye gave a slow nod. It had grieved her. "What about tagging?"

"We do some satellite tagging."

Impressive for a smaller facility. Those devices cost quite a bit. "Do you have any necropsies planned for this week?"

"When we finish your orientation, we can perform one on a young dolphin found over the weekend by a fisherman."

"A fisherman?"

"We work closely with many of them. They bring us interesting finds. A lot of the exhibits in the public aquarium across the street arrived through this collaboration." She shook her head and breathed a small laugh. "Years ago, the scientists had curious locals or tourists wander into the lab to see what was going on. Sometimes even when biologists were working with radioactive isotopes. It became apparent space was needed to provide for not only the public's curiosity, but also their education."

That was logical. Skye would much rather random people go across the street than interrupt her research. Sparrow had certainly enjoyed the small aquarium. "Are there educational programs for children?"

"We have multiple opportunities both in person and online. My favorite is the discovery excursion—a two-hour boat trip in the waters surrounding the island. They're taking one this weekend. You might enjoy the tour."

If Sparrow were along, she would particularly enjoy the adventure. "What other duties are expected of me?"

Lisa chewed her lip a moment. Not a good sign. "Well…my educational obligations are covered, but before my pregnancy, I committed to setting up our manatee outreach table at the fishing rodeo this year."

Fishing rodeo?

Skye held in a sharp reply and stared at the woman. Why had no one mentioned this in their correspondence? "Doing what exactly?"

She gave Skye a pleading look. "The event is an excellent way to collect data on the health of the waters each year and educate the public on protecting the marine mammals at the same time."

That made sense, but Skye had read about how large this event was. She'd had no idea she'd be expected to participate. In fact, she had planned to huddle indoors that weekend and work on a paper. Already, she could imagine the island crawling with strange men.

Being stuck interacting with them in a huge crowd? A nightmare.

~~~

Pete fought the urge to barrel beyond the low speed limit on the island. He was late to meet Hope and Olivia at the aquarium for the tour Skye had promised, but his problems weren't worth risking others' safety. Thank goodness Hope had been able to pick up Olivia from school.

Since Mom's stroke last week, the charter had only scheduled inshore trips, and Caleb had taken up the slack, running almost everything at the business.

Hope had been invaluable in caring for Olivia. While he appreciated Hope's help, she wouldn't be a permanent solution for summer childcare.

She had a business to run, and he couldn't take Olivia on the charter every day. His daughter didn't need to be in the sun that much, and there were too many chances a passenger might get drunk or use foul language. He had to protect her little ears and find a good sitter. Soon.

His heart fell into that deep abyss of *if onlys*.

If only Kenzie were still here. If only Mom hadn't had her stroke. If only Kenzie's parents hadn't blamed Pete and Olivia for stealing their only daughter. If only his own grandparents were alive and well. Any of them would have been happy to watch her while he worked.

Flipping on his truck's blinker, he waited for a group of tourists to cross before he turned into the aquarium lot. He could've said no to extending his passengers' excursion, but they'd offered to pay for more time.

After the two hurricanes last fall had wrecked the west end of the island and the quarantine which had limited tourism before that, he needed the extra income.
~~~

Working Pop's fishing charter had been his dream. Yet, after the shortfalls the business had incurred recently, everything Pop had built might be lost. How would he make a living if that happened? How would he take care of Olivia? Would they be forced to move in with his parents?

What would Caleb do if the charter went under? Could his partner go back to working on the rigs? Offshore workers had been laid off recently, so that option might not be on the table for his friend.

Bitterness and regret saturated Pete. His career path had probably cost him his wife, or at least hastened her death. All that time she'd spent outdoors with him—despite sunscreen, hats, and long sleeves—had surely worsened her melanoma. Now, that choice might have all been for nothing. Maybe he should have gone into ministry like everyone had hoped he would.

Finally, he pulled into a parking spot, fighting to gather his composure before he got out.

Lord, help me have wisdom and peace. I know my life and Olivia's are in the palm of Your hand, and You love us. You have good plans for us. I want to be a good father, a good provider. I just don't know what's best for my girl.

He'd be devastated to destroy his grandfather's legacy by not keeping the charter business afloat.

Enough. He didn't have time for gloom and doom. After scrambling out of the truck and making his way down the boardwalk, he rushed through the glass entrance doors of the aquarium and surveyed the lobby, where a few families milled around.

No sign of Skye or the girls.

Should he buy a ticket and enter? He pulled out his cell to send Hope a text.

A laugh came from the gift shop, and he spotted Skye, Hope, and the girls purchasing a stack of T-shirts and a couple of plush toys at the checkout register. Had they already finished the tour? Surely he wasn't that late.

Skye's eyes met his. A slight smile lifted her lips, then she mouthed the word *Hey*. Warmth unfurled within him.

What was that about? All she'd done was acknowledge his presence.

"Hey," he parroted, then made his way to the store. "Did I miss everything?"

Hope turned as she shoved her wallet into yet another large, fancy purse. "I didn't see you come in." She grinned. "We started with the inevitable fun part of the tour since you weren't here and probably wouldn't care for shopping anyway."

"Where's Miss Lydia?" He looked around but didn't see the older woman anywhere.

"Resting." Skye's forehead crinkled into a deep notch. "We only have an hour left before closing time, so we'd better get started. I have our passes."

"Daddy! Look at my manatee doll and the shirt Skye bought us." Olivia ran over, and Sparrow followed. Both girls held small stuffed animals and a white T-shirt decorated with a print of the sea mammal.

"Nice. I like it." He examined the gifts then looked up at Skye. "Very generous of you, but I can pay you back."

"You bought last time." She shook her head. "And it was Miss Lydia's cash, though I'll pay her back soon, I hope."

Sparrow caught Skye's hand and tugged. "Come on, Skye. Tell them about everything like you told me."

An adorable blush crept across Skye's cheeks. She was just as pretty without all that makeup, even more so. "I'm sure Pete and Olivia have been here before."

"True, but not with an *expert*." Pete couldn't help but smile at her shyness. "Come on, Skye. Educate us."

The girls pulled her from exhibit to exhibit where she shared intricate knowledge of each creature. He and Hope followed, amid other tourists. He had to admit, Skye knew her science. Passion streamed out as she spoke. The woman might love the water as much—or more—than he did. A rare find.

They looped through the rooms until they reached a door that led outside to the large tank featuring stingrays. Then they maneuvered through the crowd until they found a place to stand and view the animals.

"Look!" Sparrow pointed at the clear walls of the tank. "See how they're smiling at us."

The animals swam near, probably just hoping to be fed, their little curved mouths next to the glass.

"We often see skates in the water and mistake them for rays. They're similar, but skates don't have spines. These are rays."

Skye went on with more explanations about the difference in the species. "The ones speeding around in a circle are cownose rays. Their snouts have two lobes, which reminds some people of a cow nose. They also like to travel in schools. That one right there is an Atlantic ray." She pointed. "They are the ones that bury in the sand. You have to be careful not to step on their tails. The barbs can hurt you."

"You're already back?" a man asked from behind them, and they all turned to see who had spoken. Pete recognized the educator from their interactions at the fishing rodeo and other events in the small community.

"You know how it goes." Skye shrugged. "Watch a tour, give a tour."

"I taught you well when you visited."

"Michael, how are you?" Pete shook his hand.

"Good to see you again. Who else do we have here today?" Michael smiled down at the girls.

"That's my daughter Olivia." Pete motioned. "And you might know my friend Hope."

Michael's gaze landed on Hope and traveled over her. "Hello." His voice held a tone of awe. "Very nice to meet you. I've seen you around the island but never had the pleasure."

Hope flashed her usual huge smile. "Same here."

A bit of worry tightened Pete's abs. While he'd love for Hope to find a good man, he didn't know Michael well enough to judge if he was a good guy.

"Oh, Michael, can you do me a favor?" Hope asked.

"At your service." He gave a little bow, a flirtatious look covering his face.

She held out her phone. "Would you take a picture of all of us together?"

"Absolutely." He took the offering and aimed. "Would y'all mind if I posted a copy on our website?"

"No!" Skye blocked the lens with her palm. Was her hand shaking? "Absolutely no pictures of me or Sparrow. None at all. Not anywhere." She swung toward Hope. "You didn't already take or post any, did you?"

"I might have snapped a few shots, but I haven't posted anything." Hope's mouth fell open. "I'm sorry. I should have asked."

"Delete them." Skye's eyes shut as her entire body shuddered. "Please."

Pete stared at the woman before him. He understood not wanting photos blasted over social media, but she didn't have to go ballistic.

What had her so vehemently opposed to a few pictures?

Terror.

Terror? Pete mulled over the one word that popped into his mind. Skye was afraid?

Of what?

Not what, but *who.*

Realization flooded Pete, and shivers marched over his skin.

That had to be the answer. Skye was very afraid of *someone.*

Maybe he and Olivia should steer clear of whatever trouble lurked in this woman's past. If it were only himself he had to worry about, he could handle the danger. But putting his daughter in harm's way was another matter altogether.

Chapter 15

After the blowup with Hope over the photographs, Skye's every muscle snarled into tight coils of tension. She hadn't meant to behave like a lunatic or hurt Hope's feelings, but she'd succeeded at doing both.

Not long after the incident, Hope claimed she needed to get back to her boutique and scooted out. Skye, Pete, and the girls finished inside the aquarium and now stood outside on the boardwalk behind the building, overlooking the bay. Maybe Sparrow and Miss Lydia could leave to go back to Mobile after this tour. It would be best for everyone. Safer for everyone.

The wind whipped up, thrashing Skye's hair against her face. The girls giggled and squealed at her side. Pretending to be a giant crab, Pete teased them, his hands nibbling at their necks like pinchers.

Familiar darkness pecked at Skye's heart, threatening to pull her into those murky waters of sadness. What would her life have been like if her own father had lived? If Momma had been mentally stable? If she had never remarried?

Skye's stomach lurched and bile rose up her throat as unwanted images of the evil man flashed into her mind. His eight-year prison sentence would end this summer.

Her fists clenched until her nails cut into her palms. She couldn't take any chances, no matter how much being away from Sparrow and Miss Lydia tore her to pieces. Already, they'd risked too much, being out and about.

"We should be getting back." Skye forced her feet to aim

toward the exit. "Miss Lydia needs to get on the road before dark."

"Nooo." Sparrow's chin fell. "Why can't we stay? We didn't play at the beach or see the fort Olivia told me about."

The corners of Pete's mouth turned down as he shot Skye a sympathetic look. He placed a hand on Sparrow's head. "Olivia has school tomorrow, and Skye has work, but maybe y'all could come back another weekend."

"O-kay." Her shoulders slumped, but she plodded along with Skye.

"How are you getting home?" Pete asked. "We can give you a ride."

Oh, shoot. Skye had ridden the rental bike, and Miss Lydia had dropped Sparrow off. But the house was maybe a mile down the road. "We can walk. It's not that far." And thankfully, she'd worked out most of the stiffness caused by the wreck.

Another gust of balmy air whooshed across the water, swaying the nearby palms.

"The sky looks threatening out there," he said. "Might be a storm brewing."

Dark clouds loomed on the distant horizon. Squalls on the Gulf could pick up speed and be on top of them in no time. Air puffed through Skye's teeth. She hated to keep relying on this man, but they should probably accept his offer. "You're right. We'll take you up on that ride. I can get my bike later."

Miss Lydia could get on the road quicker that way.

Sparrow and Olivia held hands until they reached the truck, then Pete and Skye helped them in.

"All set, big girls?" Pete smiled before shutting the door.

Skye eyed him, taking in his tender care of his daughter and even Sparrow, not missing the kindness in his blue eyes.

It seemed strange partnering with someone. Partnering with a man.

But not as strange as it should. None of the normal alarms Skye experienced around members of the opposite sex were clanking.

There was a sweetness about Pete she'd never experienced, his presence settling the storms within her.

Maybe there were a few decent men in the world. It was good Olivia had a decent father, especially since the poor girl had already lost her mother.

In a few moments, they reached the house. After Pete and Olivia left, Skye helped Sparrow and Miss Lydia pack their car.

"Give me a hug, precious." Miss Lydia pulled Skye into her warm brown arms. "I love you. I'm here for you."

"I know." Skye sank into her embrace. "I love you, and I'm here for you too. Call me with the test results when you get them."

Sparrow hugged Frodo and Sam, then squeezed Skye's waist. "Please let me come back soon. I want to play at the beach with Olivia. She's nice."

The plea wrenched open a thousand regrets, and tears pricked Skye's eyes.

If there weren't such immense darkness that lay just below the surface, things might have been different. She and Sparrow could have stayed together with Miss Lydia.

But they couldn't. Reality wouldn't allow that life.

Skye bent to her knees and pulled Sparrow close and kissed her cheek. "I'll miss you. I love you all the time. Even when we're not together."

She wouldn't commit to letting Sparrow come back any time soon, no matter how much they both wanted that.

"Come on." She stood, took Sparrow's hand, and led her

to the car. "Be good for your momma."

Skye watched until Miss Lydia and Sparrow drove out of sight. Rain began to fall with fat drops splatting against the ground. Skye's tears joined them as a shroud of sadness draped over her.

~~~

"I'm here." Pete held open the glass door of Hope's shop but waited outside. He hadn't had time to change clothes yet, and even he could smell himself after another long day of fishing.

"Daddy!" Every time his daughter squealed with excitement at seeing him, warmth swelled inside his chest. He prayed she'd always feel that affection.

"Hey, baby girl. Have you had a good day?"

"Uh-huh." She scrambled to her feet, grabbed her backpack, and ran to him. "I made you a picture at school."

"Oh boy. Let me see."

After digging through her papers, she pulled out a drawing. It was little more than stick figures and scribbles with crayons. Apparently, his daughter had inherited his lack of artistic talent.

"What do we have here?" He grinned at her.

"It's me and you. That's the smiling stingray." She pointed at a lopsided shape. "And that's Sparrow and Skye."

Although almost a week had passed since they'd seen their new friends, Olivia hadn't stopped talking about them or asking when they could be together again.

Oddly, his own thoughts had fallen into the same pattern.

He didn't want to get involved with Skye or anyone else, especially if there was some kind of danger involved.

Yet, he couldn't get the woman out of his mind. How was she managing without her vehicle? Had she replaced her belongings? Was Miss Lydia feeling better?
~~~

When it stormed one afternoon, he'd wanted to pick Skye up from work. He hated the thought of her riding a bike in a thunderstorm. But he'd stopped himself. Skye had his phone number. He'd told her to call if she needed him.

She hadn't called.

"Did you hear me?" Hope asked.

"Sorry. I was caught up in this masterpiece." He did his best to cover his thoughts.

"I said I missed church last week because Mom's party ran late, and I spent the night at her house, but I should be there this Sunday. I can keep Olivia afterward if you need me to while you take out the charter."

Hope had missed church?

Good grief. He hadn't even noticed, he'd been so nervous with Skye there.

"Sorry I've imposed on you so much since Mom's stroke." He wiped his dirty shoes on the gravel. "I've been asking around to find a good sitter or daycare. I should have something worked out soon."

"I love having her with me." She led Olivia to the truck, helped her in, then turned and smiled. "You know that, right?"

He bobbed his head. "You're the best, Hope."

Stepping close to him, she took his hand. "I'm always here for you."

"I better go before I start attracting flies and run off your customers." He slipped his hand from hers. "I'll see you soon."

"You look tired." She caught his elbow. "You want to grab dinner in a bit?"

"I've been up since before dawn. I plan to shower, throw burgers on the grill, and play with Olivia until her bedtime, then hit the sack myself." He shook his head. "Maybe another time."

"Let me know if you change your mind. I'm free tonight. You can let someone else cook a burger for you."

Though annoyance squirmed through him, he bit his tongue and got into the truck. Hope had been his best friend since they were kids, but sometimes she pushed too hard. He appreciated her help, especially since the stroke. But he was a grown man. He would figure out how to take care of his daughter.

Back at the house, he made quick work of cleaning himself up and cooking dinner. After playing tea party with Olivia and reading her a slew of books, he kissed her head and put her to bed a little early, then headed that way himself.

Alone in his king-sized bed, he picked up the journal his father had given him and opened it to his last entry. He'd never imagined recording his thoughts with pen and paper, but after Kenzie's death, Dad had convinced him to try. The process helped more than he could have imagined. He and God wrestled there on the page. Pete wrote whatever was on his mind, then he'd learned to be still. To wait. To listen. To be sensitive to that still small voice that whispered to his soul.

This week, business was good. Bless you, Lord.

You've covered me with Your wings, provided bread for our table and care for my daughter. Your daughter.

Each day the skies and the seas declare Your artistry, Your glory. The sunrise and the sunsets on this island remind me of Your faithfulness. You are with me when I lie down and when I rise.

My heart was broken. My breath left me. My plea came up before You, and You sustained me.

Thank you for Hope and Caleb, my best friends who've been here to help hold me up. For my parents, who've been my rocks.

Help Mom recover. Thank you for Dad's strength, his faith, his example. Help me be a faithful servant like my father.

His pen stopped on the page, a strange feeling sweeping over him that he should get up and get dressed again.

Really? He was worn slap out.

He stared at the journal. Maybe Mom or Dad needed him. He could get dressed and doze here on the bed. No harm in that.

Rising, he stretched out his tired muscles, then found a clean pair of jeans. He pulled them on over his boxers. The T-shirt he had on would be fine to wear out to the assisted living center.

But what would he do with Olivia if he had to leave? She had a clean outfit in the dryer.

His feet led him to the laundry room where he removed the matching pink shorts and shirt, then set them on the kitchen table with her book bag.

Back in his bedroom, he laid his nice deck shoes beside his bed. No socks required with them. Was that dressed enough?

Looked good to him. He might be going mad anyway.

He lay back on top of the covers and let his eyes shut to wait and see what happened. If anything.

A while later, the phone on his night table woke him with a start. He grabbed the thing and answered without checking the number. "Hello."

"Pete?" A woman's trembling voice spoke barely above a whisper.

"Yes." He blinked against his blurred vision. What time was it? He tried to shake off the sleep and focus.

"Sorry. I've woken you. I hoped you were still up, but I didn't know who else to call."

The woman sniffled, and Pete recognized the shy voice.

"Skye? What's wrong?"

"Sparrow called. Miss Lydia collapsed at their house."

A sob broke through her words. "I dialed 911 and gave them their address. It's just…there's no one with Sparrow. And I don't have a car to—"

"I'll be right there. I'll drive you to Mobile."

Chapter 16

Darkness cloaked the streets of Mobile, the clouds sliding across the half moon, creating ghostly shadows of the gnarly oaks along the drive. A shiver scurried down Skye's spine like tiny spiders on bare skin. She pulled her thin jacket tighter and wrapped her arms around herself. They'd almost made it to the hospital, but what bad news waited there?

The earlier blood tests had come back showing a definite problem with Miss Lydia's liver enzymes, and she'd been scheduled to see a specialist next week. Any liver problem could be serious. Fatal even.

Skye shuddered. How would she manage life if she lost Miss Lydia? What would she do with Sparrow if the worst happened?

Well, not *the worst.* With men like Denny in the world, there were viler realities than death. But she couldn't think about losing Miss Lydia.

Her gaze swung to Pete—his profile, his features, the easy set of his chin—everything about him still spoke kindness despite the way she'd imposed on him. Thank goodness he'd shown up almost immediately after she'd called. Then they'd traveled in silence most of the way, Olivia sleeping in the back of the truck. She hated thinking of how upset and afraid Sparrow must be.

The lights of the tall white hospital came into view. They needed a plan, and Skye had no good ideas.

A neighbor had driven Sparrow here because the child had

insisted she needed to find out what was going on with her mother. Miss Lydia had regained consciousness enough to give permission when Sparrow refused to wait for Skye at the house and the ambulance driver hadn't allowed Sparrow in the vehicle. An ache wrapped around Skye's chest and squeezed as she imagined the traumatic scene.

Poor Sparrow. She had to be shaken up.

Skye's thoughts pulled her back to the gruesome night when she'd lost her own mother. The sweltering heat. The oppressive evil that weighed down the air, smothering her as screams ripped from her throat. The sounds had echoed a crescendo through the dump they'd called home, as if they'd come from a stranger. Then Denny's curses.

"We're here." Pete yanked her from the nightmare's talons, and Skye sucked in a gulp of air.

He turned into the parking lot and wound around until he found a spot and cut the engine. "How about we all go in? Olivia might be able to get Sparrow to come with us."

"Us?" Skye stared at him.

"Either she can come home with me and sleep with Olivia, or we can take you to get Miss Lydia's car, assuming you're not staying with Miss Lydia overnight." His head tilted to one side. "Unless you have another idea? Someone to watch Sparrow?"

Unfortunately, no good alternatives came to mind. "Miss Lydia's sister was at her son's house in Birmingham for the weekend, but she said she'd come back in the morning."

Sparrow didn't need to sit at the hospital with Gertie either, though. And since officially taking over the manatee sighting network after Lisa had gone into labor the day before, Skye's schedule was full.

How could she be with Lydia and Sparrow and go to work? Plus, she had the dogs to consider.

"Daddy? Where are we?" Olivia's sleepy voice chimed from the back seat.

"We're at a hospital to pick up Sparrow. Miss Lydia got sick, and they need our help."

"Sick like Grandma?" Her tone turned sad.

"Kind of." A crease formed between his eyes as he tilted his head.

"Okay, Daddy."

He exited the car, and Skye met him at Olivia's door. Hesitantly, she touched his forearm. "Thank you for helping us. I should've asked Hope or someone from the lab. Anyone else. I should've hired a ride, but I couldn't think. I panicked. I hate that you had to drag her out of bed and all. It was—"

"Skye." His hand covered hers, his fingers gently caressing her skin. "It's fine. We're happy to help. I offered, remember?" His compassionate gaze searched her face. "I pray Miss Lydia gets treatment for whatever is making her feel so bad."

She studied the man—the sincerity of his expression, the feel of his touch against her skin. She waited for the dangerous undercurrents of fear to snatch her breath, feelings like those she'd had whenever Denny had been in the same room. When the sick man had touched her.

Nothing.

But she still couldn't trust Pete. Her mom had trusted, and that naivety had shattered all their lives.

"We should go in." Breaking away, she took a step toward the building looming before them. Pete could catch up.

Could she send Sparrow home with him? She barely knew the man, so no. That wouldn't be safe.

Inside, they followed the signs until they reached the designated room and knocked.

"Come in," a female voice answered.

Skye poked her head around the door. Tubes ran from Miss Lydia's arms as she slept. Her face looked sallow and tired.

A young woman Skye had never met sat in a chair beside the bed. "You must be Skye. I'm Ann, Lydia's neighbor."

Sparrow scrambled from the small couch and ran to Skye, clutching her around the waist. The child's shoulders shook as she cried. Skye took her into her arms and breathed in the scents of Ivory soap and sunshine.

She held Sparrow close and whispered, "I'm here now, little birdie."

"You can come to my house." Olivia neared. "We came to get you."

"Give them a minute, sweet girl," Pete said. "Sparrow's had a hard night."

"Is that Pete the rock I hear?" Miss Lydia's words came out breathy.

"Sorry I woke you." He neared the bed. "We'll get out of your way soon."

"You stay." Miss Lydia's tired eyes blinked, and her mouth lifted in an attempt at a smile. "I want to speak to Skye, privately, then you." She directed a gaze at the woman sitting with her. "Ann, thank you for being there for me and my girl. You should go back to your family."

"You have my number if you need anything else." Ann gathered her purse and headed out the door.

The weakness in Miss Lydia's voice made Skye want to curl into a ball and pretend this was a bad dream. Surely tomorrow the medical staff could figure out a therapy for whatever was going on.

"Sparrow, give me a kiss good night and wait with Olivia and Pete in the hall while I talk to Skye."

Mouth turned down, Sparrow sniffled but complied. Olivia took her hand, and the three of them walked out.

The door shut, and Skye made slow, heavy steps to the bedside, her insides liquefying. Whatever came next couldn't be good. Miss Lydia held out her hand, and Skye took it.

"Now is the time, dear one." Miss Lydia took a labored breath. "Time for you to take Sparrow and step into the life God has for you both. Time to take courage from Him."

"Why—? What do you mean?" Words strangled in Skye's thick throat. "You may feel terrible now, but they'll find a treatment soon."

"Maybe, but no matter what happens, the light of Jesus will make the darkness tremble. Allow Him to push back your fear. Let Him give you the heart of a lion."

Not all that religious talk. It sounded like Miss Lydia was giving up, and Skye wouldn't let her. She and Sparrow needed her too much. "You're going to get better."

"I'm trying, but even so, it may take a while. This time I need your help." A smile stretched across Miss Lydia's face. "You can take care of Sparrow. His eye is on you both. He'll watch over you." She gave Skye's hand a weak squeeze. "Send Pete in before you go."

She shook her head. "I'm not leaving you alone up here."

"Sparrow needs you more than I do." She released Skye and patted the Bible on her bed. "I have the Lord and the nurses watching over me. Gertie will be here in the morning. She'll take good care of me."

Skye's insides twisted. How could she abandon the woman who'd always been there for her and Sparrow? Maybe she could take Pete up on his offer to take Sparrow home.

Or she could keep Sparrow here with her. Sparrow could sleep on the little couch.

"Sparrow doesn't need to be in this place." As if reading her mind, Miss Lydia's voice pleaded. "The doctor said I need to go to Birmingham for more tests. Plan on having her with you for a while."

A while? How bad was this? "There's something you're not telling me."

"As a scientist, you know liver problems are serious." Her solemn gaze bore into Skye. "Enroll her in public school for the rest of the spring on Dauphin Island. There's probably only a little over a month left. Find a good sitter for when you're at work. The guardianship paperwork for you has been drawn up by my lawyer."

"But..."

"Pete will help you figure out the school details and all."

They didn't need him more involved in their lives. "Why do you need to talk to him?"

"Pete is a good man. I *know* you can trust him. And it'll only take a minute, then you can go to my house and get my car. Take Sparrow to the island with you to stay. You can do this."

A sigh pushed its way from Skye's chest, but she pressed a kiss on Miss Lydia's forehead. She'd known this day might come. But she'd never expected it to happen so soon.

~~~

Pete hated hospitals.

After giving Skye the keys to his truck, he stood at the closed door of Miss Lydia's room and took a breath of the antiseptic air before entering.

So many sad nights in this place and others like it with Kenzie. Hopeless nights, despite all his prayers.

His beloved wife faded away before his eyes, him helpless to do anything but watch as life drained from her.
~~~

God, help me.

He pushed the door open and stepped inside. "I'm here, Miss Lydia. You wanted to talk to me?"

"Pete, pick up your Sword and protect my girls." Miss Lydia lifted a Bible he hadn't noticed before, laying on the sheets of her bed.

What did she mean? Pete scrubbed his palm across his jaw. Okay, he knew the Word of God was described as a Sword in the Bible, but the meaning seemed to go deeper. "Protect them from what?"

"The evil that's hounded Skye most of her life, both inside and out. The details are not for me to share." Deep lines on Miss Lydia's forehead formed the first frown he'd seen from her and saddened her face. "A hard life, that child's had. Things you and I can't imagine. Things that never should be." She swallowed hard. "But I've wrestled and prayed the Word over her for years. I had this feeling deep in my heart that there was a man of God meant to take my place." Her brown eyes nailed him.

A string of questions cycled through Pete's mind. Why him? What did she expect? He already had enough on his plate. He didn't understand what evil she meant, but he needed to shield his daughter from it, didn't he? And he'd failed at protecting his own wife from being taken much too soon.

Do not fear.

The words bounced in his mind, but he focused on the woman on the bed. "What's wrong with you?"

"My liver's failing. Autoimmune hepatitis. Caused by either genetics or a virus that made my immune system attack my own organs." A tear leaked from her eye, and she swiped it. "I didn't have the heart to tell Skye everything yet, because they won't know for sure until they do a biopsy next week."

Nausea swept over him. He understood not wanting to share bad news like that until it was confirmed. Wanting it not to be real. "Is there no treatment?"

"A transplant." Her serious gaze held his. "I'm not afraid to die. My husband was hit by a car helping a motorist whose car had broken down. I decided I'd never love another man after Leroy. I fostered children since we didn't get to have our own. I ended up finding Skye and Sparrow to love permanently. I'll be with Leroy and my Savior when I go home." She heaved a sigh. "But, Pete, I was wrong when I decided to close my heart. I've not known you long, but I have the impression you are making the same mistake."

She's the one.

The phrase that had come to him the first day he'd met Skye drummed in his mind. The way she'd flinched at his touch, the fear that had frozen her soft brown eyes. What had happened to make her so skittish?

Protectiveness surged through him. No woman should be made to feel like that. God help him, he'd do his best not to let anyone hurt Skye again, while still protecting Olivia.

Loving a woman again? Was it possible? He didn't know.

"What do you say, Pete?"

"I'll do what I can—with God's help."

"That's all I can ask." The lines eased on Miss Lydia's face.

He'd be supportive, but what kind of mess was he stepping into?

Chapter 17

Leaving Miss Lydia didn't seem right. Someone should be there to watch over her.

Once Skye had Olivia and Sparrow settled in the back seat of Pete's truck in the hospital parking lot, she climbed into the passenger side, reached over, and cranked the engine. How long would Pete leave them waiting? With a shiver, she locked the doors, then glanced back at the girls. Their eyes looked heavy.

It had been a long week with the move and starting the new job, so she could relate to their exhaustion. Letting her head fall back against the seat, she shut her eyes. At least she'd enjoyed working at the lab. She knew what she was doing there. But keeping Sparrow for an extended visit?

Lists. She'd need to make several when she got home. Thankfully, she had access to her bank account again and started replacing some of her belongings.

A knock on the window sent a jolt through her. She stifled a scream and snapped her head to find Pete standing beside the driver's door.

That had been quicker than she'd expected. Skye hit the unlock button, her pulse still scurrying.

The *talk* with Lydia hadn't taken long. But what in the world had she said to this man they barely knew? With the girls in the back, Skye didn't dare ask.

Pete slipped in and shut the door. Leaving the vehicle in park, his lips lifted in a kind smile. "Everyone okay?"

His tender gaze roamed her face as though he understood what she was going through. Losing his wife and being left a single parent had perhaps given him compassion for others. He probably would have made a good minister if he'd chosen to follow his father's path instead of becoming a fisherman.

Skye's mind traveled to her mother. Momma had gone through losing a spouse too.

Maybe the loss and the responsibility of it were what caused—or at least amplified—Momma's depression. That and the financial strains of being flat broke most of their lives.

Yet, life happened, and Skye had to learn to deal with it. She refused to end up like her mother.

Pete still waited for the answer to his question. Was she okay? Was Sparrow?

No. Not with Miss Lydia lying in that hospital room, sick and alone. What else could be done though? "It's late. I've got the directions punched in my phone for you. Her house isn't far."

He gave a single nod, and they wound the short distance from the hospital to Lydia's neighborhood in Mobile with no sound other than the GPS instructions.

"This is it." Skye pointed at the light gray ranch-style home on the left side of the cul-de-sac. Though the porch light glowed, she dreaded going in alone. It had been a long time since she dared visit this house. Denny's search for her those early days after Momma's death had left few stones unturned. Until he'd found someone new to terrorize eventually.

Pete pulled near the garage door and parked. "Sparrow can wait in here while you pack if you want, since they're sacked out back there." He thumbed over his shoulder toward the sleeping girls.

"Probably best."

The child had gone through enough drama for one night.

She exited and quickly unlocked the side door that opened to the laundry room. The floral smell of detergent met her, and an acrylic painting lay on the counter with paper towels beneath it. Sparrow loved to do crafts, and homeschooling allowed her plenty of time for them. She often sent pictures of her creations to Skye from Miss Lydia's phone. On this piece, she'd painted a green background of leaves, then a branch with a fairly good attempt at a bird sitting on top, looking to one side.

An ache wove through Skye's chest. She'd missed so much of Sparrow's life. Shaking her head, she dismissed the thought. Now wasn't the time to get bogged down in regret. She forced her steps farther inside Miss Lydia's spotless house, and after locating a suitcase in the hall closet, made her way to Sparrow's bedroom. How long would Sparrow need to stay? With no good answer to that, Skye wedged as much as she could into the bag.

On Miss Lydia's desk, she found the legal guardianship papers that had been prepared months before and tucked them in. Miss Lydia must have known something bad was going on with her health.

Why hadn't she said something sooner? Probably because she knew the danger of Skye coming to this part of the world. What would Denny do if he saw her? Or even if his horrible parents saw her? Saw Sparrow? Did they still live in the area?

The air in the house shifted. The atmosphere transformed into something evil and revolting. Like those nights when Denny had slipped into Skye's room.

Panic skulked up from Skye's belly, and her hands shook. What if he found her? What if—?

Stop. She didn't have time for a breakdown tonight.

She closed her eyes and focused on her breathing, taking in the sound of the air whizzing through the AC vents. She noted the sensations of her feet in her shoes against the floor, the feel of her clothes against her skin.

Focus on the present. Feel the breath enter and the chest rise. Release the breath gently.

Skye swallowed the fear clawing at her throat and opened her eyes. One step at a time, she would handle whatever arose. She couldn't let her frenetic thoughts control her. Couldn't lose sight of the mission Miss Lydia had given her.

Miss Lydia had asked for help. It would be wrong to let her down after all she had done. If only Skye had the strength and bravery Miss Lydia possessed.

His eye is on the Sparrow.

Those words. Faith in God made Miss Lydia brave—gave her the heart of a lion. But Skye had never had such courage. And she had difficulty accepting such faith. Though the intricacies of nature might indicate a Creator, she found it hard to believe that the Being cared enough to get involved in the everyday lives of humans. It seemed much more likely that, once the earth had been set in motion, the Creator had gotten busy elsewhere.

Otherwise, why hadn't He protected her family?

After shutting the suitcase, Skye grabbed a picture of Miss Lydia and Sparrow from the nightstand. Skye had captured the moment in Florida when they visited at Christmas. She studied Miss Lydia's smile. They stood on the pier near the research facility. Miss Lydia had seemed tired on the trip, but she'd attributed it to the bustle of the holiday season and the homeschool events they'd helped organize before arriving.

Had Miss Lydia known even then that something was wrong with her health?

Skye tucked the picture in the front pouch of the bag and made her way outside, an ache heavy in her chest as she locked the door.

Pete waited in the garage and motioned to the suitcase. "Let me get this for you."

Though she was perfectly capable of lifting the bag into Miss Lydia's car herself, she didn't have the energy to argue. Too many other details clogged her mind.

She pushed the trunk release, then asked, "Do you have a sitter you recommend for after school? Looks like I'll be registering Sparrow at the elementary and keeping her with me for a while."

He tilted his head as he tucked the case in and came back to stand in front of her. "I just found one. Her name's April, and she's looking to keep a couple of children so she can stay home with their baby. Her husband, Robert, runs dolphin tours at the marina." He shifted in the stale garage air and wiped his brow. "My mom had been keeping Olivia before and after school, but since her stroke, I've had to leave Caleb to run things alone or burden Hope."

Skye's jaw tightened.

Hope probably relished the opportunity.

"And you think this woman April is responsible?" she asked

"I've known her and Robert for years. Good Christian people." He nodded. "They were at the church service you attended."

Maybe she should have paid more attention to who was there. She had no memory of a lady with a baby at the beach that day. And she knew from Denny's parents that Christian people weren't always what they seemed.

Still, she had to make a plan.

"Would you mind asking if you can share her number?"

The dim light in the garage shimmered in Pete's blue eyes, and lines crinkled next to his temples when he smiled. "I don't mind at all. Might make the transition easier for Olivia if she has a buddy with her. Would make me feel better too."

Heat singed Skye's face as the thought of making Pete feel better pleased her much more than it should.

It would also be less traumatic for Sparrow having a friend in new surroundings.

"I was just wondering…" Pete shifted his feet and scraped his fingers across the dark stubble shadowing his jaw. "I have an early charter in the morning, and…" His gaze dropped as his words drifted. "Never mind."

"What?" As she studied him, Pete seemed suddenly shy—in an appealing way she'd not seen in a man. "Just ask."

His blue eyes lifted. "Only if you give me an honest answer."

A loaded requirement. "I'll try."

"Would you be willing to let Olivia spend the night at your house since it's so late? I could carry her in when we get there. She'll be grumpy if I wake her at dawn for the charter." He held up one hand. "But I can take her with me. Done it plenty of times and survived."

Oh. Of course, he worked on Saturdays. She hadn't given a thought to his schedule when she'd called him for help. "It's the least I can do."

"You don't have anything planned?"

Did she?

Goodness, she had been knocked off-kilter with all this. Her mind filtered through her obligations.

"I have something planned, but I think the girls will enjoy coming along."

As he waited for her to continue, he showed none of the impatience or annoyance she'd expect after pulling him and his daughter from his bed.

"I signed up to go to the Sea Lab's discovery excursion on the research vessel. It's a hands-on educational boat ride for families or whoever wants to come. Only lasts a couple of hours."

His head bobbed. "I bet they'll love it, and I know you'll keep a close eye on my girl."

The last part of the sentence sounded a bit like a question, as if he needed reassurance.

Taking Olivia and Sparrow with her would be a huge responsibility. A huge responsibility she'd need to accept until Miss Lydia recovered. "I'll keep them both close to me the whole time."

Satisfied, he turned toward his truck. "I'll follow you back to the island."

Maybe he shouldn't trust her so easily. What did she know about being a parent? Pete had much more experience in that area. It looked like she was about to take a crash course.

His headlights behind her the whole way, Skye navigated to her house. When they arrived, she rushed to unlock the door and let the dogs out for a quick break. Then she turned down the guest room beds so Pete could carry the girls in. He settled them and made his way into the living room. Frodo greeted him, begging for petting.

Pete knelt and obliged, peering up at her, where she hovered near the door. "You have everything you need for the morning?"

"Like what?"

"Breakfast food? Sunscreen?" He shrugged. "Any other requirements for the boat trip?"

"I have oatmeal, but we can go by the bakery or someplace if they'd rather. The excursion isn't until nine-thirty. Oh. There's a release form though, and I don't have a printer. I was going to sign one at the aquarium."

"How about emailing the document? I'll sign it and leave that and clothes for Olivia on your doorstep in the morning. I'll throw in sunscreen and snacks too."

"You're good at this."

If eyes could make a sad twinkle, his definitely did. "Have to be."

"Any advice?"

"Expect the unexpected with kids."

"That tells me everything and nothing."

Her stomach tightened with the weight of keeping a child safe—two children tomorrow.

"Welcome to the club." He laughed easily, and something about the sound eased her worry. "I pray a lot."

That wasn't something she'd be doing.

He stood, and his gaze grew serious. "I'll pray for y'all too."

The thought of Pete speaking their names—thinking of them while they were out on the boat and maybe at other times—spread warmth through Skye. Cheered her up a bit.

It was ridiculous, really, for her to allow such a reaction, but maybe that was what Miss Lydia had talked to him about. Maybe that was what the sweet woman had seen in him—a kindred spirit. He could take Miss Lydia's place as an encourager. And she probably wanted him to get Skye to keep Sparrow in church.

"Good night, Skye."

His voice floated between them softly, the use of her name, almost intimate. As if they were close now.

She battled warring emotions over the simple words.

There was a part of her she'd locked away long before that wanted to be known—wanted to be close to someone. Miss Lydia had been the only person she'd even cracked the door for. That had been after a few years of being Miss Lydia's class assistant in high school.

Skye folded her arms over her chest. Could she trust another human? Especially a male?

Speechless, she stared at him. Maybe he'd given up waiting on her to answer, or he took her silence as his cue to leave. Either way, he trekked to the door and left.

Skye watched from the window as the truck disappeared into the darkness. Before she went to bed, she had a lot to consider. From making to-do lists for managing Sparrow's care, to what to think about Pete Thompson.

Chapter 18

Goodness, Sparrow and Olivia walked slower than sloths on a diet, their hair sticking up in all manner of angles, their eyelids drooping. Skye waved them on. "Come on. We've only got about twenty minutes to get ready, so let's see if Olivia's stuff is out on the porch."

Already dressed in lightweight cropped pants and a T-shirt, Skye darted past them down the hall with the dogs on her heels. Of course, the animals had plenty of energy. They'd gotten a good night's sleep. The rest of them, not so much. Tossing and turning, Skye hadn't been able to stop the cyclone of worry for Miss Lydia. It seemed she'd only slept a few minutes before the alarm blasted.

Now, they needed to be out the door if they wanted to eat at the bakery before the excursion, and that would be cutting it close. The girls had to dress and brush their teeth. Was there anything else they should do?

After crossing the living room, she opened the door to look for Pete's clothing delivery for Olivia. Both dogs barreled through Skye's legs.

"Wait, Frodo! Sam, no! I need my shoes and the leash."

At her command, they slowed and sniffed at the grass beside the driveway.

Skye shook a finger at them. "Sam, look at me. Come back." She lowered her tone. If Sam minded, Frodo would follow.

After doing his business, Sam made his three-legged

hobble back to the porch and whined an apology, then the bigger dog did the same.

She knelt and scratched their heads. "I would have walked you, silly boys. A short walk, anyway, until this afternoon." They hated when she left for work. Or for any period of time. She understood their angst, but at least they had each other to hang out with while she was gone.

A backpack lay to the left of the door, collecting dew in the early morning light. Good. Pete had been there. Since the dogs had been out, she just had to help Olivia and Sparrow dress. Wouldn't Sparrow dress herself at her age, though?

She took the bag inside and pulled out the clothes. He'd included two sets that looked pretty much alike. A spray bottle and a face stick of sunscreen lay below them in a zipper bag. Another held a toothbrush and kid's toothpaste.

He'd remembered to print and sign the release form too. Then, she discovered a grocery bag filled with six cheddar cheese sticks, three clementine oranges, three Goldfish packages, and three waters.

What a good dad.

The thought of Pete up early, packing healthy snacks for them, brought a smile. The sweetness and the care he took of his daughter seemed sincere. And now he'd included Sparrow and Skye as well.

"Can I have my backpack?" Olivia asked.

"Let's slip on one of the outfits while Sparrow gets dressed. Her clothes are in the suitcase I laid open in her room. Then I'll put the sunscreen on you both."

"I can put on my own sunscreen." Sparrow held out one hand.

"I can dress myself." Olivia stared up at Skye with those big green eyes.

"Okay, then. Y'all take the backpack. Everything's in there, but don't eat the snacks before breakfast. Those are for later." They probably didn't want someone hovering over them. "If y'all want to eat at the bakery, you'll need to hurry. And brush your teeth."

They trudged toward the bedroom slightly faster once they heard the bakery part of the instructions.

After putting on her shoes, Skye made sure the animals had food and water, scooped Rocky's litter box, then went to check on the girls.

"Ready?" She stood in the bedroom doorway.

Sparrow wore a pink tie-dyed tank with green shorts, orange socks, and blue tennis shoes. None of the colors matched, but what did it matter?

Olivia still wore her clothes from the night before. "I don't wanna wear what my daddy brought. I wanna wear something like Sparrow."

"I have extra shirts." Sparrow lifted several tops from a pile she'd apparently made while trying to coordinate her rainbow outfit.

The long sleeves on the sun shirt Pete had sent over probably wicked moisture, but the temperatures were predicted to be warm.

Was there some sort of road map for navigating questions like these?

Skye bit one side of her lip. "I guess that will be okay. But let's hurry so we don't miss the boat."

"We will!" Both girls answered with a smile, and Olivia quickly changed into Sparrow's clothes. A little too baggy, but they stayed on.

Once they'd brushed their teeth, they skipped to the car, and Skye made sure they were buckled for the short ride.

Just off the main road of the island, cars filled the small parking lot of the quaint, older house that had been transformed into an adorable café. More vehicles lined the street too.

"No parking spaces." Slowly driving past the place, Skye groaned. "We'll have to walk from farther down the road, unless y'all want to try somewhere else?" But there weren't many other choices that she knew of.

"No, please, Skye. I want to eat here," Sparrow pleaded from the back seat.

"They might have something at the convenience store that will hold us over until lunch."

"I like the bakery better." Olivia weighed in.

"All right, but we need to figure out your orders as soon as we go inside."

They both agreed, and Skye continued down the road. She edged onto the narrow shoulder and parked under a large oak, then helped the girls out.

"Let's hold hands since we're on the road." *Please don't let them balk at that too.*

She held out both hands, and thankfully, they accepted.

Trying to keep an easy but purposeful pace, she led them up the steps, onto the porch, and through the front door. Immediately, the aromas of yeast and sugar enveloped her.

Skye's stomach gurgled about as loudly as Frodo's did, and the girls snickered.

Smiling, she shrugged as they took their place in line. "This place smells so good, I can't help it. Do y'all want muffins or the breakfast cup with eggs? Or maybe a pig-in-a-blanket?"

"Cinnamon roll!" Olivia bounced with the words.

"Chocolate chip cinnamon roll! Two, no three!" Sparrow tugged Skye closer to the counter, nudging into the back of the woman in front of them.

"Sparrow, be careful. We have to wait our turn."

The older lady glanced over her shoulder.

"Sorry," Skye said. "They're excited."

The woman grinned. "It's hard not to be. Your girls are adorable."

Her girls. The words torpedoed Skye, releasing a torrent of pent-up guilt and fear. Of course, people would assume that. What would happen if she ever ran into Denny or his parents with Sparrow? "I can't take credit. I'm just watching them."

How many more times would she have to make an explanation while Sparrow stayed with her? Her thoughts churned, hatching more fear while they waited in the line.

"Next customer."

"That's us, Skye, come on." Sparrow pulled Skye's sleeve.

Skye's attention returned to the matter at hand. Order. Get back on the road.

"Okay." She moved them closer to the counter. "Tell the nice lady what you want."

"Three chocolate chip cinnamon rolls." Sparrow answered first.

"Three? They're pretty big." The woman shot a dubious look Skye's way. "Mom?"

Not again with the assumptions. But yes, that was probably too many treats.

She needed to order a kid instruction manual to use while Sparrow stayed with her. "Let's try two."

The woman nodded. "Something to drink with that?"

"Root beer." Sparrow quickly piped up, and the woman glanced at Skye again.

"Does Miss Lydia let you have sodas?" Skye couldn't remember what they normally ordered.

"She does when we go out to eat."

"Well…okay, I guess." If there was caffeine in it, the day was still young. Plus, they were all pretty tired from the late night.

"What about you?" This time the woman spoke to Olivia.

"I want the same as Sparrow." She gazed up at Sparrow with wide green eyes, adoration evident.

How precious. Their friendship brought back memories of playing with Star.

With Momma's depression, they'd entertained themselves most days, climbing trees, picking wildflowers… Growing up, they'd been close. Her little sister had been the only person Skye had ever been close to, at least until she'd met Miss Lydia. Skye and Star had loved the outdoors, running free without a care in the world, collecting treasures from nature. Those had been sweet times.

Until Momma married again.

"What about you, ma'am?" The cashier's voice snapped Skye's attention to the menu on the wall. For all her rushing, she hadn't decided her own order.

What did she want? Didn't matter. "Apple turnover and a water."

She turned to address the girls. "We're running out of time, so we'll have to take our food with us. We can eat it on the way." The meeting place wasn't far, but all the tables had been claimed in the restaurant, and they couldn't wait around to be seated.

Minutes later, they were back in the car and buckled with their treats in hand.

"Dig in." Skye peered into her own white sack and pulled out the turnover. Just one bite until they reached their next stop. The sugar and cinnamon aroma set her stomach to rumbling again.

Maybe two bites before they left.

A clump of apples dropped out with her first mouthful. She glanced down at her light blue shirt.

Nice. She scraped the blob with her finger and looked for a napkin in the bag. None. Come to think of it, she'd seen them on the counter when they'd picked up their order but forgot to get any.

Oh well. She licked her finger, pushed her pastry back in the sack, and rubbed her hands together. So sticky. They'd better go. She could eat later.

By the time she'd made the short drive to the aquarium parking lot, the girls had already gobbled one pastry and were working on the next. Skye got out and opened the back door beside Olivia. Sugar and icing coated both girls' hands. The white flakes and chocolate circled their mouths.

"Did there happen to be any napkins in your sacks?" One could hope.

Licking her lips, Sparrow shook her head.

"I'll look." Olivia picked up her sack but knocked over her uncapped bottle of root beer in the process. The foaming liquid spewed onto the car seat. "Oh no!"

Skye lurched for the bottle and whacked her head on the door frame. Pain spiked through her. Ignoring it, she readjusted, then grabbed the bottle.

"Uh oh." Sparrow's eyes widened. "The car is messed up."

Olivia's lip quivered. "It's on your clothes."

The liquid puddled around Olivia, and she whimpered.

"Maybe there's a towel in the trunk." Skye pressed the button to open it and made her way back there. A first aid kit and one reusable grocery bag looked to be their only options. She grabbed the sack and some large gauze pads from the kit.

They might soak up some of the liquid.

When she rounded the car, she ducked her head in, careful not to whack herself again. Olivia had moved to Sparrow's place, and Sparrow sat on the floorboard.

"What are y'all doing?"

"We traded clothes." Sparrow straightened her shirt. "Olivia was sad, and I don't care if people think I wet my pants. Because I know I didn't."

Skye's gaze popped up to Olivia. Indeed, the child now wore Sparrow's colorful garb. "That was kind of you, Sparrow." And an awful lot like Star—so strong and brave.

Nothing like me. Good.

She smiled at the compassionate child. "I'm proud of you."

"Why do you have those bandages?" Olivia's head tilted. "For your head?"

"My…?" She touched her forehead and felt a small scratch over a goose-egg. She'd knocked herself harder than she'd realized. "I thought I'd try to use them to soak up some of the soda. And this bag too." After unwrapping the pads, she wiped them over the dampest areas of the seat then put them in the pocket of the door to throw away later. It helped a little. "Maybe the gift shop will be open when we leave, and we'll buy a towel."

"Can we get another stuffed manatee?" Sparrow slid closer and climbed out of the car. "Or another toy?"

Why had she opened that can of worms? "We'll see. Let's focus on making the boat ride for now. Ready, Olivia?"

"Yes, ma'am."

Holding hands, the three of them crossed the parking lot and clomped onto the decking outside the aquarium. A cluster of people gathered around a picnic table, and Skye spotted Michael giving directions and holding a clipboard.

"Whew, we made it in time." Skye led the girls to the back of the group just as they formed a loose line to head toward the dock.

"I thought you'd changed your mind." Michael wove through the small crowd. "But you've made it and brought extras." The wind feathered through his blond hair as he smiled at the girls. "You ready for an adventure?"

"Yeah!" Sparrow practically bounced with excitement. Or caffeine.

"My daddy has a boat." Olivia gave a shy shrug.

"I bet you know a lot about the fish we'll see today then." He tapped her nose. "Y'all can be my helpers." His gaze turned to Skye. "Did you happen to bring releases?"

Her stomach plummeted.

How had she forgotten the backpack? The releases? The carefully packed snacks? The girls would be devastated now if they didn't get to go. "I left them at the house."

His fingers raked across his chin. "Since you work for the lab, I'll allow you a bit of leeway. How about you sign as the responsible party, then bring the ones from their parents after?"

Relief swept through her. "Thank you. I'm not great at the childcare procedures yet."

One of his brows cocked, and he stared at her head. "You do look like you've had a morning."

"What?"

"It's good to see you without the cap, but your head's bleeding." His gaze dropped. "You have something sticky on your shirt. I think I can find wet wipes for that and the girls' mouths."

Shoot. She'd forgotten her hat. "My head's bleeding?" Her fingers found the small lump again.

"Just a little." His nose crinkled as he handed her the clipboard. "Sign these forms while we walk down to the pier. I've got everything you need on board."

Skye let out a quiet groan. Miss Lydia had to get better. Skye had never had much of a parental example, and she had no business trying to care for children.

Chapter 19

Waves rocked the Sea Lab's research vessel, soothing Skye like the embrace of a long-lost grandmother she'd always hoped to meet. Nothing compared to the feel of warm sun kissing spring skin. The scent of brine filled her senses, and the mist caressed her face. Floating perfection. The sea was her happy place. On the water, she felt at home—one with nature. *Safe.*

A memory of sitting on the beach with her mother surfaced. Momma might have had her issues, but on her good days, it was Momma who had taught Skye to notice details in nature, the tiny things that others missed as they hurried through life. The dew highlighting the intricateness of a spider's web, the colors of the leaves in their season, the way the clouds changed sizes and shapes.

Glancing out at a cormorant diving below the water, Skye shielded her eyes against the sunbeams glimmering against the cresting waves.

How had she forgotten her cap? And everything else important for going out on the water, like Olivia's bag?

Maybe because she'd spent the past week in the office getting acclimated to the procedures and working on the computer. At the rental house, she had none of her usual possessions.

Probably excuses all, because more likely, she had just never been meant for family life.

Next to her, Olivia stood, then Sparrow, leaning on the rails of the bow.

Michael had found the wipes in the cabin and tidied up their pastry and soda issues. Now the girls pointed at shrimp boats and asked about the gas rigs dotting the horizon. They squealed when dolphins crested the surf. Shafts of light stroked Sparrow's golden locks, and Skye couldn't help but reach out and run her fingers through it.

Sparrow's gaze slid toward her for a second, and she smiled before continuing her conversation with Olivia. As Skye watched the girls together, she saw her younger self as she'd been with her sister. Inquisitive, carefree, naive. Happy.

Before Momma remarried.

The waves grew larger and rocked the ship while Michael explained how the Sea Lab had started back in the seventies. Then he went through terms like estuary, basin, watershed, and brackish water. "Today, there's a good bit of wind, so the captain decided to ride south of the island into a protected area instead of Mobile Bay."

The chop had become stronger, making it difficult for them to stand without holding on tight. Which didn't normally bother her at all, but with the girls there, worry needled Skye. Though other children had come along with parents on this excursion, this might not have been the best idea for her first day keeping Sparrow. Plus Olivia.

"Estuaries are nursery grounds for the oceans." Michael continued his talk. "They provide nutrients for sea life and habitat for baby animals."

"Aww, I love baby animals, don't you?" Sparrow turned to Skye, the corners of her lips curling up.

"I do. I've spent most of my life loving them."

"I like animals too." Olivia took Skye's hand and snuggled close, her hair soft against Skye's arm and tugging at her heart. "I like your pets."

"Thank you." Skye's throat tightened at the sweetness of the child.

"Look at all the birds chasing us." Glee evident, Sparrow pointed to the dozens of gulls squawking around the boat.

The boat slowed to drop anchor, and flocks of pelicans took notice too. They soared closer, hoping for a scrap from the net trawling behind the ship.

"Daddy calls them pests because they try to get the fish," Olivia said.

Skye laughed. "I bet they do. They can be aggressive scavengers."

"In the early 1700s"—Michael continued his lecture, his voice becoming dramatic—"Dauphin Island was originally named Massacre Island because they discovered mounds of human skeletons and thought they were murder victims."

"Gross." Sparrow stuck out her tongue.

Olivia nestled closer, obviously spooked.

"In reality, the place they'd found had been a burial ground for Native Americans, and the name was eventually changed."

One of the captains came forward and said they were ready to pull in the trawling net. Michael held up one hand. "Don't everyone run to the back just yet. We need space to safely bring up our catch, but you can watch from the top level or from behind the blue line painted on the ground."

"Can we watch from upstairs?" Sparrow asked.

Skye shrugged. "I don't know why not." They made their way toward the stern until they reached the base of the staircase.

"Careful. Hold the railing." Should she go first or follow?

Sparrow charged ahead, nullifying the question.

Olivia followed, and they climbed the steep, narrow stairs to stand on the platform near the bridge.

"This is fun!" Sparrow beamed and leaned as far over the rail as she could, making Skye's palms grow slick.

"Come back a little." She guided Sparrow's shoulders away. "I don't want you to get hurt."

Olivia nodded. "We have to practice safety on Daddy's boat."

Too bad Pete isn't here.

The thought struck Skye by surprise. She couldn't start relying on the man any more than she already had.

The hum of the hydraulic winch lifting the net competed with Michael's voice from the deck below. "Before you come over, I'll check the catch and pull out anything that might be dangerous."

"Like what?" Sparrow's eyes rounded as she turned to Skye.

"Certain jellyfish and sea life that might have poisonous stings, risky spines, and sharp teeth, I imagine." Skye patted Sparrow's shoulder. "If you follow Michael's instructions, you'll be fine."

"Eels are dangerous too." Olivia made a face. "They look like snakes."

"Momma says some snakes are good." Sparrow spread her arms out wide. "I held a long one around my neck at the library."

Olivia gasped. "You did?"

"Uh-huh. It didn't hurt me at all."

"I'm glad you're learning about science at the library." Skye tilted her chin.

How could she phrase her words without coming off negatively? "We can interact with snakes and other creatures at times, but we have to be sure we are doing so on their terms and be careful. Respect the fact that they're wild animals and often attack simply because they want to protect themselves."

"I'm not gonna go find a snake in the yard and put it on my neck." Sparrow scoffed. "That was only because the zoo guy was there. His snakes are used to being held, he said."

So much for tact. "That's exactly what I meant. Good job." Maybe that sounded better.

The net dropped the catch onto the long, rimmed table, capturing the girls' attention. Using various scoops and sometimes his hands, Michael quickly tossed creatures into separate containers, then left a good sampling on the table.

"Cool!" Sparrow jumped up and down, the caffeine and sugar apparently hard at work in her system.

"Can we go down now?" Olivia bounced, too, but came down with her lip against the metal rail. "Owie, owie. I hurt myself." Tears coated her long lashes.

"Oh goodness." Skye dropped to her knees. "Your lip's bleeding a little. Are your teeth okay?"

Whimpering, Olivia opened her mouth.

"I don't see any other damage. Let's head down to the cabin for a tissue." Skye kissed the child's head. "I'm sorry you got hurt." At least they knew where the supplies were from their earlier issues. But soon Pete would know she was a sinking ship in the childcare department.

When they reached the bottom step, Michael waved them over. "Kids and parents get the good spots so they can see. Come on."

Completely forgetting her injury, Olivia released Skye's hand and bopped forward, Sparrow close behind. They positioned themselves as close as they could to Michael along the table. Shrimp, crabs, squid, and small fish wiggled in the shallow layer of water. After the other participants joined, he picked up and explained each catch, one at a time.

Then, from one of the containers, he lifted a ray. "I've handled a lot of stingrays, so don't try this yourselves. His tail won't sting, but the barb beneath can. It's a defense for them in case a shark or another animal tries to eat them."

"Cool! Can we touch him?" Sparrow inched out her hand.

"Yes, they're quite slimy. Be gentle." He wrapped its tail around his finger for a better hold and moved it close enough for the girls to reach. "Its mouth and gills are on the bottom, but you probably remember that from your visit at the aquarium."

"Neat! It is slimy." As she felt the creature, Sparrow's jaw hung open, and then she craned her head to see the underside. "They always look like they're smiling."

"Does anyone else want to touch it before I put it back in the water?"

Other children and adults took turns before he moved on to explain several types of crabs. In the meantime, a little boy picked up a small white squid, twisting and tugging its tentacles.

The way he stretched the thing as if it were a toy sent a cringe through Skye. Although she knew the creatures were often used as bait, she had to bite her tongue to keep from being too stringent in correction.

"Be gentle with the sea life," she said finally, and Michael shot her a knowing look.

He probably went through these situations quite often as an educator. "Let's trade places and give everyone a turn at the front. The boat will begin the journey back toward the dock while we continue learning about our catch."

All too soon, the pier came into view, and the deckhand reached out to steady the boat and tie it up. But Sparrow and Olivia stayed close to Michael and the observation table, pelting him with questions.

"You sure are smart girls." Michael grinned at them.

Sparrow and Olivia beamed at the compliment. Maybe the day hadn't gone so bad. They'd seemed to enjoy themselves.

"That includes you." Michael aimed a smile Skye's way, and heat swam across her cheeks.

The phone in her pocket chimed with a couple of texts, saving her from saying something awkward. She read the messages. One from Miss Lydia claiming she was doing well. She said her sister had arrived to care for her.

The next came from Pete, saying he had a break before his next charter and could meet them for lunch.

"Do we have to leave now?" Sparrow asked.

"It's time, plus Olivia's dad wants to eat at the cafeteria nearby."

Sparrow frowned. "Cafeteria?"

"It's good." Michael nudged Sparrow's shoulder with his elbow. "I'm headed there as soon as I finish cleaning up."

"Will you sit with us?" Sparrow asked.

"If it's okay with Skye, and you're still there." He shifted his attention her way. "I'll be a few minutes behind you."

Skye plastered on a pleasant expression. "We'll save you a seat. Let's go, girls."

"See you there." He winked before turning back to his duties.

The idea of carrying on conversations with multiple people—especially men—more than lacked appeal, but it appeared to have become her lot since she'd arrived on this small island. Michael was a colleague, and they could discuss marine science. Perhaps the girls could keep up the conversation with Pete.

They headed down the boardwalk that passed the aquarium, where Skye paused. "How about we go inside and wash our hands. We've been touching the sea life and all."

Right away, Sparrow perked up. "Can we go in the gift store?"

"We don't need anything," Skye said.

"Aww." Her shoulders slumped. "I wanted another shirt."

"Girl, you already have ten times more tops than I do," she teased as she held the door for them to enter. The cool air rushed over them.

"That's because you wear the same thing every day."

"What?" Skye scoffed. "I don't."

"It looks like the same thing."

As they neared the restroom entrance, Skye glanced down at her outfit, then chuckled. "Maybe they do look similar. But they're different clothes."

Olivia tugged Skye's sleeve. "My skin hurts."

Turning her focus on the child in the light of the building, she couldn't miss the pink blotches that marred the pale completion of Olivia's face and arms. "I thought you put on the sunscreen."

"I put it on my legs." On one calf, a white handprint stood out, surrounded by bright red. A few other white fingerprints dotted the other leg, but the rest…sunburned.

"I showed her how to do it." Sparrow huffed. "I don't know why that happened."

Fear gnawing her insides, Skye tried to imagine Pete's reaction when he saw the damage to his precious daughter.

This was not good.

Chapter 20

Love is patient. Love is kind.

For the tenth time today, those two sentences from First Corinthians ran through Pete's mind.

Okay, okay. I get it. Be patient and kind.

Had he been rude to anyone? He'd tried to be polite to his customers, despite a few of them using rough language on the charter. There was that one know-it-all guy too. The morning trip had gone well otherwise. No issues. Maybe this afternoon, he and Caleb would end up with a drunk, and he needed to be prepared.

Though he'd changed clothes after the morning trip, he scuffed his shoes on the sidewalk outside the cafeteria—an ingrained habit, in case he'd brought fish guts along for the ride. A huge yawn slipped out.

Good grief, he was tired. Leaving Olivia with someone other than his parents had proved much more difficult than he'd imagined.

All night, he'd tossed and turned, imagining terrible scenarios where his baby was injured or even abducted if Skye didn't pay close attention.

Would being a father of a daughter always drive him this crazy?

"Chill. She'll be here any second." Caleb bumped Pete with his elbow. "You'll see Olivia's okay, eat some chow, and we'll head back out for our next crew. The day will be over before you know it."

"I hope you're right. Skye's text said the excursion had finished. Seems like they'd be here by now."

The aroma of meat roasting in the restaurant had his stomach rumbling. In his rush to get Olivia's bag packed and over to Skye's, he'd neglected his own breakfast and forgotten his sunglasses.

Squinting against the bright sunlight, Pete swiped his fingers over the growing stubble on his jaw. He hadn't shaved in days—too busy to worry with the task. No doubt Kenzie would have been much better at all this parenting stuff. And much more organized.

Finally, three figures turned the corner and rounded the blue cinderblock building. Pete strode toward them, his eyes locked on Skye. No hat or sunglasses today, and strands of her light brown hair floated in the strong breeze. As he came closer, though, he spotted a knot and a small scrape marring her forehead. His heartbeat ramped up, and he quickened his steps. Had someone hurt her?

"What happened to your head, Skye?" Then his gaze fell to Olivia, and his abs clenched.

Dear Lord, help me.

"Baby, what happened to your lip? Where are the clothes I sent you?" Fear swamped him as he took in her scorched skin. "You're sunburned." When he reached them, he knelt in front of her to examine her face.

Her lips turned down and trembled. "I'm sorry, Daddy."

He drew her to his chest as her tears began to fall.

"She hit her lip on the boat railing, but we cleaned it off." Brown eyes rounding, Skye pressed her forearm to her head. "I whacked myself on the car trying to keep her root beer from spilling all over her."

"Root beer?"

Olivia's head lifted. "Skye bought me two chocolate chip cinnamon rolls and a root beer at the bakery."

A slew of sugar, chocolate, and caffeine to start the day? Even his mother would have cut out at least one of those. "But why didn't you wear your sun clothes?"

"She wanted to dress like me, so I loaned her some of mine." Sparrow answered for Olivia.

Steam piped through Pete. Why couldn't Skye follow simple instructions? He'd sent sunscreen, clothes, and snacks. All she'd had to do was use them.

"Is everything okay?" Caleb neared to stand beside him.

"Can you take over this afternoon?" Pete ground his teeth as he spoke. "I need to get Olivia home."

"Aww. No, Daddy." His daughter's pink brow puckered. "I don't want to go home. I wanna stay with Skye and Sparrow."

Sucking in a deep breath, Pete held in the angry words clamoring to spill out. There was no way he'd leave his daughter in this woman's care.

"Why don't I take the girls in for lunch while you and Skye talk?" Caleb motioned toward the cafeteria entrance.

"Get it to-go. I'll need to treat her sunburn right away."

With downcast expressions, Olivia and Sparrow followed his partner.

"I'm sorry." Skye's voice floated on the wind, barely above a whisper.

Sorry? "It wasn't your place to decide to let Olivia wear something else."

"I should have put the sunscreen on her myself. I know mammals need to be protected from the rays. I've even covered whales that have beached themselves, but the girls said they knew how to do it so…I let them."

"Whales?" Pete's jaw dropped.

So much anger pulsed through him, he could barely get the words out. "My daughter isn't some sea creature. Her mother died of melanoma. A sunburn in childhood for Olivia could… You're a scientist. Go research it."

"Hey, am I too late for lunch?" Michael closed in on them from the sidewalk.

"Pete, I'm so sorry." Skye's voice trembled. "I didn't know." She covered her eyes with her fingers. "I'm terrible at this."

"I've obviously interrupted something." Michael's steps slowed.

"Nope. You're not. I have to take care of my daughter." Pete turned and marched toward the cafeteria, leaving them behind before he said anything else he'd regret.

Inside, he found Caleb and the girls at the checkout counter. They stood in silence, waiting for their food to be boxed up. Every time he looked at the pink covering his daughter's skin, he saw Kenzie's frail form those last days, the sadness in her hollow eyes when he laid their tiny daughter on the bed beside her. She'd barely even gotten to hold Olivia, she was so weak.

Skye and Michael made their way through the line to stand near them as the food Caleb ordered was delivered.

His partner separated Sparrow's meal and handed it to Skye. "We'll see you soon."

Gaze downcast, she took the box then pulled Sparrow close and nodded.

Love is patient.

A niggle of guilt tugged at Pete as they left.

He'd been hard on Skye, but if she planned to care for a child—for Sparrow—she needed to know they required more attention than some sea mammal.

At the truck, he helped Olivia in, careful of her burned skin. Once he shut the door, Caleb met him, blocking his path.

His friend offered a compassionate look. "Hey, Olivia is going to be okay."

"For now." Pete kept his voice low. "We don't know the extent of the permanent damage done today."

"This isn't like you."

Grief knotted around Pete's neck. Caleb didn't understand. No one did. Sure, love was patient, but this was his daughter. This one day in the sun amped up her risk of going through all the pain Kenzie had. All the pain he had.

"I'll get you to the boat, then take her home." Pete only took one step before Caleb caught his arm.

"Did you tell Skye about Kenzie's cancer before you asked her to keep Olivia?"

Love is kind.

Pete let his chin drop. God help him, he hadn't been kind. And part of this was his fault.

Pete shook his head as the weight of the question sank in. "Nope."

Man, he was a jerk. If nothing else, he could have texted or written a note explaining everything. He could have let Skye know why it was so important for Olivia to wear the protective clothing and sunscreen.

"You're right." He glanced back toward the cafeteria. He could go in now and say he was sorry, but Olivia already waited in the truck, and he wanted to get her into a cool bath then coat her with aloe. "I'll call her and apologize once I take care of Olivia."

Chapter 21

Sunburns during childhood increase melanoma risk.

Children of melanoma survivors are at higher risk. Even one blistering sunburn could double their chances of developing the disease.

While waiting for their food in the cafeteria, Skye clicked website after website on her phone, stomach sinking at the results about melanoma and childhood sunburn. Every site repeated similar information.

Pete's blunt research suggestion made sense now. No wonder he'd been so distraught.

What were the risks for the children of melanoma patients who hadn't survived? Even higher? She could only hope Olivia wouldn't blister.

Forcing her gaze to Sparrow beside her, she searched for any hint of injury or other wreckage from the morning. "Are you all right?"

"Yeah." She shrugged her tanned shoulders. "Except, I wish Olivia didn't have to leave. I feel like we all got in trouble."

"Me too. I should have made sure—"

"Don't keep beating yourself up." Michael patted Skye's back and offered a compassionate look. "We weren't out all day or anything. She'll be okay."

Maybe. Maybe not.

"Our order's ready. I'll grab it." Michael slipped past them to the cashier and took the bags. "Want to eat here?" His blue gaze looked hopeful.

"Can we?" Sparrow asked.

"We better take it with us. I'd like to visit your mom in the hospital."

Sparrow's head bobbed, obviously eager to do the same.

"I'll take a raincheck on lunch then." Michael mussed Sparrow's hair.

"A raincheck?" Her forehead scrunched.

Chuckling, he winked. "That means we'll do it at another time."

A smile lifted her cheeks. "Okay."

He left them to take a seat at a table with someone he'd waved to earlier, and Skye led Sparrow out to the car.

At the vehicle door, Sparrow gave Skye a sideways glance. "Do you think Michael is cute?"

The question hit like a wave of cold water to the face. Did nine-year-olds find adult males attractive?

Sure, he had the blond surfer-thing going. Tanned and in good physical shape, but little girls didn't need to think of grown men that way. "Why? Do you?"

"I thought he might..." She pivoted and pulled the door handle. "Never mind."

"Wait." Skye caught Sparrow's shoulder. "Whatever it is, you can tell me." She stroked her hair. "I'm here for you."

Sparrow's eyes lifted, tears rimming her lashes. "He has hair like mine. And blue eyes. Do you think my daddy looked like Michael?"

Dizziness swarmed Skye as though she was teetering over a deep pit. The wind died down, and beads of perspiration formed on her temples. How could she even answer that?

"It's...not likely." When had Sparrow started wondering about her parentage? Her father?

Was it her age?

Maybe hanging around Pete and Olivia had brought this on. Surely Sparrow's homeschool group had fathers who participated at times.

Skye's appetite evaporated. "Let's change clothes and check on the dogs, then go see your mom."

If Skye could manage to get a moment alone with Lydia, she'd ask how to field those questions with Sparrow.

Forty-five minutes later, Skye and Sparrow walked through the chilly hospital halls. The pungent smell of cleaning fluid flooded Skye's nose. She was accustomed to such odors in the necropsy lab, but someone had been a little heavy-handed in here.

They reached the room, and the door stood open.

"Hey, babies." Miss Lydia sat on the edge of the bed, dressed in a pantsuit, her sister Gertie in the nearby chair.

Hope sprung to life in Skye's chest. "What are you doing up? Are you better?"

The sisters, who looked so similar, both offered sad smiles. Miss Lydia shook her head, and Skye's hope crumbled.

Whatever was going on, the news wasn't good.

"Come give Momma a hug." Miss Lydia held out her arms, and Sparrow ran into her embrace. "You too, Skye."

With heavy steps, Skye neared, her muscles rigid. "What's going on?"

Miss Lydia brushed a kiss on Sparrow's forehead. "Will you go with Aunt Gertie to the gift shop and buy me some scented lotion? Maybe find something you like too?"

"I just got here." Sparrow's voice sounded small as she clung to Miss Lydia.

"It won't take long." Miss Lydia smiled and clasped Sparrow's cheeks. "You know how dry my skin gets and what scents I like."

"Okay, Momma." Finally withdrawing, she followed Gertie from the room.

Once they were out of earshot, Miss Lydia patted the bed. "Sit."

Skye sagged onto the mattress, her shoulders slumping. "Tell me the whole truth."

Taking Skye's hands into hers, Miss Lydia squeezed. "They're sending me to the hospital in Birmingham. One of the specialists thinks I need a transplant. Soon."

"For your liver?" The air in the room thinned, and ice flowed through Skye's veins. "Can they give you a lobe of mine?"

"I don't want to take one from a living donor. It feels too risky for any of y'all. I'm high on the list. I've never drunk alcohol or smoked, and my health was good until this."

And the need must be urgent for her to be bumped up on a transplant list. Surely someone would match to be a living donor, but staring at the woman before her, Skye knew. Miss Lydia wouldn't ask anyone to sacrifice on her behalf.

Just because Miss Lydia wouldn't ask didn't mean Skye couldn't try.

"I'm getting tested." Skye stood and strode toward the door. She'd find out where and how to do it right now. "My liver will regenerate, and I don't want to be without you. Sparrow doesn't either."

Skye would never forgive herself if she didn't do this for Miss Lydia.

"No!" Miss Lydia's voice cracked, and the sound of her feet shuffling turned Skye around.

"You shouldn't get up." Frustration welled in the form of tears burning behind Skye's eyes. "Please, stay there, and let me try to help you."

With a slow but determined shake of her head, Miss Lydia sat back down. "You can test all you want, but I will not take that chance. Sparrow needs you."

"With the advances in technology and my good health, the risks—"

"Not another word about this." Her hand held high and using her sternest teacher voice, Miss Lydia ended the transplant discussion. "Come here, precious, and sit by me."

Skye complied but stared at her feet to keep from bawling.

Miss Lydia's arms folded around her shoulders and pulled her close, like they'd done after Momma's death. "God will take care of me one way or another. He will do the same for you and Sparrow. Put your faith in Him. He loves you more than even I do. And that's a lot."

All Skye managed was a sniffle. If only she could believe the Creator of the Universe cared.

"Put on a happy face now, so Sparrow will feel secure. You can do this."

Miss Lydia sounded so confident. But what if she was dead wrong?

When Sparrow and Gertie returned, Sparrow told Miss Lydia about their morning on the boat while Skye fretted. Hadn't she already proved she couldn't do this? What if she screwed it all up? Too soon, they all went on their separate ways.

Back on the island, night settled outside the windows of the rental house. Down the hall, Sparrow read a chapter book in her room with Sam and Rocky at her side. Fatigue glued Skye to the couch. Frodo stretched his large body next to her. As usual, his stomach issues fogged up the room. Poor dog. Her poor nose.

Poor all of them.

Sometimes, darkness tapped at Skye's psyche like a limb scraping a tin roof in the wind. Other times, an unexpected black wave crashed over her like a tsunami dredging out everything in its wake and dragging her out to that sea of hopelessness.

This was one of those times.

Her pulse thudded in her neck, her skin grew clammy, and her thoughts jumbled like sea kelp on the beach after a storm. All signs she was on the verge of an impending episode. Tears blurred her vision, and she felt she would tremble into pieces.

She couldn't, though. Not now. Not when Miss Lydia was counting on her.

Still, the sense of doom enveloped her. First, the failure with Olivia's sunburn, then her inability to talk sense into Miss Lydia about the transplant. She didn't even get to ask what to do with Sparrow's questions about her father.

The thought of walking into the Gulf until she was no more haunted Skye. If not for the child… She didn't wish to die, only to not be here anymore.

If she could just make everything stop.

But she would never do to a child what Momma had done to her. To Star. Leaving them the way she had, right where they would find her in such a state.

More black thoughts smothered Skye. They pounded against her, taunting her to give up. To bring Sparrow to Gertie and leave this area for good.

Someone, help me.

A knock on the door jolted her upright. Her heart thrashed in her chest. There was no reason for anyone to come over tonight. It was almost bedtime.

Unless someone had brought more bad news.

Chapter 22

This probably wasn't the best idea.

Pete's grip on the vase of flowers tightened. He glanced down at Olivia, who held a single tulip for Sparrow. Her pink face lit with a smile as they waited for Skye to answer the door. *If* she would answer the door.

Moths fluttered around the porch lights, and the drone of crickets filled the air.

No sound came from inside. No footsteps. But the house was lit up when they'd arrived, so he'd assumed they'd still be awake. Night had only just fallen on the island.

"Are they home, Daddy?" Olivia's forehead furrowed.

"Maybe they didn't hear us. I'll call Skye." Maybe she was afraid to come to the door. He'd seen her react in fear more than once, so that seemed possible.

Or she'd noticed him drive up and, after the way he'd behaved at lunch, decided to ignore their knock. Balancing the bouquet in the crook of his elbow, he pulled his cell from his pocket and finagled until he pressed her number.

He'd wanted to text or call to say he was sorry, but his father had convinced him that using his phone to do so was no way to treat a lady. Dad was generally right. The problem was, in this case, the lady didn't seem to enjoy the company of humans.

"Hello?" Skye's voice quivered.

Yep. He'd terrified her.

"It's Pete. Olivia and I are at your door."

She puffed a loud sigh. "Be right there."

A minute later, the door swung open. Hair disheveled and her expression hollow, Skye's gaze brushed over them, landing on the bouquet. Seeming confused, she blinked hard as if her eyes deceived her. "What's going on?"

"We brought you and Sparrow flowers," Olivia said.

"Why?" A notch creased Skye's forehead.

"My dad wants us to 'pologize."

"*A*pologize." Pete corrected then focused on Skye. "We came to say we're sorry about today and to bring you these."

She stared at the offering as if it were catfish barbs instead of tulips and snapdragons. "For what? I'm the one who screwed up."

Olivia's mouth twisted. "I knew I was sposed to wear my sun-suit on a boat."

After stepping out and kneeling in front of his daughter, Skye tipped Olivia's chin up. "You're a good girl. I'm so sorry you got sunburned. I should have helped you."

"Olivia." Pete cleared his throat. "Why don't you go inside and find Sparrow, if that's okay with Skye?"

"Sure. She's reading a book in her bedroom." Skye stood and opened the door wider, allowing Olivia to scuttle through.

"Shoo wee." Olivia looked back at them, holding her nose. "Why does it stink like rotten shrimp?"

Rolling her eyes, Skye scoffed. "Frodo and his digestive system."

"He poofs a lot." Olivia giggled then ran down the hall.

"May I set this vase inside on the table for you?" Pete quirked a smile. "Or will I be in peril?"

She stepped inside and motioned for him to follow.

A noxious odor assaulted his nose. "*Shoo wee* hardly describes this agony."

"You're telling me." She groaned. "I'm still waiting for the delivery of the special kibble his system requires. I'd brought some, but it went up in smoke with the van. I don't know what's taking it so long to arrive."

"Can I go fetch it for you—charter a plane before Nana and Pop's house dissolves?"

An adorable laugh spouted from Skye, maybe for the first time since he'd met the woman. He liked the sound of it.

Then she grew serious again. "Sorry. I'll find a good deodorizer."

"I'm joking, but I'd like to talk with you." He wrinkled his nose, but still smiled. "Maybe on the porch?"

Chewing her lip, she nodded. "I'll tell the girls and then join you in a sec."

After leaving the vase in the center of Nana's kitchen table, he returned outside and took a seat in the chair farthest from the door. He crossed his knee over his other leg, leaned back, and shut his eyes. Now that he was here, what should he say?

Dad had all but insisted that he open up and be honest with Skye about his life with Kenzie—about her death and his fears. Dad didn't normally interfere in his personal life, only offered a listening ear. But tonight, when Pete reached out, Dad had been persistent in encouraging him to bring a gift and acknowledge his part in today's misunderstanding.

It might be the right thing to do, but he hated dredging up all that wreckage. All that pain.

Pete's phone dinged with a text. He stood to drag the thing back out and read who it was from.

Dad. Again.

Pete leaned against the railing and opened the message.

You can do this, son. It's important. I just know it. This verse from Isaiah keeps coming to mind when I think of you.

"I am making a way in the wilderness and streams in the wasteland."

Praying.

Pete loved that Scripture, but this wasn't like Dad to be in their business. Could it be the stress of Mom's stroke? Could Dad want to pawn off his widowed son to a woman neither of them really knew because he had too much on his plate?

Mom had never held back suggesting that Hope would be a good mother to Olivia if Pete could ever think of his oldest friend in a romantic way. But not Dad. His father had always been the one to say *be careful and take your time. Marriage is too fragile. Don't let yourself be led into a union borne of desire or convenience alone.* Probably because, as a minister, Dad had overseen hundreds of weddings, and he'd counseled hundreds of couples in marital disasters.

The door creaked as it eased open, and Skye stepped out. "Hey." Her gaze bounced around like that of a timid animal, unsure of what to do next, but ready to bolt if need be.

Pete rose and took slow steps toward her, stopping an arm's length away. "Today was my fault. Not yours, Skye. I should have given you specific instructions and explained why it mattered so much. You didn't know about Kenzie's cancer or the fact that Olivia is accustomed to having me douse her in sunscreen."

"Any idiot should know to at least watch to make sure a first-grader puts the stuff on correctly." She covered her face with one hand.

"None of this was your fault. It was mine. Please forgive me." Blowing out a sigh, Pete reached over and touched her arm for a brief second. "Can you?"

"If you forgive me too."

"Of course. Let's forget today and start over. I'm Pete Thompson, a worrywart widower."

He'd offer to shake hands, but he doubted she'd like that.

Her gaze peeked around her fingers. As she dropped her hand from in front of her teary eyes, she offered him a hint of a smile.

Like a lightning bolt, a storm of feelings blazed through him. More than attraction or affection, though those were there. But also a tenderness that cracked open his locked-up heart and ignited a passion to hold and protect this fragile spirit.

She's the one.

Could it be possible for him to love this complex woman?

~~~

Skye took in the man before her. His dark hair, the deep color of a raven, laid against his neck, teasing the edges of his white collar. His Caribbean blue eyes shone bright, even with only the porch lights and stars to illuminate them. Kindness lingered in his gaze—no rage stiffening his posture. He appeared sincere in his apology.

How could he not blame her for Olivia's sunburn? She'd been stupid. And what was this warm-fuzzy feeling skittering over her skin?

She tried to collect her jumbled thoughts.

"April will be at the service in the morning if you'd like to meet her." His deep voice caressed her.

"What?" His words made no sense. "April?"

"The babysitter we talked about. She said you could meet after our little sunrise service. If you and Sparrow go, that is."

"Oh, right. Church." As much as she'd prefer not to attend, she'd do what Miss Lydia wanted for Sparrow.

"Is it religion in general you don't like? Or preachers?" Shoulders sagging, his expression turned somber. "Because it's obvious from your expression you don't relish attending."
~~~

"My mother's husband was a PK, as you called them." The words came out as a scoff. Did she really just admit that to a near stranger?

"Her husband? Not your father?" He studied her, bringing a burn to her cheeks.

She might as well finish the story. At least part of it. "My dad died when my sister and I were very young. Momma didn't remarry for several years, but when she did, it was a nightmare. For all of us."

"I'm sorry. That's one of the reasons I've not dated anyone since I lost Olivia's mother." His gaze held hers, his sympathy obvious. "I wouldn't settle for anyone who didn't love her as much as her mother and I do…her mother did. If that's possible."

Maybe he could sympathize with a scrap of what her family had been through. There'd be no way he could imagine the heinousness of the situation, though.

But didn't Pete date at all? Because Hope sure seemed to be waiting on the ready. "One of the reasons? Are there others?"

He lifted one muscled shoulder. "I guess I haven't found… the one."

"I don't know much about relationships—I've never gotten involved with anyone myself—but wouldn't you have to date to find her?"

"Maybe. Maybe not." His eyes had a twinkle to them. "I'm trying to allow God to be my leader. Sometimes, I'm too thick-headed to listen."

"You and Miss Lydia." She shook her head. "I don't get that listening for God expression. How does that work, exactly?"

"First, I study His written Word—the Bible—so I know

His character. Then I pray. I listen. Not as well as I should—life gets busy. I'm stubborn."

"But how do you know? I mean, what do you hear?" This never made sense to her when Miss Lydia tried to explain either.

"Let me give you a bit of background." He rested a hip against the porch railing, and Skye moved over to do the same, leaving a foot of space between them. "I was a bit of a wild child in high school. Tired of following rules, sick of the scrutiny of being a PK, I gave up trying to be what everyone expected. I could never be as good as my father.

"Though I committed to attend a Christian college and major in Christian ministry, all I wanted to do was work for Pop in the charter business. Because I didn't want to live under the constant scrutiny like my parents had. I only went to the college because that was what everyone expected of me."

"So, you *are* a preacher?" Skye held his gaze.

"I probably would have ended up being kicked out of the university, and I wouldn't have cared. But early on, a couple of things happened."

"You met your wife?"

"That was part of it, but not enough. At chapel one morning, I had a hangover and cottonmouth. I was so thirsty. The student minister told a story about trying to cure thirst with water from a bucket full of holes. Nothing ever satisfied that thirst. I felt that way. Kind of half empty and leaking. Then he said Jesus could repair my bucket and give me living water." He scuffed the boards of the deck with his shoe. "A simple lesson, but something clicked. Nothing I could do on my own would ever fill me. Nothing would make me feel whole. I gave my life to Jesus then and there."

Something inside her yearned for more of his story.

She could certainly relate to feeling empty and leaking. "Then what?"

"I started listening for His voice. Sometimes it comes like a nudge to do something. Other times, a phrase pops into my mind. Occasionally, advice from another Christian strikes a chord in my heart. I consider the feeling, the phrase, or advice. I pray. I check to see if it lines up with God's good character and His Word. If it does, I try to follow. Obey."

"Have you heard something lately? Can you give an example?"

Looking away, Pete's Adam's apple rose and lowered with a hard swallow. "Yes." He took a step closer and faced her. "I came to apologize to you."

He reached out his arms, and she froze. "What are you doing?"

"Right now, with all you have going on in your life—the wreck, losing your stuff, Miss Lydia—I feel like you need a hug." His lips quirked into a smirk. "I haven't prayed about it yet, though, so I could be wrong. May I?"

His offer didn't set off the alarms she'd expect. Still, she tucked her chin to her chest. "I'm not really the touchy-feely type."

"I noticed." He laughed, and the sound of it floated through the air like the cool spray of the sea on a sunny day.

Be brave, precious. Miss Lydia's words echoed through her mind. Now she was hearing voices.

"Okay." She squeezed her eyes closed and braced herself, as if for an unexpected blow. "You can."

Another chuckle tickled her ears, and Pete's arms gently slid around her upper back.

His chest felt firm, and he smelled of a woodsy soap. "I'm sorry for my bad behavior on top of all you've gone through.

All you're still going through."

His chin rested on her head a second, as if it were the most natural thing in the world. Skye's muscles relaxed, and she savored the strange sweetness of the moment.

Then he stepped back. "I should go. It's Olivia's bedtime, and I'm sure you're tired too."

Olivia probably wouldn't sleep well tonight with a sunburn, and she'd have to go out in the sun again if Pete had to work. The least she could do was try to make up for her mistake. If he'd let her.

"Do you…? If you want, I can…" Words fumbled in her mouth, but Pete waited for her to regain the use of her tongue. "I could try watching Olivia again tomorrow, that is, if you have a charter. After the service. I'll keep her out of the sun."

His gaze bounced between her and the house, then back. "Sounds perfect. I'll text any instructions I can think of. I know you'll take good care of her." He smiled, and all felt right with the world.

She'd never spent so much time in the company of a man, never willingly anyway. Certainly, never without stifling the desire to bolt. And for good reason.

But she'd never known a man like Pete Thompson.

Chapter 23

Bird songs filled the unseasonably cool spring morning air as Skye and Sparrow left the house. Sleepy-eyed, Sparrow yawned and climbed into the car. Once Skye made sure Sparrow buckled in, she lingered to take a sip of her to-go cup of coffee and soak in the sounds.

"What are you doing?" Sparrow stared at her as if she'd lost her mind.

"Listening," she whispered.

Sparrow tipped her head to one side. "That's a lot of chirping."

"The island is one of the first migratory stops where multiple species of birds rest after flying across the Gulf. That's why so many bird watchers come."

"What are the ones I hear tweeting?"

"Warblers and cardinals." She pointed to the limb of a nearby oak. "I spy an indigo bunting."

"He's pretty! So blue." Her eyes widened.

An ache began in Skye's chest. "Those were my mother's favorite. They remind me of her."

"Momma loves red birds. I wonder what my other mother's favorite was."

Air congealed in Skye's lungs, and dizziness blurred her vision. Now Sparrow was wondering about her birth mother?

Had this started because of Miss Lydia's illness?

That had to be the reason. At the hospital, the situation with Miss Lydia hadn't allowed an opportunity to ask how to deal with Sparrow's question about her father. Now this.

The answers would have to wait. The truth would do nothing but cause pain.

Skye forced in a breath. "We should get going or we'll be late to church."

After the short drive to the beach, they exited the car. Her nerves pulsed at the thought of being here for this service without Miss Lydia. She spotted Pete's form, but he faced the other way, talking to Hope. Now her heart rate fluttered as she recalled the tenderness of his embrace, the clean scent of his shoulder next to her cheek. Warmth rippled across her body as she relived the silly event for probably the hundredth time since last night.

She was being ridiculous. The feeling could be attributed to brain chemicals overreacting to stimuli. Hormones released from the hypothalamus and pituitary into the bloodstream during social contact accounted for feelings of bonding in mammals.

"Come on. I see Olivia." Sparrow took Skye's hand, and they trekked down the boardwalk to the beach.

The sun barely peeked over the Gulf, spraying magenta and gold against the sky. A few wispy white clouds hovered above the water. Ten yards from the circle of people gathered on the sand, a lone gray heron, with his spindly legs and broad wings, struck a lovely pose in the surf. He stared out at the sea, searching for breakfast, his silhouette dark against the sunrise.

Tension dissolving at the view, Skye's steps lightened, and they reached the sand. She'd observe nature while this church business went on. Miss Lydia would know how to handle the birth-parent questions with Sparrow. The wise woman always had a way of giving the best answers to make things right. If only she would receive a transplant and get well.

Please, let her get one.

Skye held in a groan. Who was she talking to? As if she'd accepted that a Creator intervened in the lives of humans.

"Skye! Sparrow!" Olivia spotted them, jumped from her beach blanket, and ran their way.

Hope followed not far behind.

"Careful." Skye's voice squeaked. She sure didn't want Olivia to stumble or step on a fishbone before the day even started. Pete had the child dressed in another long-sleeved sunsuit and hat. She'd no doubt been fully slathered with SPF 50.

After a quick clomp across the sand, the girl reached them and hugged Skye's legs. "Can Sparrow go for a walk with me and Hope?"

"Is it okay with your dad?" Weird that he'd let them leave.

Olivia bobbed her head. "He's going to talk to the adults for a few minutes while Hope tells us kids a Bible story, then we'll come back together for the rest. We do that sometimes."

Blue gaze colliding with Skye's, Pete smiled and gave a nod. His dark scruff had grown a little fuller each day since she'd met him. Not something she normally noticed, but the beard looked nice on him.

Especially when he smiled that way.

"If that's what Pete wants, yes, but I could walk with you too."

Hope held out both hands. "Pete would like you to stay. Come on, girls. Maybe we'll find shells while we're out."

A few other young children followed, and Hope began speaking about some men in a boat.

"I have a seat for you." Pete motioned to a lawn chair beside Caleb.

Holding in a sigh, she took her place. Why did Pete want her to be here while they left?

Eventually the wind faded out Hope's conversation with the kids. Pete paced a few steps in the sand before speaking. "Over the past week, I've had a Scripture pecking away at me from Romans eight. Not an easy chapter. The writer talks about how our present suffering can't compare to the glory waiting for us. How all of creation is frustrated and groaning to be liberated from this bondage of decay."

He pinched the bridge of his nose. "Sorry. This is hard for me to talk about." He blew out a long breath. "Most of you know I lost my wife to melanoma. At sixteen weeks pregnant, she began having seizures. She'd beaten cancer in her early teens, but we were shocked to find out it had come back. I was so angry when she refused treatment during her pregnancy, unwilling to allow any risk to our unborn daughter. She had such a great love for our child that she was willing to sacrifice anything to give Olivia life."

Every muscle in Skye's body tensed, and nausea flooded her.

What an awful dilemma. How unfair. His wife must have wanted a baby so badly. And people had children every day they didn't even want.

The harsh thought barbed her, sending a splintering pain through her core.

Stop. She closed her eyes and tried to imagine she was like the heron. Just a bird standing on the shore, the wind ruffling through its feathers.

"I'm not much of a scientist." Pete's voice broke in. "But I think there's a law in thermodynamics that implies that complex, ordered arrangements tend to become more disordered with time."

That piqued her interest. Opening her eyes, Skye nodded. The second law of thermodynamics.

"The layman's version is that everything is going from order to disorder—wearing out. We are decaying in our physical bodies because sin entered the world way back near the beginning of time on earth. It released a curse and set that law of decline into motion. But the thing is, we have a Creator who loves us so much, He was willing to allow His son to die so that we could be free of that curse. And, out of great love, His son was willing to endure that pain of a death on a cross."

All of creation is groaning.

Pete's words leapt into Skye's dark thoughts. He'd said that to her before. This message was aimed at her. That was why he'd wanted her to stay. Was it because Miss Lydia was sick—maybe dying?

It would be amazing if somehow God allowed her to live.

Amazing but doubtful.

Pete continued. "We have hope that, despite heartaches, despite the loss of our loved ones in this life—and despite our own illness or pain—nothing can separate us from God's love. I've come to understand a tiny portion of that love as a father, because now that I have Olivia, there's nothing I wouldn't give up for her."

Another realization nailed Skye. Miss Lydia would do the same for Sparrow or her. In fact, Miss Lydia would probably give up her life and possessions for almost anyone, if they truly needed it. She'd lived that kind of love since Skye had met her back in high school.

Perhaps Pete had shown a hint of something similar.

Self-sacrifice wasn't natural. Most people behaved selfishly, little better than wild animals. Not Miss Lydia or Pete. How did they do it?

"The only way we can love like our Creator is to give Him our life and our love. Then His Spirit guides our hearts."

Aiming a look at Skye, he said, "In Christ, we have a hope that the rest of the world can't understand. Because we believe what we see here is not the end. It's only a fraction of our journey."

Was he reading her mind? Maybe he and Miss Lydia had the right idea, believing that this life wasn't all there was. Because this life could be downright ugly.

"In Isaiah sixty-five, the writer describes a time when God will create a new heaven and a new earth, where the wolf and the lamb will feed together, and the lion will eat straw like an ox. The former pain will be forgotten."

The way Pete spoke the words from the Bible painted a beautiful picture in Skye's mind. A new world where animals didn't rip each other apart. Wouldn't that be amazing?

Pete was really good at this preaching thing.

"The kids are coming back." Pete moved to stand in front of his chair. "I thought this a little too much for Olivia and the children to take in, so I'll end there." He nodded to a young man seated beside a woman with a baby. "Can you lead our singing?"

The man agreed and started a song Skye had never heard. She stared at the woman with him. Could she be the lady who might babysit for them? Dressed in blue jeans and a casual top, she looked normal enough. Not fancy. She had a pleasant expression looking at her child in her lap. The baby chewed on a plastic ring of toys and smiled with chubby cheeks. He was cute and appeared well cared for.

The kids returned, and the girls settled onto Olivia's blanket. Each had their hands full of shells and rocks. Now Skye couldn't help but notice Hope's outfit. She wore a short jean jacket over a black dress that met her ankles over gold sandals. Dangly gold jewelry accented it all. Perfect as usual and staring at Pete all gooey-eyed.

A twinge of annoyance bit at Skye. Pete had said he hadn't dated since his wife passed away because he hadn't met the right person. It appeared Hope's continual infatuation hadn't received the memo. Supposedly, they'd been friends for a long time.

What in the world? Skye gave herself a mental slap. Pete's love life was not her concern. Refocusing elsewhere, she stared out at the heron instead. After standing still for a long while, it finally thrust its beak below the surf and snagged a good-sized fish. The bird rotated its head to swallow the catch.

All of creation is groaning.

The circle of life could be harsh. Could she believe that a Creator would provide a new earth where only good prevailed?

Someone said *amen*, and people began to gather their belongings, so Skye stood. At least these meetings were short.

Hope made a beeline to Pete. "Want me to take Olivia? How did she get so pink? Did your sunscreen expire?"

Maybe Hope *should* take Olivia. And Sparrow. A black feeling rooted in Skye's midsection and sprouted more doubt. She shouldn't be caring for children.

"Skye's got her today." His gaze swung her way, and that warm fuzzy feeling flowed over her again. "They're going to meet with April about childcare. I was about to introduce them."

He appeared confident in Skye's ability and had avoided answering the sunburn question.

Hope's cheeks drooped. "We could get a teen to watch Olivia at the store. I'd be right there."

He waved her off. "Thanks, but I think this is what we're going to do, if Skye agrees."

Chin dipping, Hope glanced at Skye, then turned back to Pete. "Okay."

The woman reminded Skye of a scorned puppy, and the sight pricked her heart. "You're welcome to go with us." Had she really just said that?

Hope offered her a sad smile and heaved her handbag over her shoulder. "Thanks, but I always have business I need to take care of."

Once Hope left, Pete made the introductions to April and her husband, Robert.

"Great sermon, Pete," Robert said. "We love you ministering to us, but are you sure you haven't missed your calling? You should be on a podcast or something, at least."

Pete's gaze fell. "Thanks for the encouragement." His feet shifted in the sand. "I better get to work."

Once the guys took off to start their day at sea, Skye loaded the girls in the car and followed April to her house.

She couldn't help thinking April's husband might be right though.

A few minutes later, they arrived at the brown wooden home and parked. The structure looked about as old as the one Skye rented, but the yard was well-groomed. The location wasn't far from the Sea Lab, and once they stepped inside, a yummy aroma hit Skye's nose. "What is that? Something smells wonderful."

"Just my pot roast in the slow cooker with some carrots and potatoes." April chuckled. "I'm all about using that thing since I had this little man." She dug her fingers into one of the baby's belly rolls, and he cackled. "Jack keeps me busy." She turned to smile at Olivia and Sparrow. "I bet these big girls can help me keep him entertained."

"Aww. He's so cute." Sparrow held her arms out. "Can I hold him?"

"Me too?" Olivia asked.

"I don't know…" Skye hedged.

"It'll be fine." April sounded so self-assured, even as new mom. "He's a chunk, so let's start by having you sit on the couch, and I'll set him on your lap. It'll be safer for both of you."

Patiently, April began a lesson on holding and caring for babies. She explained how they put everything in their mouths and other safety information. The girls cheered every time they got Jack to make his toothless grin. Then April explained that she'd been a high school math teacher until she'd had Jack, so she would gladly help with homework. Robert worked long hours on his dolphin cruises, a lot like Pete with the charter, so he'd rarely be around.

Skye liked the sound of that.

After another hour hanging out and talking over the logistics and a daily rate, Skye led the girls back to the car, her spirits lighter. Maybe, just maybe, this could work, and Sparrow would be okay here on the island. At least until Miss Lydia was well.

She *had* to get well.

Chapter 24

What could she do next to occupy the children?

Skye cleared their lunch dishes, placed them in the dishwasher, and wiped the counters while the girls bounced around the kitchen beside her, already bored.

She'd fed Olivia and Sparrow a healthy meal that didn't include sugar, chocolate, or sodas. They'd played a few games they'd found in the hall closet and taken the dogs for a walk.

"We wanna go to the beach." Sparrow tugged on Skye's shirt. "Please."

"With Olivia's sunburn still healing, that's not an option today." While Skye understood the draw of the sand and the waves, there was no way she'd chance it.

"Can we watch TV?" Olivia asked, and Sparrow's brows took a hopeful arc.

"Miss Lydia isn't a fan of letting Sparrow have too much screen time."

An audible sigh came from both girls, and their shoulders slumped.

Great. Only half a day in, and she was already failing. There had to be something fun, and maybe even educational, to keep two children busy for the afternoon. What had she and her sister done to pass their time as kids?

Her thoughts veered back to her days outside while growing up with Star. They'd spent hours pretending to travel on adventures. They'd always been on the lookout for hidden treasures.

That's it. Skye snapped her fingers. "I've got an idea." She tried to mimic the excited expression Miss Lydia used when teaching classes. "We'll start a list for a treasure hunt. We can work on it all summer."

"A list?" Sparrow's mouth twisted. "Are we just writing things down?"

That did sound dull. "If we find a shady place, we could start searching out the treasures once we come up with what we're looking for."

"What kind of treasures?" Olivia bounced on her toes. "Dollars? Jewelry?"

"Not really, but if you find some of that, you can add it to the collection. I was thinking more like things in nature. Pretty seashells, special rocks, rare birds…"

"We're going to catch birds and keep them?" Sparrow's jaw dropped.

Unable to stop a chuckle, Skye reached over and mussed the child's hair. "That would be illegal. We'll spot them and take a photo."

"The whole hunt is for a photo album?" A groan growled from Sparrow's throat.

"We'll keep the things we can and take pictures of the things we can't. Maybe even decorate a treasure chest for each of you." She tried for an overly happy expression. "Does that sound better?"

The girls gave hesitant nods.

"How can we find seashells if we can't go to the beach?" Olivia asked.

There had to be someplace outdoors that had shade.

Where was the map of the island she'd gotten from the bike rental company? Probably in the drawer of the end table. "Let me think a second."

She crossed the den and found the map. A quick look gave her the answer. "The bird sanctuary trail would be a good place to start. How does that sound?"

After exchanging glances with Olivia, Sparrow shrugged. "We'll try it."

Not as excited as she'd hoped, but they'd agreed. Skye brushed her hands across her shirt, knocking a few loose crumbs that had attached to her during lunch. What would they need for the trail? Binoculars, the phone… *Think childcare, Skye.*

There might be mud, so closed-toed shoes and wipes. Mosquitoes would be out, maybe ticks too. She had insect repellent, but did kids need a special kind? A quick stop at the store could answer that question.

A skitter of anxiety trickled over her. "Olivia, are you allergic to bugs, wasps, or anything else that lives outdoors?" Because something much worse than a sunburn could happen.

"No, ma'am. I'm not allergic."

"Okay, y'all go put on socks and tennis shoes."

She'd better shoot a text to Pete, just to make sure the information was correct before they left. Better yet, she'd ask his permission to go on the trail with his daughter. Would he be too far out in the Gulf to get the message? This could go wrong in so many ways. A cloud of gloom fell like dense fog over her. Why had she thought this would be a good idea?

Grabbing her phone from the coffee table, she texted Pete. A few seconds later, he replied. Holding her breath, she swiped to read the answer.

Sounds perfect! No allergies. Have fun but watch out for the gator in and around the swamp. Maybe don't take your dogs.

A breath stuttered in her chest. She'd been in the vicinity of plenty of reptiles, but never with children. Tension coiled in her neck, and she shot a text back.

Are you sure it's okay?

Yes, ma'am.

"We're ready!" Sparrow ran in, Olivia right behind her.

No backing out now. They'd just avoid the swamp. No reason to tempt fate. She pushed on her own shoes and led them out the door.

After a quick trip to the store, they stopped by the lab to print off a scavenger hunt she'd found which was made for kids and to borrow a set of binoculars. Then, they parked on the gravel-and-shell lot by the sanctuary. Only a few other cars there, thankfully. She'd rather not be in a crowd.

Once they doused themselves in an insect repellent labeled that it was safe for kids, they entered the path. Dead leaves, sticks, and pine straw covered the ground. Thick green bushes, palms, and pines lined both sides of the trail. This vegetation and natural mulch made the perfect place for birds to rest or feed, but also an ideal area for snakes to camouflage themselves.

"It's like being in the jungle." Imitating sounds resembling an orangutan grunting, Sparrow jumped up and down, making funny faces. She ran ahead, and Olivia followed.

"Wait." Skye ran after them. "Keep an eye on the ground for snakes."

"Okay," they answered but kept going, not watching much of anything.

"And you don't want to scare the birds." She'd need to find some other way to catch their attention. "Look! I see one." She saw a flutter in the leaves anyway. "Who wants to use the binoculars first?"

That did it, finally. Once they stopped and began sharing the field glasses, they spotted several interesting species. The photos wouldn't be great from this distance, but they'd work.

"Another yellow warbler!" Sparrow whispered.

She was really getting into it. Maybe they should invest in a good camera for her.

"I believe that one's called a Cape May Warbler," Skye said.

"Let me see." Olivia held out her hands, eager for her turn.

They stood silently observing, no sound but the whisper of wind rustling leaves and the twittering songs of the birds.

A flutter of wings to their right had them swiveling to check the source. Skye pressed a finger over her mouth, hoping the girls would remain quiet.

They stood and watched as a painted bunting lit on a scrubby palmetto bush only a couple of feet away. The stocky male had a vivid blue head, a green back, and a red torso.

Truly spectacular.

Wouldn't her mother have loved to see this one? Skye's gaze fell on Sparrow. Eyes wide, she smiled up at Skye and mouthed, "A treasure."

Then Olivia took Skye's hand, awe evident on her face.

A dam cracked open inside Skye. So much love flowed through her, it swept her breath away. These children were the true treasures.

No matter that she was terrible at parenting, it would still tear her apart when the time came to say good bye.

Chapter 25

Please, God, let everyone be safe and unharmed.

Pete whispered a prayer for at least the hundredth time today as he exited his truck. When Skye had messaged about going on the trail at the sanctuary, he'd refused to let fear rule his spirit. Throughout the day, he'd had to use God's Word to battle anxious thoughts that assailed him. Crazy thoughts popped up, like Olivia, Skye, and Sparrow being swarmed by bees, or a gator attack, even though, to his knowledge, none living there had ever gone after a human. A recent social media post about a water moccasin came to mind. But he had taken Olivia to walk that path before and hadn't been nervous.

He sure seemed to be under attack today.

"Daddy!" Olivia ran down the steps of Skye's porch, the smaller dog, Sam, following on her heels. No apparent damage.

Relief swept over him as he took her in. He loved the sound of Olivia's voice when she called him Daddy. If only she'd always stay this eager to see him. When she reached him, he knelt and pulled her into his arms. "Hey, sweet girl. How was your day?"

"Skye started a treasure hunt! And we're gonna work on it every time we're together."

"Really?" He glanced up at Skye, who'd left her seat on the porch when he'd driven up. The bigger dog whimpered beside the chair she'd vacated. "That should be fun."

The timid smile on Skye's face captured his attention. The dwindling light reflected in her soft brown eyes.

His pulse quickened, and something in his chest stirred, reminding him of emotions long buried.

"It is fun, and we can work on it all summer." Olivia slipped from his grasp but tugged him by the hand toward a cardboard box that Sparrow held at the top of the stairs. "Come see the blue feather we found, some pretty oyster shells, and rocks that have fossils in them."

"I can't wait."

Night birds crooned quiet songs to the chorus of frogs croaking. His heart seemed to join with its own drumbeat while holding Skye's gaze as he walked. "How about we find another treasure tonight?" The words slipping out of his mouth took him by surprise. "Unless y'all are tired. Or have other plans."

The offer had Skye's jaw dropping for a half second. "No plans, other than preparing for the morning, but it's getting dark."

"That's right. Sparrow starts school tomorrow." Dumb idea. Olivia had school, too, but the air felt so much like summer already, he'd let it slip his mind. "We'll do it another time."

"Aww." Sparrow groaned. "Do I have to go to school? You could homeschool me at night."

"It's what Miss Lydia said to do." Skye captured her bottom lip for a moment then continued. "We might have time to do one last hunt tonight. What did you have in mind?"

Her gaze landed on him, and his brain went blank. Maybe he hadn't drunk enough water this afternoon in the heat because he sure felt off. What did he have in mind?

"Yeah, Daddy, what can we look for at night?"

Night…what could they find? What had he been thinking? It would be dark. Stars came out after dark.

"How about we get my telescope and take it to the beach.

Find a few constellations? Maybe a shooting star if we get lucky."

"Oh, cool!" Sparrow set aside the box and scampered down the stairs toward him, a grin lighting up her face. "That sounds fun. I love using Momma's telescope."

Her smile faltered.

Poor child. He'd been there—felt the guilt for having fun when a loved one was ill. Pete patted her shoulder. "In that case, I bet you'll know just what to do. You can help me set up."

That seemed to cheer her a bit. Pete checked Skye's reaction. Worry creased her brow as she watched Sparrow. "Does that plan work for you, Skye?"

She gave a single nod. "I'll get the dogs in and lock up." After disappearing for a few minutes, she returned carrying Olivia's backpack. "You'll need this."

"Yep. I'd be looking for it in the morning. Want to take my truck?"

"Okay." She shrugged, and the girls ran toward the back doors.

"We'll swing by my house for the telescope."

Her muscles visibly tensed, and her eyes widened. The scared doe-eyes again. What had some man done to her?

"Y'all can wait outside in my driveway." He tried to sound reassuring. "It won't take me a second to run in."

Her chest rose and fell as if she'd just caught her breath after a long swim underwater, but her fears appeared relieved. For now.

In fifteen minutes, they'd retrieved what they needed and driven to the end of the road on the east side of the island, just past Fort Gaines, the old garrison used in the Civil War.

Once he'd set up the telescope on the beach, he aimed the

lens at the rising moon. The last of the sun's rays evaporated into the inky darkness. While the girls chattered about what they saw, he and Skye sat behind them on a large quilt. He'd intentionally grabbed the biggest one he had, suspecting she'd want her distance.

About a foot away—closer than he'd expected—she tucked her knees to her chest and wrapped her arms around them. Her slender neck arched as she stared into the heavens. He should be looking for the brightest star of Leo, the Lion, so he could point out the constellation to the girls, but he couldn't seem to tear his eyes away from this woman beside him.

Skye possessed her own kind of light—a treasure—which was quickly etching a place in his heart.

"What do you see?" he asked, his voice barely a whisper, just for her.

"I was thinking of my sister. Star." Her gaze dropped to meet his. "Watching those two play together reminds me of us when we were young."

"Skye and Star." He chuckled. "They go well together."

"Yeah, Momma was a bit…unusual." She stared at the sand, lips pinched. "She died when I was eighteen."

"That had to be hard." The rhythm of waves and wind filled the air between them. What more could he say? Losing his wife left a giant whole in his life. "Where's your sister?"

Her shoulders lifted. "Haven't talked to her in years. She ran away when Momma died, so she wouldn't have to live with…" Despite the warm breeze, a shiver made her entire body tremble.

"Your mom's husband?"

"The psychopath." Though her voice was low, she spit the words out. "Miss Lydia would have taken Star in, too, but my sister had always been determined. And tough. Nothing like me." That last sentence came out barely above a whisper, wrenching his insides.

What had the man done? Was he the one who'd hurt Skye? Based on her expression, the answer was yes.

"Where is the guy now?" He'd love to teach him a lesson in pain—like give the man a fist to the face the way he'd stopped a high school bully. Bad idea for more than one reason, though. And it would probably be even more of a scandal as the adult son of a popular minister than it had been back in the day.

"Jail, not far from here, but he's scheduled to be released this summer."

He didn't like the sound of that, but it explained her skittishness.

She chewed her lip. "I would've never come back."

Never come back? She'd abandoned her home because of this man?

"Couldn't you get a restraining order or something?"

"That would've only highlighted my presence to him, and I've worked hard to stay off his radar." Skye continued. "But I could tell at Christmas that Miss Lydia wasn't feeling well. That's why I applied for a grant to move my migration study to this area until the end of July."

"When did you leave this area?"

"Not long after Momma died, Miss Lydia helped me move to Florida for college."

"And you've not been in Alabama since?"

Her head made a small shake. "She visits me on holidays. Brings Sparrow."

Good grief. She had been too afraid to set foot in this state. "What's he in for?"

"Daddy, you have to see this crater on the moon!" Olivia waved for him to come.

Staring at the girls, she swallowed and spoke quietly. "It's not a term I'd ever want them to hear, much less understand." Suddenly rising, her feet sank into the sand, and she trekked to the telescope. "Can I see?"

A ball of dread anchored in Pete's gut. This guy had to be disgustingly evil.

And Skye, Sparrow, and now Olivia might all be in his line of fire when he got out of prison.

~~~

On the porch of her rental house, Skye couldn't stop staring. Millions of stars glittered in the night sky overhead, but none compared to the way Pete's eyes shimmered like crystal blue waves cresting in the summer.

"Thanks for going along with my last-minute intrusion into your treasure hunt."

Weird how she relished hearing his deep voice. "I wish we could've stayed longer." *Really?* Why would she say that?

"How about tomorrow night?" His eyes shone brighter—if that were possible. "We can set up out here, and I can grill fresh fish. There used to be an old charcoal grill out back."

A flash of heat crawled up her neck. Dinner tomorrow? Was he asking her on a date? Or did Pete feel he owed her for watching Olivia again and not letting any catastrophes happen this time? Maybe this was all part of some promise Miss Lydia pinned him with.

"Hey, Daddy." Olivia held the door partway open but didn't step out. Sparrow stood behind her.

"Hey, Olivia."

She spread on a big smile and batted her lashes. No doubt a request was on its way. "Can I spend the night?"
~~~

Holding up one hand, Pete shook his head. "This is a weeknight." He bounced an apologetic look Skye's way. "And I don't believe I heard anyone invite you."

"I did," Sparrow piped up. "I don't want to walk into school by myself not knowing anyone. *Please,* Pete." Now she tucked her chin and made a sad puppy face. "I've never been in a school like this. Only homeschool."

Skye couldn't help but feel sorry for Sparrow. Apparently, Pete felt the same, because he seemed speechless.

"It's okay with me," Skye said, "if it's okay with you." Of course, he might not trust her to get them to school on time and unscathed.

"I'd planned to drop her off at April's, since I have to have the boat out so early, but I wouldn't want to impose on you." His gaze searched Skye's, releasing strange currents swirling within her. But in a good way. A way she'd never felt before.

"I'm still ahead on the *imposing* chart, I think." She couldn't stop a smile. "I'll need very specific instructions, though."

"I can do that, no problem. And I'm definitely cooking dinner." The grin he returned soothed some of her broken places like the estuaries nourished sea life. "You do eat fish, right?"

"I will enjoy your fish." Her cheeks flamed. What a dumb thing to say.

"The pressure's on now." He chuckled. "I'll run to pack a bag for Olivia and leave it on the porch like last time. But with instructions."

Skye nodded. No reason to risk blurting out something else stupid.

"Give me a hug." He held out his arms for Olivia, but both girls ran over and wrapped their arms around him. A precious sight. "You girls be good for Skye."

"We will," they said together.

"Good night." His gaze landed on her. "I'm a phone call away if you need anything. You know where I live now."

His tone felt intimate, and suddenly she longed for one of his sweet hugs, too, but she didn't dare initiate one. That would be ridiculous.

She swallowed the lump in her throat before attempting to speak. "I do."

Lines crinkled his temples when he gave her one last smile. "See you tomorrow then."

Tomorrow.

She'd seen him for days in a row. And she'd see him the next. The girls would go to school together and spend their afternoons at the same babysitter.

And then they'd have dinner. Together.

The ground shifted under her feet, and her starving soul latched onto his promise and held tight. Because, other than Miss Lydia, no one had ever been there for her.

Chapter 26

Excitement pulsed through Skye's veins, and a warm breeze skimmed over her skin. In the passenger seat of the boat, she breathed in the scent of spring and the honeysuckle blooms filling the air. Thankfully, the movement of the vessel gave relief from the eighty-percent humidity. Multiple sightings of manatees had been reported this morning, so she and the marine veterinarian headed out in one of the smaller research vessels in the Dog River in search of the creatures. They could perform routine weekly sampling, and if they were fortunate, observe the animals foraging.

As the weather warmed, some manatees migrated from Florida into the Alabama waters for the summer. Her study of their diets indicated they enjoyed the vegetation in this area.

No sightings so far, though.

A boat zipped by, leaving a huge wake and jostling them. The jerks were traveling much too fast. Obviously, that vessel didn't have a designated marine mammal spotter. Didn't they realize the slow-moving animals were endangered?

"Is this the inlet where you received the most reported sightings?" Ignoring the annoyance, Dr. Courtney Boleware pointed ahead to an area in the water shaded by trees with an abundance of plant life.

Skye checked the map where she'd loaded the hotspots on her phone. This area held the highest occurrence of sightings, probably because it presented the habitat preferences like fresh, shallow water and submerged aquatic plants.

"Looks correct."

"How about we anchor, take our samples, and watch a while?" The forty-ish woman's accent gave away her Northern roots. Was it odd for her to live in such a small Alabama town after growing up in New York City? Not something Skye would venture to ask, as it was none of her business.

"Sounds good," Skye said.

The boat slowed near tall water grasses beneath a tree, and Skye lowered the anchor, while Dr. Boleware cut the engine. With the motor quieted, the songs of birds and the rippling of water kept the silence at bay. Someone must have been doing construction downriver because the occasional pound of a hammer and buzz of a saw rent the air. In the distance, a dog bark echoed every now and then, but other than that, blessed quiet reigned.

One of the great things Skye had already figured out about her colleague was that Dr. Boleware didn't require unnecessary conversation. They both took various samples and then settled in to observe their surroundings.

Over an hour passed, and perspiration beaded on Skye's nose. A dragonfly zipped between the boat and the water, wings shimmering in the sun. With the red and pink abdomen, it was probably a male Roseate Skimmer, from what she recalled in Miss Lydia's science classes. Miss Lydia had often had her students complete studies of the insects.

Remembering Miss Lydia dampened her spirits. Were things going well at the hospital in Birmingham? No one wanted to wish another's death, but they needed a transplant soon.

All of creation is groaning.

Pete's words tumbled through her mind. If everything in the world was decaying, what good did prayer do?

Precious child, prayer isn't a want list. It's a conversation. A relationship.

Now Miss Lydia's words echoed from way back to that summer after high school—the summer of Momma's death. She'd encouraged Skye to pray. But it never seemed logical. Why would the Creator of the Universe want to talk to humans?

Her stomach decided to complain loudly about skipping lunch, so she pulled a pack of almonds from her supplies. She should probably be polite and offer some to her coworker. "I have extra if you'd like."

Gaze shifting, Dr. Boleware examined the snack before nodding and extending her hand. "Thank you."

Skye handed over the package, then retrieved another. "You're welcome."

"I hear you're in charge of the educational table at the fishing rodeo this year." She spoke between crunching.

"Looks that way," Skye said. "Unless you'd like the honor, since I don't know anything about it."

That brought a rare chuckle from the doctor. "You appear competent. Besides, the student interns and grad students will help. There should be notes from last year to guide you."

"So that's a no?" Skye popped a nut in her mouth.

"I'll volunteer for a shift, but no." She quirked a smile. "I think you'll be amazed at the information we glean about the marine food webs. The three days of the rodeo are by far the lab's largest opportunity for scientific sampling each year. We gather weights, measurements, tissue samples, and even otoliths from the fish."

The ear bones could provide a wealth of information. She used them from deceased manatees to discover their age and diet.

A rustling noise snagged Skye's attention.

A few feet away the reeds shook and bent. "Something's there." She pointed to ripples in the water, then a large body became visible, and her breath caught. They'd found one.

"Yes," Dr. Boleware whispered and pointed. "There's another following."

A snout lifted from below the surface, and Skye aimed her camera to document the scar pattern on the manatees' backs. The scars from nonlethal propeller encounters identified the individual animals like a fingerprint, and seeing an animal she recognized from Florida would be a treat.

A few fish swam away from the vegetation. The manatees' foraging created a small cloud in the river.

Spotting her and Dr. Boleware in the boat, one of the animals flapped its tail to slowly swim closer, lifting its head to check out the humans.

"You're a beauty," Skye whispered, "and so curious." The creature's eyes roved over them. Skye's excitement never faded working with these gentle giants.

"That's Gina." Dr. Boleware began recording a video. "I recognize that scar pattern. Four vertical marks above one horizontal. She's been a regular since at least 2017."

The manatee measured maybe eleven feet, possibly weighing thirteen hundred pounds. A nice size.

Both she and Dr. Boleware made notes and took pictures.

Obviously, a boat propeller had slashed the animal's back to form the design. If only she could ask when and where that accident had happened. In fact, she'd love to be able to communicate with these creatures. Or any animals, really. Growing up, she'd carried on plenty of pretend conversations with them.

Prayer is a conversation.

Something in her mind clicked as Miss Lydia's words repeated.

As much as Skye loved all the animals she encountered, perhaps a Creator also would love His creation.

Would a super-intelligent Being also like to communicate with them? Communicate with humans? But how did that work?

Pete had described his methodology. Perhaps she needed to question him more.

"Would you like to join me for the next few days to do a dolphin survey?" Dr. Boleware's voice interrupted Skye's musings. "Dr. McLeod will be tagging fish. And we've had several confirmed reports of a few manatees venturing miles offshore. We're still trying to understand what that means. One of the grad students can cover your calls."

"That would be wonderful." Being out on the water beat sitting at the computer any day. "Which vessel will we take?"

"I've chartered a fishing boat for the rest of the week."

"A fishing charter?"

"We often hire Captain Thompson to take us out to do tagging or sampling when the other boats are booked."

"Pete Thompson?" Skye's pulse skittered.

They'd be spending an awful lot of time together.

"You already know him?" Dr. Boleware's gaze swung to Skye.

"I'm renting a house from him. Or rather, his family."

Dr. Boleware breathed a laugh. "It can be a small world down here."

True.

Or else there sure were a lot of coincidences. What would Pete and Miss Lydia think about *that*?

~~~
~~~

Pete threw on a button-down shirt and his nicest pair of jeans, then made his way back to the bathroom. After wiping the fog from the mirror, he finger-combed his hair.

It needed a trim, but he hadn't had time, and he didn't want to impose on Hope again. He scrubbed a hand over his stubbly chin. Should he shave?

He hadn't been this nervous about cooking fish in years. Was this a date? Or simply a friendly dinner? What did Skye think it was?

While she'd seemed afraid of him initially, the way she looked at him the night before when he'd left her porch felt…different. As if she'd like him to embrace her again.

And he'd wanted to. Almost had. Then, he'd chickened out.

Memories of their last hug still lingered. The simple gesture had churned up a sea of jumbled emotions—protectiveness, yearning, vulnerability…a connection.

Could he release the sails of his heart back into stormy waters? The whole idea frightened him worse than watching a waterspout drop down over his boat. He'd only ever loved one woman. Losing Kenzie had almost destroyed him.

While he'd cared about Hope as a friend, things with Skye felt different. Different from Kenzie too.

Why did life have to be so complicated?

Thank God, Caleb had volunteered to clean up and prepare for tomorrow's run so Pete had time to think before he set out toward Skye's. His best friend had been forced to carry a lot of the burden over the years for Pete, but even more so since Mom's stroke.

Good grief. He needed to quit idling and get a move on. Skye and the girls already waited at her house. Grabbing his wallet and shoving it in his pocket, he headed to the kitchen.

From the table, he gathered the ice chest with the fish and the sack with charcoal and everything he'd need to grill, then flew out the door. Eight minutes later, he pulled into the drive at Skye's to find them all hunkered over a bucket by the porch stairs.

A cute sight.

"What have y'all got over there? A new treasure?" he asked.

"Daddy!" Olivia waved furiously. "Come see before we let him go. Skye caught a bullfrog."

He threw back his head and laughed. "Really?"

"What's so funny?" Skye lifted a fat amphibian, its legs and webbed feet dangling. "Would you like to take a look before I release him into that gully by the bike trail? The dogs had him cornered over here. Scared him to death."

"Sure." Pete had seen and held plenty, growing up, but he'd play along. "I guess I shouldn't be surprised by you, nature girl."

Olivia and Sparrow giggled at the name, but a line creased Skye's forehead. "Nature girl?"

"Makes a fitting nickname," he teased. Coming close, he checked out the creature. "Nice. Want me to add him to our dinner menu?"

"No!" All three of the females shrieked.

Winking at Skye, he held both hands up. "Just kidding. I'm grilling, not frying."

Her nose made the most adorable crinkle. "Way to ruin dinner, but I cleaned the grill and got it ready for you."

"Even nature girls won't be able to refuse this delicious meal." Pivoting, he returned to the truck to fetch his supplies. "Tell them how good your daddy cooks, little minnow." He threw a grin at Olivia.

Too enamored with the frog to care, she ignored him.

No worries. Once they got a whiff of the grilled Spanish mackerel, zucchini, and all that garlic roasting, they'd pay attention. For a petite child, Olivia loved her dinnertime.

He'd gathered everything and set to work mounding the coals just right, then lighting them.

While he waited for the briquets to turn white and glow, he rejoined the girls.

"We'll release Mr. Bully safely into the ditch now." Skye stood, still holding the frog.

Now that Pete really looked at her, he noticed Skye had splatterings of mud dotting pretty much all of her clothes. And she seemed perfectly comfortable that way. Not many women would be, and he couldn't help but respect that.

"Aw, can't we keep him overnight?" Sparrow made puppy eyes.

"That wouldn't be healthy for him, and we wouldn't want to cause him distress, would we?" Skye gave her a parental look.

"No, ma'am," the girls answered in unison.

"Can I watch?" Pete asked.

"You can do the honors if you like, Captain." Smirking, Skye stretched her arms and the frog close to his face, its beady eyes staring at him.

"Gotta keep my hands clean for cooking your dinner, ma'am."

She lowered the frog but gave him a knowing look.

He grinned at their banter as they walked toward the ditch. Skye hadn't appeared this relaxed since he'd met her. "Did everyone have a good day?"

Sparrow nodded. "I liked school, and Miss April is really nice."

"And she helps us do our homework, then we get to play

with Jack." Olivia's voice held excitement. "He's so cute. I wish I had a baby brother."

Well, that wasn't happening. He hurried to change the subject. "How about your day, nature girl?"

Skye shot a narrow glance his way. "I'll only tell you if you promise to never call me that again."

Huffing, he rolled his eyes. "Okay. I'll have to find a nickname you like."

"Or not." She chuckled before kneeling at the edge of the culvert. "Bye, Mr. Bully. Have a good life."

The girls watched him hop away then ran back toward the house.

"Wash your hands well," Skye called after them. Then her gaze landed on him, and a smile lit her face. "I spotted a manatee today. Two, actually."

"That's amazing. Where?" Seeing her happy sent a spike to his pulse and warmed his heart way too much, but he couldn't stop staring. Couldn't stop reveling in the beauty of it.

"On the Dog River. They were spectacular. I can show you pictures once I clean up."

"I'd like that." He smiled down at her, taking in the curve of her jaw, the slope of her nose…those caramel brown eyes with flecks of gold.

So mesmerizing. He swallowed hard at the thickness swelling in his throat. His thoughts tangled like a backlash of fishing line.

"And guess who's going to be on your charter the rest of the week?" Cheeks pinking, she turned her gaze toward the ground.

He blinked to clear his head.

Who was going on his charter? "Oh, um. Dr. Boleware and someone from her… You?"

Her shoulders made a shy shrug. "Looks like you're stuck spending more time with me."

"That is a nice surprise." Really nice. "I'll get to prove fishermen aren't all bad. We care about the health of the marine ecosystem. It's where we make our livelihood."

"We'll see." She flicked her gaze toward the house and quickened her steps. "I better clean up and make sure the girls did the same."

"Dinner will be ready soon." If he could just reel in his spinning thoughts.

Skye disappeared into the house, and Pete got to work. The pleasant night passed much too quickly as they ate and talked and laughed with the girls. He hadn't enjoyed an evening that much in a long time.

Skye cleared away plates while he packed up the leftovers.

"I'll put these in the fridge for you." He took the container across the kitchen. "They'll still be good tomorrow night." Tomorrow night after they'd spent the day together. The thought of that kept floating through his head, sending a tingle of excitement and a bit of angst.

He wished he had time to check over the boat tonight to make sure everything was perfect. But he needed to get Olivia in bed.

"We enjoyed it. You're a good cook." Skye tucked the last plate in the dishwasher and turned it on.

The compliment sent a burn up his neck. "We better go. It'll be an early day. Thank God for April."

"Yeah, seems like she's used to our crazy schedules since her husband has a similar job." They both walked into the living room where the girls played with stuffed animals, and the dogs looked on. Rocky the cat batted at the smaller dog's tail.

"Let's go, Olivia. You'll see Sparrow bright and early tomorrow."

His daughter scrambled up, ran to Skye, and embraced her legs. "Can we eat together again? And find more treasures?"

Bending down, Skye pulled Olivia into a hug. "You and Sparrow will be together at April's and can look for special things every day, but your dad and I will have to let you know about dinner, okay?" She pecked a kiss on his daughter's head.

Olivia considered the answer a moment. "Okay. But I bet we can, right, Daddy?"

He scooped her up into his arms and nibbled her neck. "You're a sneaky little critter, aren't you?"

"Stop, that tickles!" She burst into a round of giggles.

He turned his gaze toward Skye. "See you tomorrow." Part of him was relieved that his arms were filled, so he didn't have to decide about hugging her.

Part of him was much too disappointed that he couldn't hold her.

Chapter 27

At the dock, the morning sun crested the water as Skye stepped onto the boardwalk. Ships of various shapes and sizes filled the marina. Pelicans stood on pilings and stretched their wings. She could almost taste the brine in the air, and excitement built in her chest. Not only about spending the day offshore in nature. What would it be like on the water with Pete Thompson?

Her thoughts lingered on him the rest of the night. How did that look he'd given her before he'd left ignite such a flame in her heart? It was as if the man had broken through a lifetime of her self-defense mechanisms with a gaze and a smile.

She'd let her guard down. Around a male. And she hadn't been shredded to pieces. But that didn't prove she was safe with him all the time. It didn't prove she'd be safe with him if they were alone. Today, though, there would be other scientists along for the ride.

Passing the boats parked in slips, she couldn't help but smile at the vessel dubbed *Therapy*. The sentiment fit. A day on the water might be worth more than counseling sessions for some people. People like her.

Despite her hat and sunglasses, the rising sun glared into her eyes as she tried to spot the *Sea of Grace*. Ahead on her right, a man waved from aboard an enclosed-bridge yacht. Maybe a sixty-footer. Nice.

"Morning." Caleb stood on deck, placing a fishing rod into a brace. "We're about ready. Dr. McLeod is in the cabin with his grad students. We're just waiting on Dr. Boleware."

"Hey, I thought I saw you." Pete climbed down the ladder from the cockpit and hurried toward the gangplank. Tucked in his jeans was a light blue fishing shirt that highlighted the color of his eyes. And his dark hair.

Stop the weird thinking, Skye.

Smiling that welcoming way he'd done the night before, he reached out. "May I help you?"

She slipped her hand in his waiting one. Fingers rough, calloused, and strong held hers, and it felt as though a school of fish swirled in her midsection. His gaze fastened on her, those oceans of blue, washing her in warmth.

"Coffee's ready in the galley if you want a cup," he said as she stepped on deck.

Did she? Her brain fogged.

A breeze slipped between them, and he released her hand. "You're awfully quiet." He quirked a dark brow. "Even for you."

Yeah, she'd not said a word to either man yet. "I guess I do need caffeine."

"Come on." He waved her forward. "I'll give you the five-minute tour."

She followed him inside the cabin, where Dr. McLeod had already begun work on a laptop with two students, one male and the other female.

"Good morning," Skye said quietly.

Her colleague glanced up over his wire-rimmed glasses. "Looks like perfect weather today."

"Yes, sir." Nodding, she followed Pete to the counter, and he poured the steaming brew into a cup.

"Here you go. Nothing fancy, but we have creamer."

"Black's fine." She took the offering, then followed him farther into the boat.

"The others have been aboard the *Sea of Grace* before, so they know their way around." He pointed to a closed door on the right. "The important stuff. Here's the restroom." Then he nodded left. "Life jackets are under the benches." His feet halted, and he stared beyond them as if pondering his next move. "You can look at the rest if you like. Just bunk rooms for overnight trips. Or if someone needs to take a break. Make yourself at home."

Dr. Boleware strode in and made a beeline to the coffee pot. "Sorry I'm late, Captain."

"Only a few minutes." Pivoting, Pete took off toward the deck. "We'll set out." His steps were agile, confident, as he left to climb back up the ladder.

Skye's stomach made a little somersault as she followed him out and watched until he disappeared above. Over the past five years working on her doctorate, she'd ridden on numerous boats with numerous captains. Plenty were excellent, some arrogant, a few creepy, but none of the captains had ever made her feel so safe.

She'd learned, riding with Michael on the discovery excursion, that boats had to be careful to stay inside the buoys to go into the Gulf. The two hurricanes the year before had dumped large amounts of sand off the island and into the Mobile Bay and the Intercoastal Waterway, creating a multitude of issues, including vessels running aground.

Once their boat cleared the marina, they passed through the channel and under the bridge with no problems, then picked up speed. The sun beamed down on Skye while she watched for dolphins in the wake churning behind the boat. Caleb set to work baiting hooks for trolling as they moved.

Dr. McLeod and his students prepared to tag fish. Looking through binoculars, Dr. Boleware scanned the waters for common bottlenose dolphins and Atlantic spotted dolphins. A large stranding event the prior year had caused terrible losses of the creatures, due to exposure to low salinity after heavy rains and watershed flooding. The information they gleaned would track the population as well as the species' range and migration.

The morning passed quickly, and at lunchtime, Caleb climbed upstairs to relieve Pete. The others went inside to eat, but Skye's gaze kept wandering to the ladder. It was silly, feeling this way—the anticipation of his return tickling her senses. But she couldn't seem to stop.

Finally, he climbed down and closed the distance between them to stand beside her at the stern. "Did you bring lunch?" His deep voice floated over her like a gentle wave.

Her thoughts fumbled. Again. Had she?

"Must not be anything too tasty," he said when she still hadn't answered. "Caleb brought me a pizza, if you want to share." He gave her a playful nudge with his elbow. "It might not meet your eyelash test."

"You don't have to. I brought trail mix and a peanut butter sandwich in my backpack." Remembering her lunch preparations for herself and Sparrow the night before, she shrugged. "It was easy."

"Want to bring it out on deck to eat?" he asked.

The idea pleased her more than she would have expected. Yes, she'd rather be outside. With him. "I'd enjoy that."

"If you don't mind my looking in your pack, I'll bring everything out for us with a couple of soft drinks or waters."

"Okay."

He took a step then turned back, that smile landing on her again. "Any preference?"

She shook her head.

All around her, the music of the sea played its song, but all she heard was the beating of her heart as she stood in the warmth of his gaze. Her preference? Only him. And that realization scared her to death.

~~~

"How's Miss Lydia? Are you able to talk to her?" Pete took another bite of pizza, then regretted asking. Was it okay to bring up such a sensitive topic while they worked?

"No better. Still waiting on a transplant, but we video chat or talk on the phone every night." Skye breathed a sigh. "We can't visit, even on the weekends, since she's in isolation."

"That's got to be hard on you and Sparrow. I'm sorry." He studied her face, searching for some clue as to how to help. "I'm praying for her. For all of you."

"I know she appreciates that." She lifted her gaze to meet his, earnest and tender. "So do I."

Was she being polite, or had her thoughts changed on spiritual things?

She glanced down at her food, her voice low. "I've been considering what you said about talking to a Creator and all. Perhaps there could be some validity to it." She must have read his mind. Then she lifted her gaze again. "By the way, how is your mother?"

She'd changed the subject when he would have liked to question her further. But he shouldn't push. God could work on Skye's heart. "Dad says she's improving. I hope to visit soon."

"I'm happy to watch Olivia when you go." She pushed a stray wisp of hair behind her ear, the small movement mesmerizing him. "Any idea when that will be?"

None, unfortunately. "Our schedule's packed this time of year, so I'm still trying to figure that out."
~~~

Guilt whacked him in the gut. This job, though he loved it, swallowed enormous amounts of time from April to August. Even working in a ministry position would have allowed him more family time. But he wasn't going back down that rabbit trail right now. "Caleb is a captain too and can handle things alone with a deckhand, but he probably regrets ever going into business with me."

"I don't know him well, but he appears to be a compassionate person."

"He is." Pete took a sip of his soda. "Too often, I feel like he gets the raw end of the deal."

"How did you end up in business together if this was your grandfather's charter?"

Those dark times gusted into the present like a gale-force wind, stirring up grief. "We'd known each other since high school. When Kenzie got sick, Caleb was one of my deckhands. He worked offshore two weeks on, two off." Stomach twisting, Pete shook his head. "He knew I was falling apart, offered to help, then eventually quit his job and bought in when I became the single parent of an infant daughter."

Her hand reached toward his, paused, then finally, her fingers slid over his skin, soft and gentle.

"I'm sorry." She breathed the words, and they wrapped around his heart like a tourniquet to the pain he'd ripped open in front of her.

His gaze dropped and clouded with moisture. Sharing something so intimate with her felt natural. As if she understood his sorrow.

Perhaps because she'd had a hard life, too, from what he'd gathered. "How did you lose your mother?"

Her fingers flinched but still held his. "Depression." She shifted toward him, checking his reaction.

Bringing his gaze back to her face, the meaning dawned, and nausea swept over him. "Oh, Skye. She…"

With a small nod, she visibly swallowed before continuing. "I found her not long before I was supposed to leave for college. That's when Miss Lydia took me in."

He slid his hand from under hers and slipped an arm around her, pulling her close.

She let herself collapse into him for a minute before straightening. "I'll clean this up if you need to get back to your post, Captain." Picking up their trash, she stood, obviously finished with the heavy emotions he'd drummed up.

A cool wind rushed between them, and Pete checked the horizon. "Looks like a cloud's blowing in. Shouldn't be too bad, though." He added that last part since many passengers feared being on the water in a storm.

"Probably just an afternoon shower." Skye offered him a smile that felt private, her soft brown gaze meeting his.

What was happening on the horizon was nothing compared to the storm of emotions raging within him over this woman.

Maybe the Voice had been right. Maybe Skye was *the one.*

Chapter 28

The beautiful day on the Gulf passed much too quickly.

Sitting in the cabin, Skye and Dr. Boleware looked over the observations and information they'd gathered.

The grad students and Dr. McLeod finished their work and left the vessel. Outside, Caleb cleaned the stern and wiped down the counters. Pete must still be upstairs.

"Let's call it a day." Dr. Boleware shut off her electronics and packed her laptop into a black bag.

"Sounds good." Skye followed her lead. "I need to speak to Pete—Captain Thompson—before I go."

Gaze homing in on Skye, Dr. Boleware gave a single nod before standing.

Though her colleague didn't question the awkward, unprofessional statement, Skye felt the need to explain. "We use the same babysitter."

"Small world indeed." The tone brought heat to Skye's cheeks as Dr. Boleware pushed on her sunglasses. In the ensuing quiet, her shoes squeaked as she walked out.

Oh well. People had to have friends and acquaintances on this small island. It was normal, right? And offering to pick up Olivia along with Sparrow seemed like a nice thing to do, in case Pete would be awhile longer.

"Want to come up and see the cockpit?" Pete's voice caught her unaware. He stood in the doorway to the cabin. "Normally, I don't allow passengers up there, but I wanted you to check it out so you could decide if it would be okay to bring

Sparrow up the ladder one day. Maybe if we go fishing?" He shifted his weight as if he were a little nervous. So cute. "With Olivia and you, too, of course. Caleb and Hope, maybe, if you like."

A fluttery tingling began in her toes and traveled upward. The idea both intrigued and terrified her. Skye checked her watch, an excuse that gave her a moment to gather her wits.

"Caleb will still be here, cleaning up, and we won't be long."

He seemed to be trying to assure her safety.

Could Pete see how damaged she was? Was it that obvious to everyone, or did his intuition run deeper than most?

"Sure." With a nod, she followed him up the ladder, and he offered his hand to help her stand. Again, his touch soothed rather than alarmed, but she avoided his gaze. "Not an easy climb for some, maybe, but Sparrow should have no difficulty. I'm sure she'd love to go for a ride and fish."

"Olivia would enjoy having y'all along. Me too."

More giddiness enfolded Skye in warmth. She eyed the control in front of the captain's chair, hoping he couldn't read her emotions.

"Want a quick look?" Pete grinned. "I bet you're a natural."

She couldn't stop a smile. "I've spent some time driving smaller boats, but not one this large."

"We'll plan something soon." He gave a sad chuckle. "Between our jobs, childcare, homework, and sick mothers."

"It's a busy season for sure." She sighed. "I have a paper to write, the manatee hotline, and I've been assigned to help at the fishing rodeo."

His eyes lit up. "They're honoring Pop on opening night for his years of helping out." Pete blinked a few times, emotion obvious. "Probably a plaque or something."

Knowing Pete would be at the event eased some of Skye's dread. Not that he'd be with her all the time, but still. "Sounds like your grandfather was special to you."

"Both my grandparents were. Pop and Nana's place was my hiatus from the scrutiny of being a PK. I spent all my summers and holidays with them. Weekends, too, if I could talk my parents into it." His gaze traveled out the window toward the water in the marina. "If I hadn't had this place, his teaching me about the fishing and the tides, his unconditional love and acceptance, I would have been lost. Pop kept my sanity afloat."

Like Miss Lydia had done for her. Except, Skye's issues would turn Pete's stomach. If only she'd been stronger.

If only she'd spoken up sooner. If only she'd been brave.

But she'd never been courageous like her sister. She'd been weak like her mother. Skye's fingers went to the chain around her neck, and she toyed with the dangling trinkets attached to it. She missed her sister. Where was Star now?

If Skye ever did pray, she'd ask the Creator to watch over her sister, give Star at least a small measure of happiness in her life.

"So that was your mother's?" Pete's voice stepped into her dark thoughts.

"The only thing I have that belonged to her."

His fingers neared but he paused. "May I?"

She blinked more than nodded her agreement, and he grazed her collarbone as he surveyed the charms attached. Ripples of warmth spread through her, and she held her breath.

"The blue sapphire represents you, and the silver star, your sister?"

"Right. Momma rarely took it off." Except that horrible night.

"You must have been dear to her. Why is that all you have?" Releasing the necklace, he brushed a lock of her hair away from her face. "I shouldn't ask something so personal. Sorry."

Swallowing hard, her focus dropped to her shoes. "I grabbed it and got out of the house as soon as I could. Away from Momma's husband while I had the chance. I left everything else." She took a shaky breath. "Miss Lydia picked me up and took me home with her as soon as the police said I could go."

His breath warming her, Pete nudged her chin, pulling her gaze to his. "Skye, all men aren't monsters. Some of us try to treat a woman with decency."

Bitterness clogged her throat, and a tear slipped down her cheek. "But it only takes one to destroy a woman." Her chest quivered as she sniffled, then she squeezed her eyes shut. "Or ruin a young girl."

~~~

Dear God, why? As her meaning settled on him, Pete ground his teeth together, anger seething through him. How could a man be so depraved? It nauseated him to even consider.

Help me speak the right words. Your words, Lord, that offer healing and comfort.

"Skye, I'm sorry for everything you've gone through." He held out his arms, though he wasn't sure she'd allow his touch. Yet she leaned into his chest, and he enfolded her close. No wonder she'd been skittish when they'd met. "You deserved better."

"I wanted to be stronger before I went to college. To tell Momma she had to leave him to make sure nothing happened to Star, but instead, she…" A sob worked its way out before she spoke again. "When I told Momma the truth, she gave up."
~~~

Gently, he made small circles on Skye's back like he did when Olivia fell and scraped a knee. "Not because of you, Skye. None of what the adults did was your fault."

His heart ached as he held her there for long moments, and her body melted into his as her tears wet his shirt. A cyclone of emotions roiled within, splintering him into pieces. Part of him longed to be closer to the woman who'd been so happy last night at dinner. Honestly, he'd been attracted to Skye—attracted to a woman for the first time since Kenzie. Another part of him pulsed with anger at the people entrusted to care for the little girl Skye had been. A third piece of his heart agonized over the idea of drawing closer to a woman so fragile. How did a man go about loving a woman who'd been abused?

The thought took him by surprise. Love? Was he falling in love with Skye? He hadn't been able to fathom putting his heart out there again. Until now.

But what about Olivia? Could he allow his daughter to form an attachment to Skye and Sparrow? What problems might arise because of Skye's damaged past?

She raised her head and wiped her face, then her soft brown eyes lifted to meet his. "I didn't mean to dump my baggage on you. Maybe say one of your prayers for me while I'm taking care of Sparrow. As you now know, I don't have any parental examples, other than Miss Lydia." Pulling away, she shrugged one shoulder. "And watching you be such a good father to Olivia. I could pick her up for you, by the way, when I get Sparrow. I mean, if you want, but I understand if you don't."

I am making a way in the wilderness and streams in the wasteland.

The words from Isaiah floated into his consciousness as he savored Skye's compliment about his parenting. And she'd asked him to pray for her. While Pete had always believed in

God and His power to heal, his faith was surely being tested. Because he and Skye had more than their share of debris to sort through from their pasts if they were to move forward.

She needs you.

There was that still, small Voice again. Perhaps it was time he stopped fighting and obeyed. "I'd appreciate it if you would get Olivia." He managed to smile. "I'll even pick up dinner."

"I'll handle the cooking tonight. It's my turn." The way Skye's face glowed as he placed his trust in her almost quieted his fears about their future.

Almost.

Chapter 29

"Pete! Guess what?"

Running full speed, Sparrow aimed at Pete as soon as he'd parked the truck. Halfway to the house, he knelt, ready to listen, the way he did for Olivia when she had exciting news to share. When Sparrow reached him, she hurled herself into him and wrapped her young, strong arms around his neck, nearly toppling them both.

"Whoa, you found a big treasure, I bet." How precious that the child felt so comfortable with him. None of the fear that Skye held marred Sparrow's ability to love. He prayed that meant Sparrow had been spared a rough background. No one had said how old she had been when Miss Lydia adopted her.

Sparrow trapped her bottom lip between her teeth. "It's sort of a treasure, I guess, but different."

Pete glanced over to the front porch to where Skye stood just outside the open doorway, watching their exchange. Tracks of tears glistened on her cheeks, yet she smiled. This must be big news. "Did y'all see a manatee? Or rescue a dolphin?"

Shaking her head, Sparrow wrinkled her nose. "That would be fun, but no."

"Goodness." He whistled a breath through his teeth. "I give up. Tell me. I have to know."

"Momma's getting her surgery so she can get better." The child beamed. "She called us on a video chat a few minutes ago."

"Oh, sweetheart, that's wonderful." He squeezed her closer and pressed a kiss on top of her head.

"I know! I can't wait until I see her again." The girl gave a vigorous nod. "I'm going to play with Olivia. Rocky is sitting on her lap in my room. We're so excited he likes her because he hardly likes anyone."

It wasn't until Sparrow scampered happily back to the porch that he thought about how Skye might react about his display of affection.

He checked her body language for any sign of unease. Her brown eyes filled with liquid, but her smile remained, pulling him like an unseen magnet.

At the porch, he practically leapt up the steps and stood in front of her, wanting to hug her, too, but waiting. Knowing what he did—what she'd gone through—it seemed best to let her set the tone for physical touch.

"I'm thankful to God for your good news." His gaze locked with hers, and she took a step closer, removing all space between them.

Arms inching up, she seemed to be gathering courage. "Me too," she breathed, then rested her head against his shoulder. "I just hope the transplant takes."

Permission enough. He drew her closer, and her arms encircled him. He stood there, soaking in her warmth, the scent of her freshly washed hair, remembering the softness of a woman's body. It had been a long time since he'd considered those kinds of things, outside of his memories of Kenzie. A longing to know and be known by a woman—to be loved—emerged from some locked-away place that had been buried in deep waters since his wife died.

His hands made their way to Skye's hair, and he fingered a damp strand. The sensation stirred more yearning within, breaking open a dam of emotion, and a tear rolled down his cheek. It was as if he'd been sleepwalking through his days, and Skye had woken that part of him to life again.

What did he do with all these sentiments? Skye was here temporarily. Could that change?

"She wants you to call her." Skye slid back a step and swiped at her eyes. He immediately missed her touch. "I apologize in advance for whatever she says."

"Who?" He blinked, trying to catch up.

She made a small tsk. "Miss Lydia. There's no telling what she'll ask you to do, but don't feel obligated."

Duh, Pete, come back to shore. "I'll call her right away."

"You have the number?"

He patted his pocket. "She gave it to me when she was here."

"Of course she did." Waving him off, Skye snorted a laugh. "I'll get dinner on the table while you talk."

Now that she mentioned food, his stomach grumbled. "Smells good. What is it?"

Her expression turned shy. "Just shrimp stir-fry and rice."

"Just?" He made a dramatic huff. "That's my favorite. We'll enjoy every bite."

One of her brows hiked. "I thought Hope's gumbo was your favorite."

And that sounded exactly like something Kenzie had said early in their relationship. He'd learned enough about women to know not to take that bait. "I better make this call."

She stepped inside, and he eased the door closed.

Once he pressed Miss Lydia's contact, he waited. After several rings, he almost hung up, but finally, a weak voice answered.

"Pete? Can you hear me?" The words came out raspy.

Not a good sign. "Yes, ma'am. I heard the good news."

"I have three things I feel led to tell you." She wasn't wasting her breath on pleasantries.

"I'm listening."

"Don't stop writing to the Lord."

Air left Pete's lungs. He'd barely journaled since Mom had suffered the stroke, and that had been the night Miss Lydia went to the hospital. Had he even told the woman about it? Or Skye? He didn't recall doing so.

"The second is to listen to His voice regarding your life, regarding Skye." Her words came out stronger this time.

He hadn't told anyone about the strange Voice in his head. Because he hadn't wanted to sound nuts. But this message from her…

"Finally, Pete, don't be afraid to step out of the boat and walk on the water. Follow your true calling. When the waves come, He'll pull you up. He won't let you sink. In fact, even if you burn the ship, you'll start anew."

What did that mean? The line grew quiet as he pondered the bizarre words. Only ragged breaths from Miss Lydia filled the silence.

He should say something. "I'll be praying for you." He tried to sound more confident than he felt.

"And I for you all."

They ended the call, and a whirlpool of anxiety swirled in Pete's midsection. The surgery was Miss Lydia's only hope for a cure, but it would still be a long, risky ordeal. And he knew full well not all prayers were answered with an earthly healing.

Chapter 30

The pen in Pete's hand felt like an anchor. As he had every night in the week since he'd spoken to Miss Lydia, he sat at his perch at his kitchen table. He stared through the window at the puffy evening clouds beginning their transformation into a golden yellow. When had writing his thoughts become so hard?

Maybe he should call Dad and talk instead.

No.

He'd journal for the few minutes he had before meeting Skye, then he'd check in with Dad on the way. Skye had suggested they meet for a picnic at the beach once he'd cleaned up after work.

What can I write to You that hasn't been written, Lord?
What can I say about You that hasn't been better said?
Blue sky touches the green canopy of trees.
Warmth beams down through my window.
A child needs me to reach out to You for wisdom—two children and a woman.
Do not let me fail them, Lord. Do not let me fail You.
Heart, words, and feelings flounder in our broken world.
Yet, You are unfailing, unshakable. Thank You for that.
The tiniest recesses of my soul are known to You.
It hurts as You cleanse those tender places, but I ask You to continue.
Even as I draw back in pain, gently purify me of any unrighteousness and cowardice.
Sharpen my awareness in all things spiritual, I beg you.
You are my strength and shield.

Peace cascaded over Pete as he dropped the pen and sat quietly for another ten minutes, praying. The words were few on the page, but they spoke his heart, and that would be enough. Now, his responsibility would be to watch and listen for God's direction.

Pete ran his fingers through his still-wet hair, grabbed his keys, and clomped out the door in his beach sandals.

This week with Skye aboard his boat had kept his heart drumming a happy beat. Having her there felt right. None of the fears engulfed him like they had when Kenzie had joined him on the weekends, so they could spend time together. Her parents had warned them her cancer might come back. They'd never been a fan of his career choice—wanted him to stay in ministry. Her bout with melanoma had only been one of several reasons.

Being on the water and out in the sun's rays had been a part of Skye's life long before he'd ever met her. The sea was her passion as much as it had always been his. Nothing he said or did put her in danger.

Once he got in the truck, he punched in Dad's number and connected to the speaker.

"Hello, son. What's going on?" Dad answered right away, like he always did when Pete called. Or anyone in their family. Dad always made time for them.

"Can I speak to you as my minister today?" Although maybe this was too much on his father right now. Mom's stroke was burden enough.

"You know it. I've been missing our talks." Dad's enthusiasm encouraged Pete to continue.

All the way to the public beach, Pete explained everything that had happened since he'd met Skye, Sparrow, and Miss Lydia, including the Voice in his head and the recent messages from Miss Lydia.

In the parking lot, he waited for his father to respond. Did he sound like a complete nut?

Finally, Dad cleared his throat. "While I've never personally had the experiences you're having, I've felt His nudges urging me to take a step of faith—or to not accept a position at a certain church. I've had someone—even a stranger—say something to me that was an answer to exactly the question I'd been asking God. I've had a parishioner send me a verse that fit a current dilemma perfectly when they had no idea I was struggling."

"Okay." Pete took in the information, glad that Dad could identify with what he was saying. "So what do I do?"

His father chuckled. "You're asking me?"

"Well, yeah. That's why I called. And to check on you and Mom." Though he hadn't quite gotten to that part yet.

"Jesus said His sheep hear His voice. Listen. Study the Word. Write what you hear and see if it matches up with Scripture. I believe He is always putting the pieces in place, though we can't see the whole picture."

"But what about the risks to Olivia? Should I put her in the middle of a messy situation?"

"We Christians are simply broken people serving other broken individuals. True, Skye's upbringing was rotten, but desolation can be a training ground for good too. Does she seem like she'd hurt children?"

Skye's gentle ways with the girls, and even the misfit pets she kept, ran through his mind. He couldn't imagine a gentler soul.

"No, but I've read about generational dysfunction and how hard it is to break that cycle."

His father sighed.

"You know, there's a reason your nana didn't talk about her family. My sister and I weren't allowed to have any contact with them because they never changed their ways, but my mother did. It only takes one person to decide to break the cycle."

"Nana?" Pete's stomach roiled. "You're saying she grew up in an abusive home?"

"I found her journals when I helped her and Pop move into the assisted living. I never cried so hard in my life. Until your mother had a stroke."

"Oh, Dad." Liquid filled Pete's eyes. "I'm sorry." Guilt clobbered him. He should help more with Mom. He just couldn't figure out when. "I'll speak to Caleb and take a day off this week so you can have a break."

"All of you come visit, including Skye." Dad sniffed hard. "It will brighten our day having the children around. And I'd like to meet this special woman."

They said their goodbyes, and Pete exited the vehicle, scanning the shore for the girls. To the east, on the edge of the water, he spotted them wading with the dogs, all looking down.

With the sun lowering, the light hit them just right, wrapping them in a golden glow. What a beautiful picture they made. As he walked toward them, a rush of wind skimmed over his face, carrying with it the smell of wet sand, salt, and coconut sunscreen—the aroma of his childhood, his life.

Glancing up, Skye spotted him and gave him her shy smile. "Come see." She waved him close.

They must have spotted another treasure.

Maybe he'd found one of his own.

~~~

A burst of joy flooded Skye, seeing Pete's grin as he aimed toward her. A sensation she'd not often experienced.
~~~

It was as though she'd come alive since she'd moved here. Things seemed so very right when Pete and Olivia were with her and Sparrow—as if this was the way her life was supposed to be. Almost as if there were some grand design in their meeting that first day, the day when she'd wrecked and lost everything. It seemed like…it felt like a plan larger than she could imagine.

Could there be a caring God? One Who'd provided Miss Lydia when Skye needed her? Perhaps One who'd sent Pete and his adorable daughter during this trying time?

Could she dive into the unknown and let her heart sink or swim with this man?

"What do we have today, little minnows?" Shirking off his shoes, Pete waded into the shallow surf and hugged the girls.

"A whelk egg case, Daddy." Olivia lifted the long spiral strand.

"It almost looks like a ruffly necklace." Sparrow scrunched her freckled nose. "Except it would be gross to wear."

"That's really something. Are you keeping it?" Pete examined their find, then turned toward Skye.

"Can we?" the girls asked, droplets of water shimmering on their shins.

"Onshore like that, it's no longer productive, so it should be fine if you let it dry outdoors before bringing it inside."

"Any news?" Pete neared Skye, waiting like he'd done each night for her to extend her arms and give him permission to hug her as well.

The unspoken request had her scrambling to get her bearings. Being this close to a man was like being unmoored in strange seas. "Miss Lydia is still doing well with her new liver." She held up her hands and studied them. "I'm wet and messy again already."

"So were the minnows. Doesn't bother me."

Shrugging, she lifted her arms, and he closed the distance between them to embrace her. She held her breath then released it as she gave herself permission to move closer. An ocean of emotions for this man brewed within her. An attraction like nothing she'd ever imagined—had never allowed herself to even dip a toe into. And it terrified her.

"What's cooking?" he asked.

"Huh?" Skye backed up and looked at him, finding a silly smirk on his face.

"What's for supper? I could eat a whale." He released her and growled, running toward the girls. "Or maybe a minnow!"

Giggling, they splashed away in the surf, Pete giving chase. A chorus of gulls cackled in the air. The dogs barked and trotted behind them.

"I better set up our picnic right away." Playing along, Skye chuckled and headed toward the basket she'd brought, reveling in their glee. "Seems like there's a hungry whale out hunting."

"Whale?" He turned to her and dug his fingers into his firm stomach. "Do I look like I have blubber?"

Running faster until he reached Skye, he started to grab at her, then instead pivoted and practically dove at the food. "All mine!"

"No, Daddy!" Olivia squealed and darted toward him, Sparrow following. "Save some for us."

Flinging himself onto one of the towels Skye had spread for them, Pete groaned. "O-kaay. If I have to, but I'm fading from hunger." Frodo shook water on him, then leaned down to lick his face, but Pete didn't seem to care.

"Goodness." Skye laughed and shook her head. "We wouldn't want that to happen. Girls, get your sandwiches, and I'll find the one I made for the poor famished Pete monster."

Squinting, he looked at Skye. "What did you make me?"

"Well, Olivia said your favorite sandwich was okra and egg, but I didn't know how to make that. I thought maybe it was one of Hope's special recipes."

"Okra?" He popped up and frowned. "On a sandwich?"

Skye shrugged and neared the basket. "That's what she said."

"Daddy, you liked the okra at Nana's one time, remember?" Olivia asked, then she and Sparrow sat together on an oversize flowered towel. Sam settled beside them. "I'll say the blessing." They quieted, and Olivia began. "Come, Lord Jesus, be our guest. Let this food to us be blessed. Amen."

"Amen." Pete echoed, then turned his gaze to Skye. "So, what did you fix? A BLT without the bacon or something?"

His expression oozed teasing drama.

"I made egg salad with olives." She should have texted and asked what he wanted. He probably wouldn't like this. She handed him a plastic bag with his sandwich. "It was the closest thing I could think of to your okra favorite. I also brought apples, hummus, crackers, and carrot sticks if you don't want it."

Looking slightly dubious, he accepted, opened the bag, and took a bite.

Skye studied him before she tossed Frodo and Sam each two treats and picked up her own sandwich.

"Wow," he spoke through bites. "This is delicious."

"You won't hurt my feelings if you don't eat it." Much.

"Really. I mean it." He smiled. "My new favorite."

Her face scalded at the praise, and then the heat spread through her entire body. How did his approval cause such a strong chemical reaction in her?

She turned her attention to Sparrow and Olivia, asking

about school while they ate. The sun lowered in the sky, and the girls finished quickly and headed back toward the shallow surf with the dogs.

"Tomorrow, Michael is taking a group out on a salt marsh excursion." Skye gathered her nerve to continue. "Since it's Saturday and you're working, I thought maybe I could take Sparrow and Olivia."

"I hate for you to feel like you always have to invite Olivia." He took a bite of hummus on a carrot. "Where did you find this? It's great."

Sucking in a deep breath, she tried to keep from blushing again. It was just a compliment. "I made it. It's a simple recipe. And I enjoy Olivia. She's a wonderful girl."

"If you keep feeding me like this, you may never get rid of me." His gaze pierced her, probing, waiting for her response.

And she had no clue what to say.

She bit her lip. "I…I'll have to learn how to make okra like Nana."

And that was dumb.

His laugh rumbled between them, and she couldn't stop drinking in the sound of it. "Olivia can go with you if you're sure," he said. "I know you'll take precautions. Did you mean for her to spend the night?"

"That would be easier than you waking her before dawn."

"Okay, I'll get her bag together when we leave." He checked his watch. "Probably should be soon, sadly."

"Right. They'll be tired, and you have an early day." Skye gathered their trash and then stood to fold the girls' towel.

"I'll fold ours." Pete offered, setting aside the hummus.

Ours. She liked the sound of that. "Finish eating, Mr. Hungry Whale. I made your favorites, after all."

"Not a whale, but yes, ma'am." He gave her a teasing look.

The phone in her bag rang, tearing her gaze from Pete. Probably a good thing, except this could be bad news. No one called except Miss Lydia or work.

She dug through her things until she snagged the cell and answered.

"I hate to bother you on a Friday night," Dr. Boleware said. "But we have an injured manatee near Aloe Bay. A boat strike. And I'd hoped to have your help."

"Oh no. Poor baby." Sadness swamped her. A boat strike often ended badly for the injured creature. "I'm not sure if I can come now." She glanced at Pete.

Concern filled his gaze. "What's wrong?"

"Let me get back with you in a minute." Skye ended the call and explained the situation.

"Go. I'll take everyone to your house and get the girls ready for bed."

Bed. That meant bathing, a change of clothes, and Sparrow being alone with a man. Clutching her stomach, she fought to keep her mind from sinking into dark places. But could she trust Pete with—?

"I won't bathe them." He seemed to read her thoughts again. "I'll give them each a wet cloth and send them to the bathroom to clean up. I'll stay on the couch in the living room. Or if you rather, I can ask Hope—"

"Just a second." She held up one hand, needing to think. Should she call Miss Lydia? She hated to bother her. Maybe she should pray? Would the Creator answer? "Let me talk to Sparrow privately while you put Olivia in your truck." And she'd try one of those prayers.

If You're listening, Creator of the Universe, and if You care about Sparrow, could You give me some wisdom? Can I trust this man—Pete Thompson—with Sparrow? With our hearts?

Chapter 31

"I know." Sparrow huffed and frowned. "Momma already had this talk with me. And you need to save the manatee."

Skye's mind shuffled through all the fears that pelted her about leaving Sparrow with Pete and Olivia, but something in her heart assured her that Pete could be trusted. Sparrow would be okay with them.

"If you're comfortable staying without me here…"

"Go, Skye," Sparrow insisted.

"Okay. Love you." As hard as it was to trust, she gathered a towel and her purse, then took off to meet Dr. Boleware at the marina.

Moments after arriving, Skye was in the boat with their crew of eight biologists headed toward the bay. Other than going over their plan of action, the group remained quiet, watching for the manatee and the citizens who had reported the injured animal. They'd offered to wait in their boat to keep a visual.

The sun lowered on the western horizon, and Skye's stomach churned. The capture and rescue would be much harder once darkness fell. They needed to hurry, but also maintain their vigilance in order not to cause another marine mammal injury.

At last, the smaller fishing vessel that had reported the sighting came into view, along with one from the Marine Resources Division who'd offered to join them. The boaters waved a greeting and pointed toward the location of the animal. Once they'd neared, Dr. Boleware shone a light onto its body. The good-sized manatee had a severe wound on its left side.

Skye cringed at the sight. Poor thing. If only people would be more careful.

"Thank you for the help." Dr. Boleware called to the other boaters. "He looks like he'll need rehab." The fisherman waved and took off, but the Marine Resources Officers' boat stayed.

"We're here to help any way we can," one of the officers called.

"We'll spread the net to encircle him, then pull him into our boat. Keep watch for us for now." Dr. Boleware explained to their driver which way to go and how far, then the boat made a slow arc as Skye and the other crew members gradually released the net.

Despite the waning light, they all gathered on the back of the boat and gently dragged him closer. As it became more difficult, Skye, Dr. Boleware, and the others lay on their stomachs in the open hull in the back of the vessel, pulling from the bottom of the net. Skye's wet arms strained at the weight as she tugged harder and harder. After what seemed like an hour of hard tugging, they'd made little progress.

Frustration racked Skye. They needed to get this animal help.

This was what she'd trained for, preserving as many of these gentle creatures as she could. Would she fail at it too? So many manatees had been lost this year in Florida already.

"Come on, everyone," Skye yelled. "Keep at it."

They all worked harder. Sweat poured down their tired muscles. Finally, the creature moved closer to the boat's edge. As he flailed in protest, Skye and Dr. Boleware scooted back, then stood and tugged with the others.

Though manatees were gentle, their sheer weight could easily injure humans caught in their way.

One of the officers in the other boat shouted, "I can help pull him in."

"We could use you," Dr. Boleware yelled back.

The Marine Resources boat sidled close, and the officer made an agile entry, considering the waves and the swaying of the boat.

Intense work continued as the heavy animal struggled. Perspiration beaded and dripped into Skye's eyes, but she blinked it away.

Dr. Boleware shouted more instructions amid the chaos of dragging the huge animal aboard.

The animal thrashed again, barely missing one of the men. Skye's pulse amped up, and she rushed to help secure the lower body. "Shh, it's okay, baby. We're just trying to help."

Hairs dotted the animal's leathery skin, along with soft patches of algae, normal for manatees. As the animal ceased flailing in the secure net on board, two of the guys replaced the end cover for the stern that slid down like a tailgate, closing their patient's escape route.

"Whew." Skye swiped her brow.

The light of a flashlight shone over her shoulder and onto the manatee's paddle. Oh no. Her gut sank at the sight of another propeller cut. With wounds this serious, he could have internal injuries as well. He might not make it after all this.

Water from the dripping animal circled in the hull around Skye's feet as they made a slow drive to the dock to meet the truck that would take the manatee to a critical care facility. What she wouldn't give to go along and help heal him of his pain. But she had commitments of her own. Until Miss Lydia was well enough to care for Sparrow.

Moving the animal from the boat onto a tarp took the strength of a dozen people with a lot of grunting and groaning from the human team. Once he'd been placed in the specialized vehicle, Skye poured water over his skin and watched for his adorable whiskered snout to take a breath. When the manatee responded to the stimulation, she exhaled a large sigh of her own.

Thank you. Please help him make it. She'd been praying these silent prayers more often lately. Would the Creator of the Universe listen?

~~~

Nearing eleven o'clock, another set of headlights in the window caught Pete's attention. There had been quite a few vehicles traversing the roads this Friday night. He'd tried to snooze on the couch while the girls slept in the back of the house with the pets, but he'd done nothing but think of Skye. Though manatees weren't dangerous, the animals weighed about a thousand pounds. If one flipped onto her, she'd be crushed. Rising, he made his way over to peer through the blinds. Her car parked in the drive. *She was home.* His heartbeat sped like a sail in the windstorm, and he hurried out to greet her.

Exiting the vehicle, she moved slowly but gave him one of her rare grins. "We did it. We rescued him and sent him for rehab."

"That's great news." Unable to stop a grin of his own, he held his arms out. "I was worried about you."

Her gaze locked onto him. She closed the car door and took a step closer, then paused. "I'm wet and probably look like I've been in a swamp."

"Well, I usually smell like bait, but you… You look radiant to me."
~~~

Not daring to move a muscle, he waited, his breathing stalled. The last thing he wanted was to frighten her away.

Nearing, she extended her arms, and he took that as permission. As he pulled her close, his chest expanded with the air easing into his lungs. They held each other for a long minute, her smaller form fitting perfectly next to him, his pulse racing, until she pulled her head back to look at him.

Those caramel-colored eyes caressed his. "Thank you for watching Sparrow."

"Glad to help." Swallowing hard, he fought the urge to taste her lips.

Giving into that temptation could ruin everything. Yet, she still held his gaze.

"Skye, I…" Where was he going with that?

"Mmm-hmm?" she breathed.

Was she as drawn to him as he was to her? "I've come to care deeply for you, but I'd never do anything to endanger our friendship."

Even in the dim moonlight, he knew she was blushing, but she didn't pull away. "I think I feel the same."

"You think?" he teased and gave her his best puppy-dog look.

A small laugh made its way out of her throat, and her eyes crinkled with a shy smile. "I do." Her expression wilted. "Except, I've never been in a relationship. Never dated. Nothing." Her gaze fell to his chest. "I'm too broken."

"Skye," he whispered. "Look at me." He cupped her cheeks, and she raised her eyes to his. "We're all broken."

Her gaze sought his. Searching. "What if I'm shattered beyond repair?"

"I wish I could take away your pain, but I'm just a man. God can heal our hearts. Your heart. He can lift us up and help us go on, despite what life or evil men dole out."

"I hope you're right." Her hands covered his. "Because I'd like to…"

He shuddered at the slight touch. "You'd like to what?"

Her teeth caught her lip, and she dropped her gaze to his mouth. "I'd like to try."

"I'll let you take the lead." He lowered his forehead almost to hers, so close her breath stroked his skin. "However you're comfortable."

Her face turned up, her look penetrating. Heat charged through him, but he didn't dare move.

Hesitantly, soft lips brushed his, and her fingers feathered through his hair. His pulse thudded, and blood rushed in his ears. His thinking stalled as she took her time exploring his mouth with her kisses. Gently, he kissed her back, and all at once, with every single fiber of his being, he knew.

There was no turning back now. He was hopelessly in love with this woman. With Skye.

Headlights poured their beams over them, and Skye inched away much too soon. How long had they been kissing? Not long enough. He didn't spare a glance for whoever was in the driveway. "Probably someone turning around in the drive," he whispered next to her hair, unwilling to be pulled from this perfect moment.

"Pete? I saw your truck on my way home." A door slammed, and heels crunched on the gravel and shells. "Is something wrong? It's late and I—"

Hope rounded his truck, and she gasped when she spotted them. "Oh, I'm sorry… I didn't expect…" She turned on her heel. "I should go." Her voice broke with that last word as she ran back to her SUV.

Skye's arms dropped, then wrapped around her own waist.

"You need to talk to her."

Hope? She was his oldest friend, but her timing couldn't be worse. "I'll call her tomorrow."

Skye watched as Hope's vehicle backed out and took off too fast, skidding on the sandy road. When it was gone, she faced him again. "She's in love with you. Deep down, I think you know that."

In love? He opened his mouth to argue, but… Maybe Skye was right. "I don't have those kind of feelings for her." And he wanted to continue where they'd left off.

"Are you sure?" Skye searched his face, and he battled to keep from touching her—from pulling her close and kissing away any doubts she might have.

"I'm positive," he said with confidence. If looks could express feeling, he prayed his displayed the depth of this truth. "My heart is engaged elsewhere."

Her mouth made a hesitant curve before she nudged him on the shoulder. "You should still go talk with her. She's been your friend a long time."

He hated to admit it, but Skye was right. He owed Hope that much after all she'd done for him. "I'll take care of it."

Chapter 32

Using shovels, sieves, and dip nets, Skye worked beside the girls, scooping through the muck of the salt marsh while Michael instructed them on what to watch for. About fifteen people made up the group of parents and children on the salt marsh excursion, the youngsters much happier than the parents about the whole thing as mud squished into their water shoes.

The smell of the marsh always reminded her of rotten eggs, though the odor was simply decomposing organic matter combined with brackish water. The sun beat down on their hats and the backs of their shirts, but the girls' smiles said Sparrow and Olivia didn't mind the heat at all.

As hard as Skye tried to focus on enjoying the outing in nature and watching the girls find treasures in the muck, she couldn't help reliving the sweet kisses with Pete the night before. Her lips touching his, the gentle way he'd held her, returning her affection—her passion, even. The courage she'd found to take that step baffled her. So many wounds scarred her, inside and out. She'd never imagined a messed-up girl like her would discover a good man like Pete.

He'd said he cared deeply for her. Did that mean love?

This was all so foreign and unexpected. Could God really heal her shattered pieces enough for her and Pete to try to find out? And how had his talk with Hope gone?

Did Pete truly have no feelings for Hope other than friendship?

"Have you found something, Skye? You're staring awful hard into that sieve." Michael's tone indicated he was teasing her.

"Sorry, I drifted off. I was up late last night."

A smile lifted his cheeks. "I heard."

He'd heard? Fire flamed her face. Had someone spotted her and Pete outside and spread it around the island, or had Hope somehow told Michael?

"I wish I could've been there, but I'd gone into Mobile."

Been there? That was bizarre.

"Was the rescue pretty intense?" He gave her an inquisitive stare.

Rescue? Oh, right. The manatee. Yes, she was losing her mind. "Pulling him in was difficult, but we did it. We should receive an update today."

"Good to hear." He nodded toward the girls. "Looks like you and Pete settled your differences."

"Olivia is doused in sunscreen and insect repellent."

"Good job." He stood taller and put on his teacher voice for the kids. "Remember, I told you guys about how salt marshes can be a nursery for baby animals. There's water, grasses, and other plants that keep the land from eroding. Many animals take refuge here."

"A turtle!" One of the children yelled.

"Good find!" Michael neared and peered at the creature. "That's a diamondback terrapin. Their strong back legs have nails, so let me be the one to pick it up."

"He's so pretty." Olivia gasped. "He has polka dots on his neck and legs, but his shell is green and orange."

"Each one is different too." Michael lifted it closer to the kids. "They're protected by law because too many people used to make them into soup."

"Gross!" Sparrow groaned.

"Something's in my net!" Olivia squealed.

"Let's see." Skye peered into the net. "A hermit crab. They find empty snail shells to make their home. As he grows bigger, he'll vacate it to find a larger one."

"Look at that!" Sparrow pointed to movement in front of her.

"That's a blue crab. We're having quite the discovery party today." Michael netted the crustacean then lifted it. "This is a male, and we know that because of the shape on its abdomen. They eat almost anything, even smaller crabs like the one Olivia found."

"That's mean." Olivia frowned and held her net closer to her body.

"It's just the way nature works." Skye placed a hand on the child's shoulder. "Humans eat crabs and other animals."

"Not this one." Pivoting away from Michael, Olivia jerked the net around.

"How about you release it over near those tall grasses so he can hide." Skye motioned with her head. "I'll go with you."

The girl sighed. "I hope nothing eats him. He's so cute."

"He's adorable, but he'd prefer to be free." Even though he might end up being lunch. Life could be cruel.

All of creation groans.

Pete had said something about the book of Romans and that verse. Maybe she could find answers if she read the book. There was an app for everything on phones these days, but she'd prefer to have a paper version. She'd seen a Bible of Pete's grandmother's on a shelf somewhere in the house.

By lunchtime, they'd finished the excursion. Skye helped Olivia and Sparrow clean up, showered herself, fed them all grilled cheese sandwiches.

Then she'd allowed the girls to watch a movie to rest. Once she had the dogs walked and the mud-drenched clothes in the wash, she had some time to herself.

She ducked into the bedroom with the Bible. With her head propped on a pile of pillows on the bed, she searched the table of contents for Romans. Pete had mentioned a chapter, but from what Miss Lydia had always told her, the books were better understood when read as a whole.

An hour later, she closed the pages with more questions than answers. The letter this man Paul had written left her thoughts jumbled. Some of it made sense, but other parts…

Could Pete explain? Or Miss Lydia? The woman loved to talk about the Bible. Where had she left the phone? Maybe they could make their daily call.

Scooting off the bed, Skye padded down the hall to the living room. Though the TV still played, both girls snoozed, curled up on either ends of the couch with Sam and Frodo snuggled between them. Their morning adventure must have worn them out. Skye's heart squeezed. They looked so cute there together. She couldn't help but be happy they'd grown so fond of each other, neither having a sister to be close to like she and Star had been. They could call Miss Lydia a little later.

Skye tiptoed to the table to fetch her phone in case Pete called. When she picked it up, an alert showed a text from him already. That warm, gushy feeling from the night before had her tingling all the way down to her toes.

Hey, how was the excursion? Good, I hope. I wish I could have been there. Or anywhere with you and the girls. I really enjoyed last night. A lot. Miss you! Looking forward to seeing you.

She couldn't stop a smile, and she held her phone to her chest, wishing it were Pete instead. *He missed her.* A gush of emotion swelled within her so strong that tears welled in her eyes, and she almost sobbed. She pressed a hand to her mouth. Was this what it felt like to be loved? To love? She should quit standing there about to blubber and answer the man.

Her fingers hovered over the screen.

What to say?

All is well. The girls made several interesting discoveries and enjoyed the morning in the marsh. She paused, her pulse skittering, *then added, Miss you too.*

Closing her eyes, she hit send. Her cheeks scalded over the three simple words. What a mess she was.

Good!! BTW, I tried to find Hope for that talk last night, but she wasn't at her house.

Skye's chest tightened. The Hope situation still lingered. Would it always? Pete and Hope had been friends since childhood, and he had to know the beautiful woman adored him. And Hope was a good-hearted person.

Perhaps deep down, Pete needed Hope more than he realized—felt more for her too.

Skye whipped out another text.

Why don't you connect with Hope before you come tonight?

Maybe that was too pushy, but she'd rather know Pete's feelings, one way or another. Because one thing was sure—Pete Thompson had captured her heart.

~~~

Showered and shaved, Pete climbed the staircase that led to the porch of Hope's raised-foundation home. He scuffed his shoe on the wood before knocking. Night had already begun its descent. It had been a long day, and he was ready to get to Skye—Olivia and Sparrow too.

His stomach knotted at the thought of the conversation he should have had with Hope years before. He'd been a chicken. And a bit of a jerk, really.
~~~

Though he'd never intentionally led her on, he should have made it clear that she should find a nice guy to settle down with and not to waste her time taking care of him. But he'd never wanted to hurt her feelings, though it seemed not being upfront with her had done worse.

The wind rustled the palms in her yard, and he swung his gaze up to the darkening sky. Strong currents were sweeping him into a new future he'd never imagined. A future with a woman who wasn't Kenzie. A future with Skye.

The look on Hope's face last night when—

The door opened, and Hope stared at him, her hair pulled back in a disheveled bun. Barefoot, she wore a wrinkled T-shirt with gym shorts and no makeup. He'd never seen her look so natural, so raw.

Her red-rimmed eyes met his. "Were you just standing there for a reason? I could see you on my security camera."

"I was about to knock." He cleared his tight throat. "I tried to find you last night, but you weren't here. I called, too, but you didn't answer. You had me worried." All true. He'd lost some sleep wondering if she was okay.

Cocking her head, she shrugged a slender shoulder. "Why would you worry?"

"It was late."

Her jaw ticked. "I'm out late all the time. You've never marched over here to check on me."

Maybe he hadn't been as good of a friend as he'd imagined. "I think we should talk. Do you want to go somewhere or sit out here on the porch?"

"Talk about what?" Her lip trembled.

Was she going to cry? He wasn't prepared for tears. All of a sudden, he was full-on tongue-tied. This was going to be much harder than he'd imagined.

"Pete?" She forced his name out before sniffling.

Lord, help me.

"About you and me. Our friendship. And Skye."

A tear rolled down her cheek as she took a step closer. "I should have been honest with you. Maybe this wouldn't have happened." She reached out and took his hand. "Pete, I've loved you since we were kids. At college, I saw the way you looked at Kenzie, and I knew you'd fallen for her. Who couldn't help but love her? She was perfect." She squeezed his hand. "But this girl, Skye… I know you have a big heart. You feel sorry for her. She's needy right now, but don't confuse compassion for something else."

Shaking his head, he pulled his fingers from hers. "My feelings for Skye are more than sympathy. I wouldn't lead a woman on that way."

"Really?" Her jaw ticked. "I've loved you. I've been there for you and Olivia whenever you needed me—for Kenzie, even, when she was sick. I've waited for you to see me. I've waited for you…" Her voice broke. "I've waited for you to love me. All this time." Her chest heaved with a sob.

His gaze dropped to the boards of the deck. Guilt smacked him in the gut. He should have been more sensitive. But what could he say? "I'm sorry. You've been the best friend anyone ever had. I do love you, but like a sister, and that's how I'll always feel."

"Just go." Shooing him away, she pivoted. "I can't talk to you anymore. You're making a mistake."

With that, she stepped inside, then shut and locked the door.

Chapter 33

The downward turn of Pete's mouth when Skye answered the door said the conversation with Hope hadn't gone well. The sad expression whipped up a surge of sympathy in Skye. With the girls playing in the bedroom, she stepped out onto the porch with him and shut the door. The hum of cicadas joined the frogs' and crickets' loud chirping, the chorus of summer's approach.

"I'm sorry." She should have stayed out of his business.

Shifting his weight, he shook his head. "What do you have to be sorry for? I'm the one who's been such a louse. For years."

"Pete, no. That's not true. Hope's an adult and made her own choices." Self-deluded choices, but didn't everyone lie to themselves at times? Skye took a step closer and reached for his hand. Then stopped. Maybe he blamed her for ruining his friendship.

Blue eyes pensive, he took her hand, but his chin dipped—a cleanly shaved chin that she couldn't help wanting to slide her fingers across. "I shouldn't have depended on her so much. I should've seen how she felt."

Fire raged beneath Skye's skin, but not from his touch. Hope had obviously laid a guilt trip on Pete.

"I've observed the two of you closely since I arrived. Even that first night at my house, I saw how she fawned over you. Every time, your body language and your responses let her know that you weren't romantically interested. Hope simply didn't want to accept the truth."

The corner of his mouth ticked up, and his gaze lifted to meet hers. "You've observed me *closely* since you've arrived?"

"I meant… You were there. She was there. Caleb…" She sounded creepier by the second.

Stepping closer—so close their bodies almost touched—his face brightened. "I'd like for you to keep observing me." His tone was teasing.

Their fingers entwined, and warmth radiated all the way to her heart. In Florida, her life had been orderly and quiet. Safe. But now, despite the risk, she wanted more. "I'd like that too."

"May I get a hug before I come in to get Olivia?" A wind kicked up, and his dark hair, like liquid ebony, ruffled as he gave her a tender look. "Maybe a kiss?"

Lost in that sea of blue, she closed the small distance between them and met his lips with hers, featherlight at first. He kissed her back, caressing her hair. Fire and sweetness coursed through her. Abandoning her fears, she let herself be swept out into the tides of emotions and sensations, kissing him fiercely, holding him as if he were her anchor in a storm.

For a long while, there was only Pete and her, floating in their own little world, free from the pain of their pasts.

Too soon, the ringing of a phone interrupted their bliss, and Pete pulled away breathless. "Why did they have to invent these annoying things?"

He pressed his forehead to hers, and the pad of his thumb stroked her chin.

She managed a chuckle. "Terrible idea."

"I better see who it is, I guess." He nuzzled her nose, then eased back and pulled his cell from his pocket. "My dad."

A divot formed between his brows.

"I'll fix you a plate of supper."

She needed to check on the girls, too, because she'd lost track of how long she and Pete had stood out here. Probably too long.

Still, a few more kisses would have been nice.

"Thank you." Sighing, he cupped her cheek. "More later?"

"I hope so." She turned, and he answered the call.

Inside the house, she found Olivia and Sparrow still playing happily in Sparrow's bedroom. Then Skye flitted from the refrigerator to the cabinet to the microwave, preparing Pete's supper. The colors on the walls appeared brighter, and the aromas in the kitchen smelled more delicious. All her senses awash with life, her lips and skin still tingled. She could get used to this feeling.

~~~

"Mom came home today?" Pete's attention snapped to his father's voice on the phone. "That's great news." It was an answer to prayer—hundreds of prayers he'd prayed, thousands by friends and family and his parents' congregation.

"A miracle indeed." A chuckle floated through the line. "Praise the Lord."

A tender feeling washed over Pete, hearing his father so happy. "If I'd known, I would have helped."

"It was unexpected, and you were at work." The line went quiet a moment. "I do need a huge favor."

"Anything, Dad." They'd done so much for him.

"I don't want to leave her tomorrow."

"Okay." Calling this late might throw Caleb for a loop, but they could find a good deckhand. "I'll stay with her. What time should I get there?"

"No. I mean I want to stay with her. Myself."

"Then what are you asking?"

This wasn't making any sense.
~~~

"Take my place."

Pete's vision went white. Dad couldn't be asking him to preach at his megachurch. They probably wouldn't allow it, and they had to have other pastors on staff who could fill in.

Dad sighed. "I know what you're thinking, but it's too late to ask anyone else, and considering the circumstances, the elders have given their approval. Plus, the congregation would love an update on your mother from her own son. And you're an excellent preacher."

"You know I don't do organized religion anymore, plus I have my…my people on the beach."

"*Your* church?" Dad asked.

"Well, yeah."

Where was this going?

"Son, I named you Peter after the apostle. His confession that Jesus was Christ, the Son of the Living God, was the rock on which Jesus built *His* church, *His* bride. Not *Peter's* church." Dad's voice grew stronger. "I know it was hard growing up as a preacher's kid. Your feelings were hurt. But don't let a few gossipy people tarnish your perception of something God cherishes. His body of believers. You're a grown man now. Healing is possible. Past due, even."

It was a rare thing for Dad to ask anything of him. Rarer still for Dad to scold him. But his father had taken him behind the woodshed just now.

And he deserved the admonishment. A heavy sigh worked its way from deep within Pete.

Twice tonight, the self-centeredness in his life had been illuminated, smacking him in the face. How long had his father held his tongue about this? "Well, Dad, I don't have time to get a cool hairstyle, and I don't have any skinny jeans, but I'll be there."

His father's rich laugh boomed. "Wear anything you want, preach anything God gives you, as long as I can be here at home with my Dorothy. I trust you, son."

Pete let his head fall back. "I'll do my best not to let you or God down."

They finished the call, and Pete bent to his knees on the porch. "God, give me the words to say to Your people. *Your* church."

The door cracked open, and Skye peeked out. Seeing him there, she rushed to bend at his side. "Did something happen with your mother?"

He caught her hand in his. "A miracle. She's home."

"That's wonderful!"

"Yep." He bobbed his head.

"I sense a *but*." Concern etched a crease in her forehead, and she squeezed his hand.

She had no idea how much he needed her at that moment. How much he wanted her at his side in the morning.

"My dad asked me to preach at his church tomorrow so he can stay home with her."

Her shell-shocked expression likely mirrored his own.

Seeing the fear in her eyes, he didn't dare ask anything of her.

Instead, he said, "I better get Olivia and go. I need to call Caleb and arrange help for him, both at the beach service and on the charter."

He released her hand and hauled himself to his feet. "Then, I need to write a sermon. The little bit I had prepared for our fellowship won't be nearly enough."

Slowly standing, she caught his arm. Her mouth opened, shut, then opened again. Biting her bottom lip, she squeezed her eyes shut. "What time should we be ready?"

His chest teemed with so much love for this woman, he could barely breathe.

He tipped her chin and touched a kiss to her nose. "You don't have to."

"You need me," she whispered. "I feel it in my soul."

"More than you'll ever know."

Chapter 34

"This is where Momma used to take me for homeschool PE class." Sparrow pointed to the large brick building as they arrived at the church in Mobile.

"Seriously?" Skye whipped her head toward the back seat of Pete's truck.

Sparrow nodded. "On Tuesdays and Thursdays."

"That's great." Pete pulled the truck into a parking spot and put the gear in park. "Maybe you'll know someone in the children's area."

"I hope so." Sparrow's tone held none of the uneasiness swirling through Skye.

On the way into the building, Skye's legs felt as if they were swimming in sand, and her breaths came in shallow wisps. She was taking a risk being among this many people, but Miss Lydia had encouraged her not to fear.

Once they entered, Pete took her hand. "Thank you for being here to cheer me on."

She managed a small smile. "Never thought of myself as a cheerleader."

At least, since they'd arrived early, the halls were empty. She'd have time to try to gather her wits. If that were possible.

Pete led them to an area that held offices, then to the entrance of a conference room. A few men and women gathered there, drinking coffee.

"Hey, Pete." One of the men rounded the table. "Good to see you again." He shook Pete's hand. "I mean, really good to see you. Otherwise, I might've had to preach on the fly."

A cute lopsided smile accompanied Pete's chuckle. "You might wish you had once I finish."

"I've heard you speak to the youth group at our retreats on the island, so I know you'll do a fine job. And everyone will be excited to see you."

Pete waved her and the girls in, then made introductions. Skye's palms grew slicker with each handshake, and none of the names stuck in her mind.

The guy who seemed to be the leader continued. "We'll pray over you, then give you a crash course on how to operate the wireless microphone and the necessary technology. Do you have any slides or videos for our tech team?"

"Nope." He drew in a heavy breath. "I don't use any of that with my beach group."

"All the easier for everyone." The man motioned, and the rest of the strangers neared, encircled them, then placed their hands on Pete's shoulders. "Let's pray."

Air caught in Skye's lungs as the bodies crowded around. Her arms stiffened at her side. They all stood so suffocatingly close.

Pete slipped his fingers over hers, and her tight chest loosened. Smiling, he slid a glance her way and winked before closing his eyes. Like this was perfectly normal.

She managed a small breath as the praying began.

"Lord, anoint Pete with Your Holy Spirit. Give him clarity of mind to proclaim the Good News." More words continued, but Skye focused on staying upright despite the dizziness that only seemed to be worsening.

Once they finished, a woman bent in front of the children and smiled. "I'm Karen, the children's minister. Would y'all be my special helpers today?"

Sparrow and Olivia nodded, and the woman turned her attention to Skye and Pete. "I'll keep them with me all three services, then meet you back here, if that's okay."

Three services? Goodness. Had Pete mentioned that? Skye looked to Pete for an answer, since she knew nothing about the place or the procedures.

"We'd appreciate that." Pete nodded. "They'd be bored out of their minds by the third go."

Shivers slid across the nape of Skye's neck. How would she manage to keep her sanity that long in a crowd?

The girls left, and Pete led her into the large auditorium filled with plush chairs, kind of like a movie theater. In fact, three screens hung from the ceiling over a stage. She took a seat on the front row while the others showed Pete where to stand, fitted the microphone onto him, and talked about the order of worship.

One of her knees refused to stop bouncing, despite her efforts, and she slid her shaky hands over her khaki slacks. She probably should have worn something nicer, but Pete had assured her the service would be casual and promised he would be too.

And he'd been honest. He wore jeans and that crisp blue button-down that matched his eyes. She slid her gaze over him. He looked handsome, as usual. Really handsome. If she didn't faint away from panic, she'd still have to give herself a mental slap to make herself listen to what the man said, rather than gawk over how good he looked. When had she turned into a middle-schooler?

Too quickly, the room filled, and people came to speak to Pete. So many faces and names.

Skye did her best to appear normal. Music started, and the church stood to sing, so she did the same, mouthing the words on the screen since she didn't know the tune.

Pete placed his hand on the small of her back, probably because he picked up on how close she was to keeling over. She glanced up at his face.

Tension pulled around his mouth and formed lines near his temples. He was nervous too. Leaning into him, she pressed her hand to his back and patted, hoping to give him comfort as well. Before she knew it, he stood on the platform in front of the enormous crowd and began to speak. Her hands trembled as she took her seat.

Lord, be with us both. Calm our anxious thoughts.

"Good morning. I'm Pete Thompson, filling in for my father. He wanted me to tell you how much he's appreciated the prayers, the cards, the food, and the encouraging texts during Mom's illness. God answered by providing healing. She left the rehab yesterday, and Dad is home taking care of his Dorothy. They both want you to know that they love the Body of Christ here—they love you—so much."

The church stood and applauded.

When the sound died down and the people sat again, Pete continued. "Thank you again. Since everything happened quicker than expected, you're stuck with me today." Gripping the podium, Pete grinned. "News grows legs, spreads wings, and flies around, so you may have heard the rumors about Pete Thompson, the preacher's son, or if you've been coming here a while, you might have experienced the terror. I was the kid who crumbled the crayons, colored on the walls, and drew mustaches on myself and my friends with permanent markers. Basically, the kid no one wanted in their Sunday school class."

People in the audience snickered.

"I'm the teen who slathered cheese slices all over the young minister's car one hot summer, then wrapped it in toilet paper.

Later that year, I" —he made air quotes— "borrowed someone's truck without permission at church camp. I'm also the guy who showed the youth group the secret closet with a ladder that led to the roof. Wait." He held up his palm. "Don't look for it. I'll be in trouble again."

More laughter circulated the large room.

"You're looking at the mascot for preachers' kids with bad reputations." His expression grew serious. "Somewhere along the way, I decided that, if I had to be under the microscope, I'd give people something to look at."

The church quieted, and Skye's stomach lurched. Though the awkwardness of his honesty caught her off guard, she did her best to school her features and keep a pleasant expression on her face.

His gaze tracked around the room as he thumbed toward his chest. "A train wreck, right? But deep down, I did truly love and respect my father, so I chose to follow his steps to attend his alma mater in Birmingham, majoring in Biblical studies, though I was still a big hot mess until God caught hold of me."

He paced a little before continuing. "I met a pretty girl that first semester, and I knew I wanted to marry her. I studied hard and found internships at churches every summer, preparing to go into ministry."

Skye's anxious fingers rubbed circles on her chair's edge. Pete's wife must have been a strong woman. Much stronger than her.

"The summer before my senior year, the church I served went through an ugly split." Pete blew out a long sigh. "So many hurt feelings, things that shouldn't have been said, damaged relationships. I walked out and told my fiancée I was finished with organized religion. Finished with the church. Bitterness grew and flourished in my heart. When I graduated,

I went into the fishing charter business with my grandfather. Many of you knew and loved Pop."

Several people on the pew beside Skye nodded. She wished she'd gotten to meet Pete's grandparents. They seemed to have been well-loved.

Pete slid a glance at Skye, and his face brightened. "Sunday mornings, I worship with a few Christians on the beach around sunrise. We pray for and encourage each other. Those families stood by me when my wife died of cancer, leaving me with a newborn baby."

Forehead creasing, he cocked his head. "Somehow, in my mind, I considered my little gathering superior to other larger congregations. I guess I wrongly thought *myself* superior too. But last night, Dad reminded me that the Bible refers to the Church—whatever the size of the gathering—as Christ's Bride. I don't know about you, but if anyone trash-talked my wife, they'd have been in a world of trouble."

Silence blanketed the room as Pete's chin dipped. "I was convicted. I hadn't been respectful or reverent. I accepted God's grace to cover *my sins*, but I hadn't given that same grace to people who'd made mistakes as a part of what I called organized religion. I'd chosen to be judgmental, walking in bitterness rather than mercy."

Lifting his head, Pete looked around the room, then down at Skye. "If someone dragged you here this morning and you don't feel comfortable, or you've been hurt by people in a church setting, don't let that define your opinion of Christ's beloved bride—the Church. We are just a group of flawed individuals trying to follow God together."

He held up a copy of the Bible. "This book is filled with imperfect people performing great acts of service for a perfect God. The same can happen with us if we'll trust Him."

The words landed on Skye and washed over her.

She'd been prejudiced against Christianity because of the generational dysfunction in Denny's family. She'd given up on the belief in a good Creator because of the bad things that had happened in her life. But she saw now that terrible tragedies struck all kinds of people. Pete and Olivia's loss was proof of that, yet he still had faith. Miss Lydia certainly had her share of heartache, but she'd carried on with such joy and love for others.

By the time the third service ended, tears streamed down Skye's face. Perhaps, she could learn to have faith that God loved her. And allow a parcel of trust and grace toward other imperfect humans like herself.

After a long round of shaking hands and meeting more strangers, Skye and Pete walked back toward the offices.

"You survived?" He smiled down at her with those blue eyes.

Returning a smile, she gave a small nod. "The preacher at this church set me at ease."

Slipping his arm around her, he leaned close and whispered next to her hair. "Thank you."

"You know, you're really good at this church speaking. Are you sure preaching wasn't what you should be—"

"Daddy, look what we made!" Olivia spotted them as they rounded the corner and sprinted their way. When she reached them, she displayed an open envelope she'd decorated as a church. Popsicle sticks with haphazard smiley faces drawn on them stood in it. "This is the church."

"It's perfect." Pete bent down and pulled her into a hug.

"What about you?" Skye searched Sparrow's face as she approached with the children's minister. "Did you have a good time?"

"I helped lead singing and acted a part in a skit. And Miss Karen said I was a natural." She gazed up at the young woman.

"You sure are." Karen grinned at her, then turned to Skye. "I hope y'all come back."

"Can we?" Sparrow turned her pleading eyes to Skye.

Doubts assailed Skye, leaving her speechless.

So many people had seen her today. What had she been thinking? Among all the crowds, someone could have known her—known Denny or his parents.

"Can we go see Mimi today, since she's home?" Olivia asked Pete, and Skye turned to hear his response.

"I don't know." He glanced at Skye, as if the answer were up to her.

Pete probably wanted to see with his own eyes how his mother was doing. She certainly shouldn't hold him back from that. "Okay with me," she said finally.

Though fear coursed through her, maybe relationships could be worth a few risks.

Chapter 35

Nightmares had stolen Skye's sleep, leaving her exhausted for work Monday morning. She'd barely gotten Sparrow to school on time. Now in the lab, Skye's hands hovered over the computer keys, waiting for her mind to give instructions. But she couldn't shake the bad dreams or the residual fear haunting her. Strangers' faces. Fingers pointing. They shouted, *"There she is. That's Skye Youngblood. You know, the weird loner from high school. The teachers' pet."*

These feelings had to stem from yesterday's anxiety at the church, because meeting Pete's parents had been easy. When she and Pete had picked up lunch and delivered it to their house, Mr. and Mrs. Thompson had hugged them and invited them in. A little heavier than Pete, his father had a kind face with full cheeks when he grinned. His hair was a mix of gray and black, and his patient expression showed no hurry for them to move from the kitchen table, much less leave.

His mother had seemed tired, but she kept a smile on her face and had the same bright blue eyes as Pete. They'd both been so gracious, Skye looked forward to visiting them again.

They were nothing like Denny's parents. Blinking away the brutal images his family stirred up, she stared at the screen and forced her fingers to move.

Nitrogen and phosphorous from sewage leaks and other chemical pollution runoffs are feeding algae overgrowth, resulting in Florida seagrass die-off. Manatee starvation deaths have skyrocketed, and large numbers are migrating westward as they attempt to attain food sources.

"Knock, knock." Dr. Boleware stood at Skye's office door. "Did you have a good rest of the weekend?"

The fluttering started in her midsection again as Pete's kisses came to mind. "Yes. You?"

Not one to make a lot of small talk, Dr. Boleware bobbed her head. "You haven't given your RSVP to the fundraising gala in Mobile. Will you have a plus one?"

Skye swiped her hands down the sides of her face.

This didn't sound familiar. "I'm not sure I received the invitation." Or she'd thrown it away. "Hobnobbing isn't in my comfort zone anyway."

"Most of us can relate, but we need to attend next Thursday night to raise awareness about the Manatee Sighting and Marine Mammal Stranding Networks." Her lips curled into a smirk. "Captain Thompson is capable of carrying on small talk, and you two seemed…very *comfortable* with each other on our research excursions."

A flush swept over Skye's skin. How awkward. "What does one wear to the event?"

"Generally, I wear a dress or black slacks with a formal top." Dr. Boleware scanned Skye up and down. "I could loan you something if you haven't had time to replace all the clothing lost in the fire."

Yes, her wardrobe was limited, but her replacement credit card had arrived. She'd bought a few things, just not a dress or anything formal. "That's not necessary. I'll find something."

Shopping at Hope's store was out of the question, so she might end up driving over half an hour to a big box store or something farther off the island.

"I'll email the details again. Let me know about your plus one situation in the morning."

"Will do."

Holding in a groan, Skye turned her focus to her computer screen, glad to end the embarrassing conversation. She could mention the event to Pete, but he probably couldn't finish work and clean himself up in time for a formal dinner on a weeknight. And who would keep the girls if he could?

Again, Hope would be out of the question, and April might not want to watch the girls that late.

Could she bring Sparrow with her? She brushed away that idea.

It didn't seem professional, plus they'd be seen together by more people. Questions could arise. At least Sunday at church, Sparrow had spent the morning in the children's area.

This event would likely be a miserable solo endeavor. But maybe…

Skye tugged her phone from her purse. Asking Pete couldn't hurt, could it? She shot him a text, explaining the situation. Then she put her cell away, punching down her silly fantasies about him. She had work to do.

Four hours later, her phone chimed with a message.

Got it all worked out for us. We can drop the girls off at my parents' on the way to the restaurant. I'll be looking forward to a date with you.

~~~

Thursday evening, by the time Pete scrubbed away the fish smell after work, donned his suit, and took off in his truck, he realized they'd only arrive on time at the fundraiser if there was zero traffic on the interstate in Mobile. Probably out of luck on that, but he couldn't wait to spend an evening alone with Skye.

Sort of alone. At least they'd be by themselves in the truck on the way to the restaurant. Adult time and conversation would be nice. A quick kiss at a stoplight would be even better.

Oh, man. When had he become this gushy?
~~~

For the past few weeks, they'd followed the same routine. They had supper together with the kids and the dogs, beach walks on moonlit weekend evenings. The rhythmic language of the sea, the chirping songs of the night, and stealing sweet good-night kisses when they could sneak out to the porch. The satisfying memories slid over him like a breeze on a sunny day.

He glanced in the rearview mirror and caught himself smiling. He hadn't been this happy in years.

At the house, Pete practically sprinted to Skye's door and knocked. The smaller dog's yip echoed inside, followed by the sound of scampering feet.

Sparrow yanked open the door. "Hey, Pete!" Her voice was full of sunshine. "I made something for you in art."

"I can't wait to see it."

She skipped to the table and retrieved a picture frame with small stones glued to the wooden edges. In the center, the words You Rock stood out in orange marker, decorated with a few flourishes.

"That's amazing. Thank you." He took the frame, then gave her a big hug. The affection he felt for the child and her gift caught him by surprise. Sure, Olivia made things for him every week, and he adored her. And he was crazy about Skye. He just hadn't realized how attached he'd grown to this child as well.

"Sparrow, you're supposed to wait for me before answering the door." From around the corner, Skye entered the living room with Olivia following, and Pete's heart stuttered as his breath caught in his chest.

Skye's light brown hair lay against an emerald green dress. The square line of the collar featured her slender neck, and the desire to kiss her swept over him. Pulse throttling, he struggled to speak. "You look beautiful."

Her chin dipped, but she met his gaze. "You do too."

A laugh erupted from Sparrow. "Men aren't beautiful. They're hot."

"Sparrow!" Gaping, Skye tsked. "Where did you hear that?"

The girl's shoulders lifted almost to her ears. "School."

"Do I look beautiful, Daddy?" Olivia ran to hug him.

"Always. And Sparrow does too." He pressed a kiss on Sparrow's head. Gathering his wits, he smiled. "We better hit the road, beautiful ladies, or we'll miss this shindig."

All the way to his truck, though, he slid glances Skye's way. Once the girls were buckled, he rushed to hold the door for her. She was a vision in green as she glided into the front seat. Another urge to *at least* kiss her cheek assailed him, but he stuffed it away until he could deliver the girls to his parents.

Finally, they took off down the road and across the bridge that left the island. Forty minutes later, they reached his parents' house. Mom looked so much better that it was hard to believe she'd had a stroke. She'd even prepared sugar cookie dough and had it ready to cut into shapes and bake with the girls.

At last, he and Skye drove alone in the car, and a flush of anticipation throbbed through his fingers, if only to hold her hand in his. At the first red light, he glanced her way and hesitated, finding her arms cocooning her chest.

"Are you okay?" he asked as the light turned green.

"I'm dreading this." Her voice wavered.

"Way to make a guy feel special."

That earned a laugh. "Sorry. It's not you. I'm an introvert, if you hadn't noticed by now."

"You don't say?" A snort accompanied his words. "Have you always—?"

The chiming of his low fuel alert interrupted them, and he groaned. "I can't believe I forgot to fill up yesterday."

"It's okay with me if we're a little late. Or if we skip the whole thing."

"I know Dr. Boleware will notice your absence."

"You're right about that." She sighed.

Slow-moving strands of purple clouds topped with pink layered the sky ahead. He'd rather fill up now than late tonight. "There's a station not far from here. I'll make it quick."

Four blocks away, he pulled in next to a pump and popped open the cover of the tank.

"I think I'll run in for a pack of mints." Skye unbuckled and turned his way. "Do you want anything?"

Facing her, he cocked a brow. "Maybe you can share?" His gaze locked on her mouth. "In case a pretty girl wants to kiss me good night." It was corny, but he couldn't help himself.

Blushing, she caught her bottom lip between her teeth, then blessed him with that sweet shy smile. "I'll consider your request."

"That's all I can ask." He got out to fill the tank while she grabbed her purse and headed inside the store.

After he'd pumped maybe three gallons, he looked up to find Skye running toward him, panic etching her features.

"We have to leave. Now!" Her voice was quiet but frantic. She fell into the front seat and slid down low.

He replaced the gas nozzle and cap, then jumped back into the truck. "What's wrong? Did someone hurt you?"

Her whole body trembled. "No. Just go. Hurry." Her voice broke as she hunched over and covered her face.

"That horrible woman, Mrs. Beasley—Denny's mother, was in there. She made Denny into the monster he became. I just pray she didn't recognize me."

Driving forward, Pete glanced back in his mirror to see a lean, blonde woman with a hard set to her jaw, perhaps a few years older than his mother, come out of the store. She looked familiar. He had seen something about the Beasley family on the news, years before. They'd been the talk of Mobile church circles almost a decade ago. He hated thinking of people in ministry tarnishing the church's reputation. He especially hated hearing they'd hurt children.

Once he'd pulled out onto the highway, he reached over and stroked Skye's back. "I'm here for whatever you need, Skye. You're safe now."

"No." She gulped in a shaky breath. "I can never be safe around here."

Chapter 36

A haze of darkness brooded outside the truck's windows and inside Skye's soul, threatening to swallow her up and send her into a loop of anxiety and depression.

Echoes of cynical laughter still made her skin crawl. But she hadn't seen Denny's mother in almost ten years. Maybe the woman hadn't recognized her. Miss Lydia had encouraged Skye, even in recent days, not to live in fear. To trust that God would provide.

"Do you want me to turn around? Take you home?" Pete asked. "You could tell Dr. Boleware you aren't feeling well."

That would be the truth.

Her body pulsed with those childhood wounds of fear and abandonment, the helpless feeling that no one would come to her rescue.

Whether Miss Lydia was right or wrong, going home now wouldn't change what had happened. It might change how long she remained in the Mobile area, though. "I committed to attending, and Mrs. Beasley didn't look like she was dressed for a fancy event like the fundraiser, so…" Her thinking changed directions. Had Denny's parents moved? Last she'd heard, they lived northeast of Mobile. This event was located south of the city and off the Causeway.

Miss Lydia had kept tabs on Denny's incarceration over the years, but now the responsibility fell to Skye. She needed to get her head out of the sand. "Keep heading toward the restaurant. I want to do an internet search on the way."

A few minutes into the search, she found old articles about Denny's arrest and his father's dismissal from his church after trying to help cover up the abuse.

No other helpful information.

Once they pulled into the restaurant and parked near the back of the full lot, Pete turned to her. "How can I help you?"

"I don't know if you can." She set aside the phone and rubbed her temples. "I'd like to know where they live and if Denny—Momma's husband—is out of prison and living with them."

"Did you have to testify?" His voice was gentle.

"I never came forward. Never told the police about what he'd done to me." And that fact sickened her. "If I'd spoken up, he might not have hurt anyone else."

He reached over and covered her hand. "It's not your fault. You don't have to own what he did."

Squeezing her eyes shut, she hung her head. If only she could have been stronger. Or smarter. If she'd taken her sister and run away.

A knock on the window jerked their attention. She opened her eyes to find Michael waving outside Pete's door. In the glow of the streetlight, Hope stood behind him. She wore a stunning sleeveless red dress, her expression unreadable.

Interesting duo. Despite all the thoughts jumbling in her mind, she couldn't help but wonder what Pete would think of their matchup.

Easing the window down, Pete's gaze bounced between the pair, confusion evident in the squint of his stare. "What's up?"

Did it bother him to see Hope with another man? Not something she'd ask tonight. There was enough to stress over already.

"You guys coming in?" Michael stretched his neck to make eye contact with Skye. "Everything okay?"

Trying to hide the tremor in her lip, Skye attempted a strained smile. She had to pull herself together. "Just dreading this. You know, me and social interactions." She forced a laugh and fiddled with her mother's necklace.

Michael scoffed. "Come on." He motioned for them to get out. "It'll be a blast. Food and drink. Music. The silent auction. People with money for your research."

Her laugh faded to a sigh, and she reached for the door handle. "Sure. Let's go raise funds."

After rolling up the window, Pete turned her way. "I believe in you."

Having him at her side gave her more comfort than he could know.

When she stepped out and straightened her dress—which seemed casual compared to Hope's—Pete rounded the vehicle and held out his elbow for her. "Shall we?"

She tucked her hand under his firm arm and stared toward the longstanding seafood restaurant nestled against Mobile Bay. Her mother had taken her and Star here once. They'd all three shared a single meal—a special treat.

That had been before Momma remarried. A local favorite, the restaurant had weathered many a storm, but the building didn't appear to have changed much other than a coat of white paint and a few replaced boards on the decking.

Ahead, Michael and Hope chatted, but Skye couldn't make out the words, perhaps because she couldn't help studying how perfect Hope looked. The hair, the makeup, the manicured nails, the way she walked in heels without tripping. Sure she was being trivial, yet, Skye glanced down at her own flat sandals she'd picked up on the clearance rack in a bargain store.

Paint hadn't glossed her toenails since she was ten years old. And Star had lifted the polish from someone's trash. Skye snickered at the memory.

"What?" Pete slipped his hand down to entwine her fingers in his. "Was that a real laugh I heard?"

"Just thinking about how my sister used to dumpster-dive and wander the roadsides on garbage days." She checked his reaction. "It probably sounds disgusting to you, but she found some good stuff."

Smiling, he clicked his tongue. "What's the saying? One person's trash is another's treasure."

"Exactly. Or a weapon even, in Star's case." She shook her head. "Star was tough. She found and hid an arsenal of knives, bats, and who knows what else. Even Denny feared her enough to lock her up at night, meanwhile I crouched in the bedroom, frozen in fear."

A look of horror slacked Pete's jaw. "Oh, Skye. That's so wrong."

Why had she gone there? "I'm sorry. Seeing his mother dredged up the past."

"Don't ever feel *you* need to be sorry." He stopped, letting distance settle between them and the happy couple leading the way. He cradled her face, then stroked her cheek with his thumb. "I'm here for you."

Michael reached the door and held it open, and music carried on the breeze out to them. "Come on, lovebirds. Plenty of time for that on the dance floor."

A flash of hurt tightened Hope's expression, but she quickly turned her attention inside.

Without commenting, Pete released Skye, and they entered the crowded room.

Near the front of the bar, Dr. Boleware stood with a well-dressed man and woman, maybe in their late fifties. Probably some power couple from Mobile.

Dr. Boleware spotted Skye and beckoned with her head for them to come over.

"I guess I have to work now." Skye nudged Pete with her elbow. "You still have time to run away."

"Not a chance," he whispered as they walked.

"Just the couple I've been waiting for." Dr. Boleware wagged her finger at Skye. "This is Dr. Sydney Smith, known as Skye to her friends, and her date Captain Pete Thompson."

"A doctorate?" The man raised a brow while scanning her up and down. "Impressive for someone so…young."

Skye resisted the urge to cross her arms and clam up.

Maybe she should have worn her usual khakis and long sleeves. "I only finished in December, and I've had no other life for a decade." She brandished what she hoped was an intelligent—non-irritated—expression. "I'm older than I look too."

"Ignore my husband's lack of couth." The perfectly coiffed brunette rolled her eyes. "Everyone looks young when you're over the hill. Tell us about your work. In layman's terms, of course."

Swallowing the nervous mass in her throat, Skye raced through an explanation of the manatee sighting network and the use of citizen science to track migration, then continued into her own research of manatees' diet and understanding their movements to forage for food. "The quality of water has recently declined, especially in Florida, causing an algae overgrowth, seagrass deterioration, and an unusual manatee mortality event. Over six-hundred have died this year."

"Can't they eat seaweed or something?"

"They don't eat seaweed. More and more are migrating

westward during the warm weather months for food, but they have to travel back to Florida for the winter or they'll succumb to cold stress."

"We have to help the poor creatures." The wife patted her husband's arm. "Don't we, dear?"

He gave a good-natured smirk. "I knew that was coming. Who do I make the check out to?"

Dr. Boleware flicked a satisfied smile at Skye. "Make it out to our foundation. We also have a silent auction with some amazing listings." She walked him through the donation process, then introduced Pete and Skye to other donors around the restaurant. They ended up eating finger food for dinner as they worked the room.

After an hour or more of blurred faces and names, her colleague stopped and glanced left then right. "That should do. Y'all go play."

"Really?" Skye blinked. "I'm finished. I can go home?"

Frowning, Dr. Boleware tsked. "That is not what I said." Her gaze landed on Pete. "Show this woman how to have fun."

Chuckling, Pete saluted. "On it." Then he held out one hand as if they were about to do a waltz. "May I have the next dance?"

"I don't know how." Her pulse thrashed in her neck. She'd make a fool of them both.

"I'll lead." His blue gaze met hers and flickered. "Trust me."

Maybe she could try. "Don't be mad if I step on your toes."

"I can carry your weight." His soulful expression said he meant more than her hundred-plus pounds.

He led her outside near the waterfront under the stars where the band played a slow tune and held out his arms. "I've got you. Relax."

With shaky steps, she eased into his warmth, and his strength steadied her. She rested her head against his firm shoulder and tried to follow his lead. As they swayed to the music, white lights strung along the rails of the dock reflected on the bay. A breeze took the edge off the balminess of the late spring evening. This night couldn't be more perfect.

"I'm in love with you, Skye." Pete's whisper tickled her ear and stopped her heart.

"What?" She lifted her head and blinked.

"You heard me." Light glittered in his eyes, and his dark hair ruffled in the wind like deep onyx blackbird feathers.

"Why?" It made no sense for him to fall for someone like her.

"You're obviously brilliant, after the way Dr. Boleware showed you off." His tone was teasing. "You're beautiful and kind and gentle—the whole package."

For a heartbeat she believed him, but reality crept back in. "A damaged package." She lowered her gaze.

"We're all broken." He pulled her closer and rubbed soft circles on her back. "Don't let the lies of the enemy hold you prisoner any longer."

A faster song with a heavy beat began, and the dance floor sprang to life.

"Look at y'all rocking the house." Michael strode past and pressed through the crowd, towing Hope toward the stage.

Skye nodded after them, watching the elegant and beautiful Hope capture the attention of men all around. "Someone like Hope would be better for—"

Pete's mouth met hers, quieting her, and a current jolted through her core.

When he relinquished her lips, he whispered, "You're the one."

The one?

Could she be anyone's *one*?

She wanted to believe it. More than anything. The magical night, the music, the dancing. Maybe, just maybe, she wasn't too broken for this.

"If you insist." She couldn't stop a smile. "I love you too."

She wouldn't rock the boat now, but at some point, her research here would end, and Sparrow would go back to live with Miss Lydia. Tonight, though, she'd forget all that and be Cinderella dancing in the arms of her handsome prince.

Chapter 37

Pete held open the page of his worn journal. He'd written so much that week—had so many thoughts and prayers for God since dancing with Skye at the fundraiser. The memory sent a jolt to his heart and pinpricks of fire to his skin. Tonight, he'd meet Skye and the girls to take them on a boat ride. When he had the chance, he needed to ask Skye about plans for the future. Plans for *their* future.

She'd said she loved him. If true, would she be willing to commit to him the way he wanted to commit himself to her? What would that look like?

Dad had called, telling Pete about a position as a youth minister at a church in Florida, several ministry jobs actually, and reminding him that Skye had only rented Nana and Pop's house for a few months. She'd only ever planned to stay on Dauphin Island temporarily. Was Dad hinting Pete should give up everything and move? *Like that would happen.* When Pete ignored the ridiculous implication, Dad had gone on to ask Pete if Skye was a believer.

Pete pressed his eyes closed.

That was an important question. And he needed direction on how to proceed. Skye was a tender soul. A wounded soul. She'd openly showed her disdain for religion originally, yet she claimed to be praying now and even attended church with him.

With all that he'd been through during Kenzie's cancer and death, he never would have survived without God's loving presence holding him upright.

He and Skye needed to be on the same page if they continued this relationship.

The pen beside his journal called to him. He lifted it to the paper and let his heart lead his hand.

Elements alone without Your breath?

A wasteland, a desert, a cold hollow mess,

No life, no love, no order or control,

A darkness, a blackness, a still empty hole.

Your presence brings life and light.

Your words spring colors that disperse the night

Teaming seas churn and foam,

Creatures swim, and hop, and roam,

Fruits so succulent and sweet,

Green grass, flowers, and trees,

You open Your heart, Your mouth, and blow out dear breath

Your beauty, Your love, Your life, and Your depth

You enter Your creation You designed

Please walk with Your masterpiece, Your servant, on the edge of this night.

Pete dropped the pen and bowed his head. "God, I don't know how to proceed. I need your constant guidance. Thank you for this joy I feel with Skye."

Even if it was only temporary, he'd learned he could love again.

~~~

On the deck of the anchored charter, Skye soaked in the lavenders and magentas splashed across the edges of the Gulf's western horizon. The setting golden globe of the sun sank lower as if melting into the water. She soaked in Pete's solid presence on one side and the girls' laughter on her other as the boat gently rocked.

Thank you, God.
~~~

The thought tumbled through her mind, surprising her at how easily and often the prayers had come lately. She'd reread the book of Romans numerous times, and the teachings had begun to make sense. The words seemed to come to life now, as if they'd been written especially for her. Miss Lydia had cried with joy when Skye told her about this new faith.

Now, whenever Skye ventured outdoors, God's creation whispered His love. As if He'd spoken to her heart, *Look, I made all this for you. I've left My fingerprints all over creation for you to find.*

"Daddy, can you show Sparrow how you drive the boat?" Olivia asked as the sun dipped from their view.

A smile crinkling the corners of his blue eyes, Pete looked to Skye for permission.

"I guess so." She focused on Sparrow. "If you obey Pete's instructions."

"We will," the girls said in unison, and they all headed toward the ladder leading to the bridge. Pete climbed up first, helping the girls make the top step, and Skye followed. They stood behind Pete as he folded into the captain's chair and began to explain the instruments.

"This is the chart plotter." His fingers pointed to a black instrument with small red spots dotting a green screen. "I've got radar to see other boats." He touched it to change the function. "This one sets a pin for them. I can tell the depth of the water and see the buoys to drive between in the channels."

Sparrow leaned closer. "Oh, cool. Can you see fish?"

"That would happen over here." Pete swiveled in his seat. "I've got an old-school fish finder. Works just as good as anything, but I've got the more advanced one too." He pointed. "See that loop down there? That's a big fish. Maybe a shark or something."

Eyes wide, Sparrow gasped. "Can it get us?"

Skye shook her head. "Sharks primarily prey on fish and other marine mammals."

Sparrow's fists punched her slender hips. "I've read on the internet about sharks biting people."

When had the child become so grown?

"Occasionally, that happens, but it's rare. You're more likely to get struck by lightning." And now she'd give them something else to worry about.

"Look over here, girls." Pete pulled their attention to his instruments again, thank goodness. "These are my radios. I can talk to the passengers below with this one, and I use this one if I need to call other vessels."

"How do you make the boat go?" Sparrow asked.

"I plot the GPS coordinates for my route." He put his hand on one of three gear shifts. "I have starboard and port engines. This one moves us forward. If I find a deep hole that I think will be a good spot, I hold over it and keep the boat in position so my passengers can fish there. If I'm bucking the westward current, I put the starboard engine forward and reverse with these levers."

"Do you have a special name for this?" Skye touched the wheel in front of him.

He gave her a crooked grin. "I call it the *steering wheel.*"

The girls giggled, causing heat to creep over Skye's cheeks. "I thought it might have a special nautical term."

Chuckling, Pete winked. "You can name it whatever you like."

Skye couldn't help but laugh with them. "What else do you have to show us, Captain, before we have to go home?"

"I have autopilot I can use, but I'd have to manually program the plot points."

His piercing blue gaze swung to her and held on. "If you stick around, I could give you lessons."

If she stuck around.

How she longed to say she would stay in this place forever with him. If only things were different. Tension brewing within her, she looked away.

Outside the windshield, darkness gathered, and a waning crescent moon rose. The sky became a dark velvet with pin-pricks of stars beginning to twinkle.

Olivia yawned and rubbed her eyes, then rested her head on Pete's shoulder.

"Time for the little minnows to rest, I think." Pete nuzzled his daughter.

"Aww," Sparrow moaned. "It's the weekend. Can't we stay up?"

Skye mussed her hair. "The ride back to the harbor will take a bit. Let's go downstairs and look at the sky on the way. Maybe we'll see a meteor falling."

The child's face brightened. "Okay."

Olivia perked up enough to follow them down the ladder with Pete's help. The three of them sat on a bench watching the stars while Pete drove them back. In no time, Olivia fell asleep in Skye's lap.

Nearing the marina, a streak of light blazed before disappearing into the darkness.

"A shooting star!" Sparrow jolted up and wrapped Skye in a fierce hug. "A treasure from God for us!"

With both girls cuddled close, Skye nodded. "You're exactly right. A treasure from God."

Once Pete had the boat secured in the slip, he lifted Olivia from Skye's lap. Yawning, Sparrow took Skye's hand as they walked across the lot to the truck.

They settled the girls in the back seat and closed the truck doors. Sparrow might be asleep in seconds too.

"Hang on a minute before you get in." Pete held up one finger, then cranked the engine before walking around to stand before Skye. He pushed his hands in his pockets and propped himself against the truck. "Did you have a good time?"

Skye's heart fluttered like a hungry bird, flitting around a feeder. Yes, she was starving for more time with this man. "I… I like your boat."

And she was still terrible at flirting.

A smirk spread across his lips, but his eyes smiled. "Is that all you liked? My boat?"

"You know better." Currents of affection thrummed in her veins. "I've told you."

"Good." A look of satisfaction spread across his face. "I'd like to set aside some time to talk with you alone."

"Talk?" Alone? It felt as though a pile of stones plummeted into her stomach. She'd never been in a relationship, but this sounded serious.

"About us." His chin dipped, and he cocked his head, still looking at her. "About our future. Together."

Realization dawned. They did need to talk, but she hadn't wanted to face that reality yet. "Okay," she breathed. "When?"

The phone in Skye's pocket rang.

Thankful for the distraction, she ripped it out, answering without checking the source of the call. "Hello."

"Skye?"

The voice sounded familiar but garbled and distant. Not Miss Lydia but similar.

Maybe her sister? "Gertie?"

"Yes. Oh, baby, I've been trying to call you tonight," Gertie sobbed. "Our Lydia's gone home to the Lord."

Gone?

The world around Skye spun. Her eyes couldn't focus. Dread fell like a mountain collapsing on top of her.

This couldn't be. "But she was getting better."

Pete braced her shoulders. "What's wrong?" he whispered.

"She didn't want me to tell you she'd been running high fevers." Gertie's voice quivered. "Didn't want you to worry… There wasn't anything you could do."

"I could have come to her." Tears pricked Skye's eyes, then streamed down her cheeks.

"You couldn't. They had her in isolation." Gertie sniffled. "Some complication called bacteremia."

Skye had read about the risk factors, but Miss Lydia had claimed to be doing well. Miss Lydia was their anchor. "She can't be gone."

"I know how you feel, sweet girl, but—"

Nothing made sense.

Sparrow needs Miss Lydia. I can't be a good mother like Miss Lydia is. Why couldn't You take me instead, God?

The voice on the line faded as Skye dropped the phone and fell into Pete's arms.

Chapter 38

Skye stood and stared at the flower-covered coffin that rested in front of a gaping cavity in the ground. The thought of Miss Lydia beneath six feet of dirt crushed the breath from Skye's lungs. Those sensations from her childhood—the darkness pursuing her, the paralyzing fear, the helplessness—they rose up to clutch her throat now.

She leaned into Pete's shoulder. "I don't know how to go on."

"I'm here." His voice hummed. "I'll be beside you and Sparrow every step. We'll get through this together."

Without him, she'd probably be curled in a ball back at the funeral home. After three days of tears and dealing with Miss Lydia's friends offering condolences, taking Sparrow to the family viewing this morning had vaporized what little composure Skye had left.

But Miss Lydia had left specific instructions, and perhaps that closure was important.

This afternoon's outdoor celebration of life highlighted all the beautiful ways she had ministered to people over the years, and Sparrow had soaked in each testimony with earnest attention. The child had held up remarkably well, but perhaps she was still in a state of shock and denial.

Those ghosts of grief crept up at the strangest times. At least that was how it had been for Skye after Momma died. One day in a shoe store Skye had been wrecked after spotting a pair of tennis shoes like her mother's.

The smallest memory could puncture the heart like a spike.

Hazy clouds closed in above the cemetery's tent. They threatened rain and turned the horizon to a pale silver. The humidity made it that much harder to breathe.

When would Gertie quit introducing Sparrow to everyone? When could they leave?

Her stomach knotted. Getting through this day would be only a first step. She'd take custody of Sparrow, be responsible for her wellbeing. How would she navigate school projects, dance lessons, or soccer practices? Even worse, what advice would she give to help Sparrow through dating, choosing prom dresses, or all the other things Skye had never experienced while growing up in a dysfunctional home?

Gertie led the girls back to Skye and Pete. Relatives hugged and made the trek back to their cars.

"Take as much time as you need." Pete landed a compassionate look on Sparrow then Skye.

"Thanks," Skye spoke around the catch in her throat, then turned to Sparrow. "Do you want to bring a flower home or say good bye now that we're alone?"

After a short pause, the child nodded.

"We can wait here," Pete said.

Holding Sparrow's hand, Skye led her to the ominous shiny white casket one last time.

"Pink roses were her favorite." Sparrow touched a velvety petal in one of the many arrangements.

"We can take a couple." Skye slid two of the flowers from the bouquet and gave one to Sparrow.

"Get another for Olivia, or she'll feel left out." Sparrow stated the request stoically, then, her chin quivered, undoing Skye as she pulled out another rose.

"Everyone told stories of Momma today. Except you."

"I was too…" Devastated. Heartbroken. Despairing. But she owed Miss Lydia so much. Owed Sparrow comfort. "I was in her science class in high school. Miss Lydia saw deeper inside people than most do. She could spot the students with bruises both inside and out." Skye sucked in a deep breath. "My mom suffered from depression when I was growing up, and her second husband hurt me and my sister. Miss Lydia sensed that, and she took me under her wing."

At that moment, a cardinal fluttered beneath the canopy and perched on top of a wreath of bright flowers.

Sparrow gasped and whispered, "Look. Her favorite bird."

A tear caught on Skye's lashes, then trickled down her cheek. What did seeing the cardinal mean? Was Miss Lydia a red bird now, sent to watch over them? She hadn't read anything like that in the Bible.

"Momma said God sends us hugs through His creation—reminders that He loves us to cheer our hearts."

Warmth cascaded over Skye, and she wrapped Sparrow in her arms. "You learned from the best mother in the world."

Teary blue eyes gazed up at her. "Will you take care of me now?"

Love swelled up inside of Skye, so deep and strong that it was painful. Along with it, a fear of screwing up something so vitally important. And of Denny. "I will."

They stayed there holding each other a long moment, then Sparrow slid back. "They're probably burning up out there, waiting on us." She turned toward Pete and Olivia, then looked over her shoulder once more. "Bye, Momma."

Skye's nose stung, but she tamped down the urge to sob. She had to be strong. If ever there was a time to have courage, it was now. For Miss Lydia. For Sparrow.

Help me, God.

When they reached Pete, he hugged them both and led them to his truck. "How does pizza and cookies at my house sound? April offered to drop off dinner." He smiled gently at Sparrow. "You haven't been inside our place, have you?"

"Okay," she mumbled.

His gaze darted to Skye.

"We like pizza and cookies. The dogs should be okay for a while longer." What more could she say? She was thankful for his help.

Rain fell hard during their fifty-minute drive back to the island. The girls sat silently in the back with nothing but the deluge filling the quiet.

On the long bridge where Skye had wrecked in her van, visibility was limited to a couple of feet ahead of them. Skye's clammy hands fisted. What if Sparrow had been in the van that day?

From now on, in any decision she made, Sparrow had to be the first consideration. They'd have to be that much more careful.

The folders Miss Lydia had left with her attorney for Skye gave detailed instructions for what to do with her house and her belongings. The volume of tasks that waited to be taken care of pressed in on her like a smothering weight. She hadn't read past the packet with funeral directions and bank account directives needed to pay for the service.

They reached Pete's house and, because of the heavy rain, sprinted to the porch.

Skye took in what she could of the charming blue cottage while he unlocked the door.

When they'd waited in the driveway for him to get a telescope, it had been at nighttime, and she'd been so scared of him that she'd not paid attention to the details.

Now that she was no longer afraid of his presence, maybe seeing where he lived could be a needed distraction.

Inside, pale-yellow paint coated the walls, but the photos in black frames in the entryway captured Skye's attention. Two of the pictures displayed a younger Pete grinning at a stunningly beautiful woman whose luminous eyes and long lashes mirrored Olivia's.

"That's my momma." Olivia's voice squeaked. "She died too."

Maybe this wasn't such a good idea. Skye pinched her lips together before speaking. "She's beautiful. You look like her."

The child smiled and then turned to Sparrow. "Want to see my room?"

"Okay." Sparrow followed her down a hall.

"April should be here soon." Pete motioned to a plush blue sofa that faced a fireplace in the living room. "Want to sit and rest? We can talk or not. Your call."

Nodding, Skye made her way to the couch and sank into the cushions. Pete took a seat in a matching oversize chair. He kicked his feet onto the ottoman.

Skye took in the colorful area rugs and throw pillows, the combination of nautical and coastal artwork. The cozy décor was a mix of masculine and feminine. "You have a nice place."

"Kenzie decorated when we moved in." His hands folded in front of him, but his thumbs bounced a nervous rhythm. "I've just kept things clean since then."

"She did a good job." The pictures in the hall came to mind, reminding Skye that today had likely been hard on him, bringing back painful memories.

His expression tightened. "This old house has been through a lot, long before we moved in, probably back to Hurricane Frederick in the late seventies. You see that line in the chimney bricks?" He pointed toward the fireplace. "That was from hurricane Katrina. And outside, there's a stump from the oak that crashed into the kitchen during Zeta. We were here for that one. This house has been damaged many times, but it's always repaired. We can work together to carry on for another day."

He was preaching to her now, offering an object lesson, but he didn't understand.

And now wasn't the best time. "It's different for me."

"What do you mean?"

How could she tell him? "I'm afraid some things are too messed up."

"We all have fears, Skye. Just different ones." He sighed and planted his feet on the floor. "I've been broken, too, by Kenzie's death, her parents' blame, and losing Nana and Pop. Mom's stroke. Being a single parent."

Leaning in, he fixed a serious gaze on her. "When Kenzie passed, I sat on my parents' couch, for days and weeks, dazed, numb, with a newborn. No idea how to take care of an infant. One day, I sensed God saying, *Go home, go back to work, and take care of your daughter.* I literally strapped her on my chest and took her everywhere with me. Like this old house, we can rebuild. You and I can build a better life. We can be stronger *together.* With God's help."

What would building a new life with Pete be like? She struggled to imagine such bliss. They could never live here in this area. Plus, there were things he'd need to know about her. About Sparrow. Things that might change his mind.

"What are you thinking?" he asked, his voice soft.

The girls' chatter drifted down the hall, and Skye shook her head. "I can't risk them hearing."

"We could stand out on the front porch."

She should tell him the truth. Tell him why she'd have to move Sparrow out of this town to raise her. She needed to lay all her life's debris out in the open so he could make his choice. The choice that would no doubt crush her heart.

It was the right thing to do. "Okay." Pushing to her feet, she stood.

The doorbell rang before she took a step.

"That must be April with the food." He sprang from the chair. "Can we continue this later?"

Fatigue swept over Skye, and the thought of continuing anything at all became staggering. "Yes. Later."

Chapter 39

Was Skye closing her heart to him? Pete fished the keys from his pocket and jingled them on his fingers. They hadn't spent any time together in the two weeks since Miss Lydia's funeral. And not from his lack of trying. When he reached out, she answered in texts with barely three-word answers, and she'd not answered his calls. Sure, she had a lot to deal with, but she didn't have to shoulder it alone.

Heavy rain claimed the morning, so with his charter canceled and the girls in school, he'd drive to the Sea Lab, to her house, or even to Miss Lydia's in Mobile until he found Skye and got her to talk to him. Something was going on.

She needs you.

The thought battered him. He hadn't heard that voice in some time now. He made quick steps out of the house, through the deluge, and into his truck.

After checking both the lab and Nana's house, he drove toward Mobile. The wipers pounded a heavy beat as the storm worsened, and the muscles in his neck knotted. What if Skye wasn't at Miss Lydia's? With the bad weather, it was doubtful she'd be on the water.

He blew out a long breath. If he didn't find her, he'd go by his parents' house. At least he could make good use of the time. Pressing a button on his phone, he played his father's latest sermon through the truck's speakers. Dad always offered plenty of wisdom, and Pete made a point to listen to each one. At least he listened now, as an adult. Growing up, not so much.

Funny how time changes one's perspective. The day he'd preached at Dad's church hadn't been as bad as he'd expected. In fact, in some small corner of his heart, he'd enjoyed it. Pete huffed. But that didn't mean he should give up his business and go into ministry again. He knew how ugly things could get.

After more than an hour of sitting in traffic due to accidents on the slick highway, Pete pulled into the driveway of Miss Lydia's. The garage door was closed, but lights shone from the window.

Maybe he'd found Skye.

He shook off the tension nagging him and exited his vehicle, running up the sidewalk to the front door. Water dripped from his hair and ran down his arms despite the short path. His finger neared the doorbell, but he stopped himself. She might be frightened here alone. He'd text first.

I'm at Miss Lydia's and would like to speak to you. I see a light on, and I'm about to knock on the front door. I hope you'll answer so we can talk.

If Skye wasn't here, he'd look like an idiot—maybe even like a stalker—but he couldn't turn back now.

A moment later, the door eased open, and Skye peeked out. She wore a cap, but from the looks of it, her hair had been cut and dyed blonde. "Is something wrong? Are the girls okay?"

Lightning singed the earth with an earsplitting thud and clap of thunder. They both flinched.

"Can I come in?" he asked.

She eyed the dark clouds, then nodded and let him pass her to go into the entrance hall. "I'm trying to prepare things…for storage."

Boxes filled the narrow space, loaded, and taped shut, the contents labeled with a marker. A section of plastic containers just inside the living room had been labeled *Florida.*

The sight gutted him. So that was it. Skye planned to take Sparrow and go back. And she hadn't bothered to tell him.

"When are you moving?" He couldn't stop his sarcastic tone.

When she turned to face him, her eyes misted, and she looked away. "We do need to talk. I've been putting it off."

Sure, she'd been through a lot, but he deserved some sort of explanation. "I've got time now."

Sighing heavily, she motioned toward the sofa. A tag on it read *For Gertie.*

Another wave of reality slapped him. "You've been busy." His feet felt like cement as he plodded over and took a seat.

On the other end of the couch, she slipped onto the edge of a cushion, put her fingers to her forehead, and massaged below the bill of her cap.

A niggle of compassion pricked through his pain. None of this could be easy for her. Losing her adopted mother…taking in a child. "Are you okay?"

"I've been having migraines again."

"Again?"

"I had them growing up, but they were better in Florida."

"Anything I can get you?"

"Pete…" Her chin lifted, and she leveled a solemn gaze on him. "I don't have a choice."

"We always have choices." A current of indignation rose in his chest. How could she just discard the relationships the four of them had built? "You're running away."

"I don't know how to explain." A tear leaked from the corner of her eye.

"Try. I need to understand." His voice came out weak and desperate. He was being pathetic, but he couldn't help himself. He couldn't let her go that easily. "Please."

Scooting back, she sank into the cushions and shut her eyes. "Okay."

~~~

She was going to disgust him. Skye swallowed the bile rising and gathered what courage she could muster. *Truth.* Pete deserved the truth.

"My sister fought life head on. I, on the other hand, hid in my made-up world, with animals as my only close companions. I studied everything I could about them, about science. The rest of what went on in my life, I pretended was some bad dream—the desolation and despair. My mother lying in bed, sad and broken."

She took a deep breath and continued. "Star and I would find treasures outdoors. Each shell, each piece of driftwood, sea glass, sea bean, or bottle, we dreamed they'd been sent by our real father who would come back one day. We dreamed he wasn't really dead. He'd cheer up our mother. He'd tell Denny to leave and never come near us again."

A vision of Denny's face, his cigarette breath—the paralyzing fear swimming inside her.

Bending over, Skye covered her eyes with her fingers. "But Denny always stayed. I remember lying there, terrified. I didn't want to move. I didn't want him to know I was awake. I thought, 'I can't go through this anymore.' I threatened to tell the police, but he swore to hurt my mother or Star if I ever said anything."

Weight shifted on the sofa, and she knew Pete had scooted close, felt the gentle pressure of his hand rubbing her back. "I'm so sorry. It's awful, but we can work through it. Get a restraining order if he comes after you. I'll protect—"

"No." Sobbing, she shook her head. "People like the Beasleys don't respect the law or restraining orders, and it's not
~~~

me I'm protecting, Pete. I warned Momma to run away from Denny, go to a shelter or something, anything to protect Star. Because I was leaving for college. I wasn't going to have *that monster's* baby—never wanted to be a mother. Didn't want a child to come into the hellish world I'd lived in."

She felt him tense, but she had to keep going. Frustration simmered within her at the unfairness of it all. "He's like this ghost haunting me that wants to devour me. Would want to get at Sparrow if he knew. His parents too."

Her chest shook so hard, she could barely speak. "Momma killed herself the night I told her about what Denny had been doing to me. Miss Lydia came. She convinced me to keep the baby. Said she'd raise Sparrow as her own. We moved. I went to college pregnant, gave birth near spring break, gave Sparrow to Miss Lydia, and went right back to classes not long after."

Finally, Skye found the courage to lift her eyes to Pete. Tears soaked his lashes, but a muscle in his jaw ticked. His posture stiffened.

Exactly what she'd expected. He could never get past her reality.

"Miss Lydia brought Sparrow back here to raise as her own. I pursued my education there. They came every holiday. I became like a…big sister."

She clenched her fists and battled against more tears. Even if Pete didn't understand, she'd do what was necessary to fight for her child. "I can't ever let Denny or his sick parents near my daughter. They can never know about her. They can't see us together. She looks just like him. Her blonde hair and freckles, her eyes. If they guessed her age… From everything Denny told me, his mother was an abuser like he was."

Motionless, she stared at Pete, this good, gentle, honorable man. So unlike the man who haunted her nightmares.

Swells of clashing emotions smashed against her resolve. She'd love nothing more than to stay here with Pete, the four of them a little family, and have a fairytale life. But she couldn't risk it, even if Pete could move past her truth. A restraining order would never stop someone like Denny or his parents.

Something in her DNA must be flawed. Because it seemed she'd been destined for sorrow.

"You have to see why you and I can't work—why Sparrow and I can't stay."

Turmoil contorted Pete's face as he stood and rubbed his hands on his jeans. "I just need a while to think." Turning, he walked toward the door.

Watching his back, her heart broke. She'd expected him to walk away, but the sight of it… Soon, he'd be gone. Like everyone else in her life. He'd leave another gaping hole in her heart, but she refused to let him undo her. Sparrow was all that mattered now.

Chapter 40

She never wanted to be a mother.

Raindrops splatted on Pete's shoulders and back, dripped off his cap, and ran down his cheeks, but he kept his brisk pace along the empty western shore of the island. Seaweed cluttered the beach, the disheveled scene resembling his own state of mind.

He needed time. Needed distance. Needed quiet—only water and sky, the sound of the surf, the seagulls, and his breath in his lungs. In front of him, three plastic grocery bags took flight in the gusts, in search of a place to spread their mayhem. Mayhem like the bomb Skye had just dropped.

Why had she let them all become so deeply involved, knowing she wouldn't stay? It hadn't been fair to any of them. True, she'd been through inconceivably horrific circumstances, things no girl or woman should have to endure. But he couldn't help but think of Kenzie.

As hard as Kenzie had battled—she'd traded her own life to give birth to Olivia—hearing Skye say *she never wanted to become a mother* unraveled him. He had a daughter, after all. Then there was Sparrow, such a precious child.

God, why? Why did You put this woman in my path? I'm not that strong a man.

But what kind of man was he? The kind of man who discarded a damaged woman and her daughter because of his own grief? The kind who wouldn't show compassion and grace because the truth of the circumstances hurt him deeply?

A pelican swooped into the storm's waves and scooped up a fish. The bird spent its days that way, and that was all Pete wanted to do. All he wanted to be—a fisherman. A father and a fisherman. He'd given up ministry because of its turbulent nature. The sea could be rough and fickle, but the sea never promised to be steady. Now this woman—God help him, this woman he'd fallen in love with—had Pete's entire world raging, and he had no idea how to navigate these waters.

Skye had made it clear that if he wanted to be with her and Sparrow, he would have to leave this area. It meant leaving his parents, his church, his home, Caleb, and his business behind. Even then, he'd be keeping constant guard, at least until Sparrow turned eighteen, to make sure neither the child molester nor his parents had any part in the girl's life.

And what about Olivia's safety?

Although he didn't know how long Skye planned to stay on Dauphin Island, he needed time. There was too much to consider. He and God would have a lot to wrestle through with this one.

Another lightning bolt crackled, closer this time. His feet halted in the wet sand. The last thing he needed was to get himself injured. Or worse. His daughter depended on him.

By the time he'd driven home, stripped off his wet clothes, and cleaned up, his exasperation subsided. In its place, exhaustion swamped his every molecule. Sitting at the table with his Bible and journal, he rested his forehead against his palms.

I don't know which way to turn, Lord. I need Your guidance.

After reading through Scriptures, he lifted his pen, tears blurring his vision.

Like Moses in the desert, if Your presence will not lead me, I am lost.

I must have You with me or I cannot go on.

I wait for Your wisdom, yet beg...

Let me not have to wait.
Lead me gently and clearly.
Help me grasp hold of Your path for me—for all of us.
I am learning to trust—two steps forward, how many back?
You are patient and kind and compassionate in heart.
Inside and out, mold me to Your pleasing, to Your glory.
I am vain and bullheaded but long to be humble for You.
I am selfish but yearn to be generous in Your name.
I can be gruff but desire to be gentle, as You are with me.
Forgive my arrogance, I beg You.
Hold me steady as You tenderly teach me Your ways.

He dropped the pen and exchanged it for his phone. Of one thing, he was sure. Calling Skye was the least he could do after running out on her that way.

After three rings, she answered, her tone hesitant. "Hello."

"I'm sorry I left you like that." He breathed a long sigh. "I was caught off guard."

"Now you know I can't raise Sparrow here as my daughter. And why. Denny or his parents could see her with me, see how much she looks like him, and make the connection. They could try to insert themselves into Sparrow's life." This time, her words sounded much firmer. "It's best we separate ourselves, before…before the girls become more attached. I'm just not sure how to go about it since we share a babysitter."

The finality of her statement swallowed him in a thick layer of sadness. She'd made the decision for them all.

"Pete?"

It was his turn to speak, but nothing seemed right. "My parents normally keep Olivia in the summer. With the longer days, my hours are late, and Mom already asked if she could." Although, at the time, he'd thought he and Skye had created a better routine. A routine he'd miss. "School's out in a week."

"Okay." Her tone softened. "Thank you for everything you've done for us after the wreck and during Miss Lydia's illness. We would have been lost without your help. We needed you."

She needs you.

Those words from that first day they'd met kept echoing through his mind.

Was that it, God?

Skye and Sparrow had needed them, and now it was over? But what about the rest of those impressions on his heart? What about her being the one?

No answers came, and she still waited on the line.

He fought to speak past the sadness swamping him. "I'm glad I could be there for you and Sparrow." But God knew he'd miss them.

Chapter 41

Sweltering July heat pressed down on Skye's back, despite the lowering sun. Cocooned between a chain-link fence, other information booths, and a table full of information about manatees, Skye tried to keep a pleasant expression on her face as people strolled by to view the literature and pick up swag. And this was only Thursday night, the opening evening of the festivities. The fishing rodeo lasted the entire weekend.

At least her colleague, Lisa, planned to return from leave in two weeks, meaning this event ended the bulk of Skye's duties with the lab. And April had been willing to babysit Sparrow for this thing.

By the first of August, she and Sparrow should be settled in their new home in Florida. The position as a post-doctoral scholar at another lab five hours away was fully funded for four years and included health insurance. While she'd prefer something even farther from Mobile, she looked forward to collaborating and seeking ways to recover ecosystems in Apalachicola Bay. She and Sparrow would make a new life together there. When the time was right, Skye would tell Sparrow that she was her biological mother. She and God would have a lot of conversations about that first.

She'd miss Pete and Olivia, though. Already missed them these past weeks.

"Hot enough for you?" Smirking, Michael stood in front of her table. "No need to move to Florida for scorching temperatures."

"You're correct about that." She needed to pay attention. She hadn't noticed his approach.

"But seriously." His mouth twisted into a one-sided smile. "I'll miss you around the island. You and Sparrow are some of my favorite people, the only people who've attended *every one* of my excursions and boardwalk talks."

"We don't have much of a life." She lifted a shoulder and tried to keep her expression nonchalant.

"Gee, thanks."

Chuckling, she wrinkled her nose. "I'm kidding. We really enjoyed your tours." She'd say they'd miss him, too, but the sentiment felt too mushy and awkward, him being a coworker, after all.

Pete and Olivia, on the other hand… Losing their presence in her and Sparrow's lives had left a raw, gaping vacuum. One Skye had tried to fill with activities, like the ones Michael provided. They'd visited Gertie and her family, met a few times with Sparrow's homeschool group, too, since the public school had let out, trying to stay occupied without taking too many chances.

"Do you have interns lined up to help you this weekend?" Michael still lingered, lifting the skull of the marine mammal on display.

"As long as no one gets sick or forgets."

Please, God, don't let that happen.

The smell of beer mingled in the air with the odor of raw fish and the aromas of the many food booths. Multitudes of men mulled around drinking alcohol, sending goose bumps down her spine. Already, she'd imagined she'd spotted someone who looked like Denny in their midst.

The less time she spent there alone, the better.

After setting the piece back down, he rapped the table with

his knuckles. "You survived last week's children's fishing tournament. You'll do fine."

That event lasted part of *one day* with mostly local kids. "This is already a whole other animal."

Snickering, he nodded. "You're a smart one, Skye. If you want, we can snag dinner together and watch the opening ceremony."

"Maybe. If things are covered here." The idea triggered a spasm of angst. She'd heard Michael and Hope had still been spending a lot of time together. But maybe Pete realized Hope was a much better match for him and had come between the two. The thought sent a spike to her heart.

None of that mattered. Over a month had passed since she'd let him go. She and Pete couldn't have worked out in a relationship, even if he'd accepted her past. He'd never leave his family, his little beach church, or his business.

During these quiet weeks, she and Sparrow had spent time reading the Bible together and talking. Miss Lydia's words often came to memory as encouragement. Skye's prayer life had grown too. Despite everything that had happened, a new sense of peace and belonging walked with her through it all. Perhaps, her Creator did care. And perhaps, like Miss Lydia had said, His eye was on her and Sparrow.

Not long after a couple of interns arrived and settled in, Michael made his way back to her booth, carrying a paper sack in one hand and supporting two bagged lawn chairs on his shoulder. "I bought dinner. We can watch the start of the liars' contest." His voice competed with the sound of a woman singing the national anthem through the PA system.

The idea seemed a bit silly. Grown men competing with tall tales of their adventures in catching fish.

"Come on. It's all in fun." He motioned for her to follow.

A bit of hunger fanned through her, and Michael had already done the hard part by standing in the food truck line. "Okay, if we stay out of the fray. Someplace near the back."

"What else would I expect from you, Dr. Introvert?"

She couldn't help but laugh. Michael had gotten to know something about her. After making certain the interns were comfortable without her, Skye stepped out from behind her table. "I can carry a chair or the food."

He raised a brow. "Can I trust you with my fries?"

"Nope."

"Figures." He laughed and handed her the bag. "Luckily, I bought extra. You quiet types can't be trusted."

Sadly, Pete might agree with Michael's assessment.

They wove around the throng of people until they found an opening parallel to the stage. Once Michael set up the chairs, they settled in, and Skye let Michael divvy up the food.

"Has anyone told you about all of this hoopla?" He took a bite of his shrimp po'boy.

"The event provides massive amounts of research for the lab." She stared at her own overfilled sandwich, trying to decide how best to bite it without blobs of anything falling on her shirt.

"Yeah, but it's fun too." He dabbed a shred of lettuce from his chin with a napkin. "They'll shoot the cannon at five a.m. tomorrow and throw this year's rodeo chairman into the water to start the tournament. Besides seeing all the cool fish being brought in, there are the vendor booths, the prizes, the food, and partying with the bands at night."

That last part sounded like a nightmare. "I'll plan to be out of here before that starts, but I hope you have fun."

"I saw you dancing at the fundraiser." He darted a teasing glance her way before grabbing three fries from their container.

"You and Pete could—"

"That's not happening." She held up her palm.

"Because you're moving?" He slipped the fries into his mouth and studied her.

"Basically." There was no way she'd continue this line of conversation. Was he asking because of Hope?

A man on the microphone began speaking kind words about a charter captain who'd passed.

Skye's heart stung as Pete stepped onto the platform. Olivia, his parents, and another guy followed him, but she couldn't take her eyes off the man she still loved. They must be talking about his grandfather. She'd forgotten he was to be honored at this event.

Pete and his father accepted the plaque honoring their patriarch and offered thanks on behalf of their family, but she barely heard the words, only remembered the way Pete's voice always wrapped its protective arms around her. Then Pete and his father took seats at the judges' table for the contest. Not far away, Hope stood, wearing a jean skirt and white tank, smiling and chatting with Mrs. Thompson and Olivia.

As Skye took in the entire scene, a groundswell of anguish mushroomed inside her. She couldn't imagine a sweeter life than what she'd have here on Dauphin Island with Pete and his family, and though she couldn't be the one to share it, she prayed he'd find happiness.

Chapter 42

By Sunday night, Pete's back ached after the intense weekend of fishing. At least this was the last evening of the rodeo and his customers had already weighed in their catch.

"Skye! Wait!" Olivia slipped away from Pete's mother, scuttled around the weigh-in tent, and sprinted into the crowd.

"I've got her," Pete said to his mom as he took off after his daughter. Though panic gripped him, at least he knew *who* Olivia was running to. He quickly caught up, offering apologies to those he'd had to nudge past in the process. He'd avoided this area all weekend, knowing she'd be manning the booth. Knowing being near her would make him ache with longing. Because right now, everything within him wanted to slide his arms around Skye, pull her close, and tell her he'd take care of her and Sparrow forever.

Olivia flung herself around Skye. "I've missed you."

Face tense, Skye looked down at his daughter then scanned the area, probably aware he or his family would be worried. Michael stood at her side but bent down to say something to Olivia.

Finally, Skye's gaze found Pete, and her posture relaxed, but those eyes…so hauntingly sad when they met his.

His feet wanted to stop right there, but he kept going until he neared.

Her eyes flickered with emotion before she looked away. She knelt beside Olivia, listening to his daughter speak words too quiet for Pete to make out over the noise of the festival.

"How's the fishing been this weekend?" Michael stepped up to shake Pete's hand.

In the distance, thunder rumbled, and the wind kicked up. Pete thumbed over his shoulder. "Good enough. Caleb and I avoided the squalls with our passengers." Acting casual was killing him when all he wanted was to step closer to Skye, to hear her sweet voice again.

Michael bobbed his head. "You know what they say."

"Yep. The rodeo is always the worst weekend for popup storms." Pete shrugged. "At least we've made it to Sunday without anything too rough."

About the same time his family caught up with him, Hope appeared from around the canvas of one of the booths. Her gaze bounced from him to Skye, then she took Michael's arm and smiled before he pecked a kiss on her lips in return.

She'd hung out with the family the past few days at Pete's brother Andrew's request. They'd all been buddies growing up. Of course, his brother knew nothing of the tension between them. Andrew didn't know much that went on here since he'd left for college years ago. The fact that he'd flown all the way in from the West Coast to attend the rodeo floored Pete. Something might be going on with his brother, but Pete hadn't had any spare time this weekend to find out what.

As for Hope, worry squirmed through Pete when he saw her interact with Michael. They seemed awfully familiar. Was Michael a nice guy? A Christian guy? There was nothing for Pete to do but pray the man would be good to her.

Skye enveloped Olivia in a long hug, then she stood and turned to him with a sad smile. "Sorry. I didn't mean to cause a problem."

Ripples of the fading light reflected in her gaze, those swirls of brown capturing his attention. "Not your fault."

"I wish I could play with Sparrow," Olivia whined.

"It's good to see you again." Mom directed a warm gaze at Skye, and Dad did the same.

"You too." Skye nervously fingered her necklace. "I was just about to leave, before the nighttime mob takes over. Take care." In a flash, she turned and disappeared through the mass of people swarming in. Her departure cracked through his hull of resolve, allowing the sadness to flood in. He felt as if she'd taken half of his being with her when she'd walked away.

Dad held out a hand to Olivia. "Let's all get some of that frozen lemonade I saw. I'm parched."

She agreed, and they made their way toward a food truck decorated with lemons. The line extended so far that Pete squinted to figure out where it ended.

Great. They'd pass out from dehydration before they ordered, and he needed to get Olivia home and ready for bed. "This won't work."

"Andrew and I can buy it while you walk Mom and Olivia to the car." Dad shooed them away.

Pete shook his head. "We can find something else."

"I want a frozen drink." More whining. His girl was tired.

"If it takes too long, we'll buy you a slushie on the way home." Dad tried to console Olivia, but her lip still poked out.

Pete lifted her to his chest. "Be the sweet girl I know you are."

Burrowing her head in his shoulder, she sniffled. "Ok-ay, Daddy."

By the time they reached the car, she'd sacked out in his arms. Mom cranked the engine and turned on the AC while Pete strapped Olivia in the booster then shut the back door.

"As usual, thank you for taking care of us." Somehow, he'd been blessed with the best parents anyone could ask for.

After a glance back at Olivia, Mom got out. She inched the car door to almost closed but left it cracked. "What happened with you and Skye?"

The question caught him off guard. "Long story." He'd talked with Dad, but obviously his father had kept their conversations private.

Checking to make sure Olivia was still asleep and no one stood close enough to hear, he gave her a condensed synopsis of their relationship and her past.

Her shoulders sagged when he finished, and her face screwed into a frown. "I never was big on corporal punishment with you boys, but right now, if I could pull you over my lap, I'd spank you, then rest, then spank you some more."

"What?" He gawked at her. Why was he in trouble? What had he done?

"If you love her that much, none of *this* matters." She flicked her hand back and forth between the rodeo and the marina. "You boys make me want to pull my hair out sometimes. It's high time y'all quit putting your careers above everything else. We taught you better than that."

Apparently, Andrew was in trouble, too, but Pete still didn't understand. "What are you saying?"

"Pete," she huffed. "Deep down, you know you've always had a calling on your life. A mission. A ministry. I don't know why you and Andrew thought following Jesus would come without hardship or pain. You don't think I hurt when someone gossiped about our family or grumbled about a sermon your father preached? Jesus warned his followers to expect adversity." A sigh worked its way through her. "And don't you imagine that I'm saying this because I don't want to take care of that precious child in there."

Realization fell on Pete like a sledgehammer to the heart.

Of course, Mom and Dad had to have suffered heartache in ministry. Careless or harsh words had hurt them, but they hadn't quit. They'd persevered.

He, on the other hand, had walked away from the church when things got tough. He'd tucked tail, walked away, and denied his calling.

Now, he'd let Skye walk away too. And for what? A boat? Fishing? His parents would be fine without him.

They'd probably be a lot less tired. And Caleb might even prefer to buy out the other half of the charter.

Pick up your sword and protect my girls.

Miss Lydia's words pressed in on him with an urgency. "Mom, I have to go."

"We'll take Olivia home for the night."

~~~

Fatigue and sadness weighing her down, Skye pulled her car into the marina parking lot. April had come out to the boat to help her husband, Robert, clean up after their busy weekend, towing Sparrow and little Jack along with her. While Skye hadn't been crazy about the idea, she'd had little choice. When they moved to Florida, she'd make a concerted effort to avoid having to work weekend events like this.

She'd ended up having to stay at the rodeo longer than she'd intended after one of the interns had caught her on the way out, wanting to discuss a research paper. At least, the threat of severe thunderstorms had caused the band to cancel their show, so the crowds had left the small island. But, by now, the dogs would have made a mess at the house.

She got out of the car, and darkness enveloped her. The nearest streetlight must have burned out.

The marina had been packed because of the rodeo all weekend, but it felt deserted now. Something rattled in the
~~~

distance, and her heart rate ramped up. Was someone out there? Making a quick scan, she saw no one.

She was being paranoid, again, because of Denny. With the heavy clouds blackening the sky, she kept a quick pace, though. Fat raindrops began splatting down on her.

Lightning flashed across the inky waves. She'd feel better when she had Sparrow off the water and back at the rental house.

The crunch of gravel behind her sent a bolt of terror up her spine. Before she could react, a hand clamped over her mouth, muffling her scream. An arm shackled around her waist and dragged her toward the churning water's edge.

Polo cologne mixed with the odor of sweat and the stench of cigarettes, filling Skye's senses. Panic clawed in her throat.

"Momma said she saw you. Followed you down to some fancy restaurant. Said you looked good." Denny hissed the words, his hot breath next to her ear. "Thought she was crazy, but there you were at the rodeo, plain as day. Have you been missing me?"

No! This can't be happening. Help me, God!

She fought with all her might. Kicking, she struggled against the iron grip that bit into her flesh. She wasn't a child anymore. She wasn't going to take whatever he dished out. Not again. Determination rose within her. Even if he hurt her, even if he killed her, she wouldn't give up. She jabbed at his chest with her elbow, smashed her heel on his foot.

He cursed. "Stop that." His fingers grabbed her throat. She couldn't breathe. Still, she fought.

A blow struck her face, leaving her momentarily senseless. Before she could stop him, Denny hoisted her into the air and threw her inside the hull of a boat.

Chapter 43

The bottom dropped out of the clouds, and rain pounded down on Pete as he ran through the parking lot that had turned into a pond. Almost to his truck, his phone rang. Not now. He didn't have time for this, but the call might be from his parents. He dragged the device from his wet pocket to check.

April? Worry niggled in his chest. "What's up?"

"I'm sorry to bother you, but I don't know who else to call." April's voice sounded hesitant. "Have you seen Skye? She said she was on her way to the marina over half an hour ago. She hasn't shown up, and I can't get her on the phone."

Alarm blasted like a foghorn. Something was wrong.

"She was meeting you at your boat?" He jogged to the truck and got in.

"Yeah. We had a mess down here from our last bunch of passengers on the dolphin tour, and Robert needed help, but we're ready to go now."

"You still have Sparrow?"

"She's been entertaining Jack for me."

A wisp of relief eased through him, knowing Sparrow was in good hands. "Keep an eye on her. I'll find Skye."

Please, God, help me find her.

Water dripping all over, he stretched on his seatbelt. No time to care about a little moisture in his vehicle. Once he started the engine and put it in drive, he hesitated. Should he go to Skye's house? Or could she still be here at the fishing rodeo? She'd said she was leaving, plus it was pouring rain.

If he knew Skye, she'd have gone straight to pick up Sparrow. April and Robert's boat was closer than her house, and he could look for her car along the way.

Minutes later, he drove through the marina parking lot, his wipers battling to keep up with the pouring rain. When her dark vehicle loomed in his headlights, a sinking feeling swamped him.

He pulled close. Empty. Just to be sure, he got out and looked inside. Still nothing. She'd made it here, so why wasn't she at April's boat yet?

Back in his truck, he pressed the contact to check with April again. "Is she there yet? Her car's here."

"No, and she still hasn't answered my calls." Worry crept into April's tone. "This isn't like her. I'm not sure what to do."

"I'll call the police station."

They probably had their hands full between leftover rodeo traffic and visitors in this weather, not to mention their normal duties. Dauphin Island's population, sans the tourists, didn't afford much more than three officers on duty. But a woman was missing. They'd need to make time.

Once he'd made the call and the dispatcher promised she'd alert the officers to keep an eye out for Skye, he opened his truck door and climbed out. He'd look more closely around the lot and the piers.

Blinding rain splattered his face, and he tented a hand over his eyes as he sprinted from one end of the parking lot to the other. He looked behind the office building and checked inside the bathrooms.

Wind rattled and moaned against the buildings and the anchored ships. The palms dotting the road's edge swirled in chaotic circles.

No one with any sense would be out in this squall.

His mind churned with one bleak possibility after another.

Had Skye fallen into the water? Been struck by lightning and taken off in an ambulance? Surely, the dispatcher he'd spoken to would know if someone had been taken to a hospital from this small community. With the close proximity to the festival, he would have seen flashing lights too.

Unless no one had found her.

He turned toward the rows of boat slips and sprinted to the pier nearest her car. As he took a step onto the boardwalk, something shiny caught his eye. Probably nothing important, but he had to check. Bending down, he scooped the item from a puddle.

A broken necklace. Blue sapphire and a silver star. Skye's necklace.

Blood pounded through his veins. Pocketing the broken chain, he ran down the pier, eyes peeled for any sign of her, scanning the dark water. The first boat he came to that had lights on, he boarded and knocked on the cabin door.

A man in his late sixties answered right away, gawking at Pete as if he were crazy, which he might be. "Can I help you?" The guy's face was familiar—a local retiree.

"My friend is missing." He described Skye, explaining about her car and necklace. "Have you seen anything that seemed off in the past forty minutes or so?"

He stroked his whiskered chin. "A guy had been cleaning a smaller craft. It left not fifteen minutes ago. Thought it was odd they'd go out before this storm cleared."

No! "What kind of boat?"

Once the man described it, Pete thanked him and took off, anger boiling through him. If there was any chance Denny or someone else had Skye on a small boat in this storm, he had to help her. He ran back to the parking lot, then two piers down, scrambling onto the *Sea of Grace*. Thunder cracked not far away, but he'd steered through rough water plenty of times. If Skye was out there, he'd find her.

~~~

Dim awareness crept over Skye. An ache throbbed in her head. The smells of mildew and fish invaded her nose.

Squinting, she tried to make out her surroundings in the darkness. Roiling movement churned her stomach. With great effort, she hauled herself to a sitting position. Rain splattered her arms.

A boat? It creaked and moaned beneath her. Water sloshed onto the floor as one wave after another slammed against the hull. Then the past came crashing back. *Denny*. How he'd twisted her arms, dragged and then slammed her in.

God, no! Help me.

Where was the monster? Turning, she spotted a dark form at the helm in front of her. No one else sat in the open bow. Denny faced forward, focused on navigating the stormy channel. Where was he taking her? She crawled to the edge of the boat and struggled to find something to grip so she could stand, but her knees slipped beneath her. Finally, she found a bench and clawed her way onto it.

Black sky and water surrounded them. The bow dipped in the huge swells. How could she escape? Her body quivered with both the bone-deep chill and the terror of seeing her worst nightmare again.

She fought the urge to lie down, close her eyes, and drift into that place she used to go in her mind as a young girl when Denny crept in. Those nights when her mind floated out on a raft in the surf. She'd imagine clouds, pelicans, grains of sand, or a dragonfly hovering over the marsh. She'd become a dolphin in the waves.
~~~

No!

She was a grown woman. An educated woman. She wasn't that girl in castoff clothes, living in whatever dump Denny moved them to. She'd jump ship and swim for shore before she let that man touch her.

The boat slammed hard against an enormous swell, rolling her to the back of the stern and whacking her legs against the fiberglass.

She gasped. Denny had completely lost his mind to go out in this storm. He'd drown them both.

Anger ripped through her. She couldn't leave Sparrow alone. *Think, Skye!* She took a deep breath. There was no way out of this mess on her own.

I don't know what to do, God. Please send help.

Tears burned, but she refused to give up. If her sister were in this situation, she would have found a weapon by now. Skye glanced around for any ideas, but she had never thought like Star and doubted a weapon would be of help. Yet, there had to be something. Maybe a flare gun or an oar? A handle to a compartment on the floor caught her attention. There might be something there. If not in that holding area, then in another. While Denny was occupied at the wheel, she'd search every single one or die trying.

On her knees, she scooted over and slid her cold fingers over the latch. The door flapped as they hit another wave, but she held on.

The humidity-laden air became tumultuous, alternating between warm and gusty with a cool undercurrent. Definitely a bad sign. The pressure in the air dropped.

Not a tornado. Not now.

Her focus drew back to the contents in the hatch. Nothing but fishing line. She clawed open the next one. Still no luck.

Maybe under the bench seat. Struggling to stay upright on her knees, she pushed up the lid until she could feel inside. Her fingers found a strap and fabric, and her heart leapt. She yanked the life preserver out and wrestled it on, buckling it around her middle.

The air thickened around her, then seemed to evaporate. A loud noise of wind roared. Her ears popped. Cold terror pulsed in Skye's veins. The boat went airborne and flipped onto its starboard side.

Chapter 44

This couldn't be happening. According to his instruments, he'd almost caught up to the other boat. To Skye. The tornado hit the water and formed a waterspout. It lifted and spun The *Sea of Grace*, then dropped it back down hard on its side. Pete's hands slipped from the steering wheel. His body slammed hard into what felt like solid iron. Pain shot through his side. Water filled the boat around him, and he fought to find his way upright. He had to get out!

As the darkness and murky water closed over him, panic exploded in his chest. He ran his fingers along the edges of the wall trying to gain a reference point.

His right arm throbbed with each movement. He had to break free and find the surface. *Come on!*

At last, he felt an opening, tugged himself closer to it with his left arm, and swam out.

When he popped up to the surface, his lungs burned. Eight-foot swells dipped him up and down, angry waves crashing over him. He had to keep his head up. Not drink too much sea water. Get his bearings.

Find Skye.

The wind still blasted. The salty spray filled his nose and mouth. Groaning against the pain in his arm and chest, he treaded water, searching for any sign of life. Had she gone into the water too?

"Skye? Can you hear me?"

He called over and over until his throat became raw.

The Dauphin Island Bridge loomed about a hundred yards away. Maybe he could swim toward it and find something to hold onto. If he could just find Skye first. Was she aboard the smaller vessel he'd been tracking? Had that boat continued on without damage? Or had it gone under? Was she trapped below the surface?

Please, God, let her be okay.

The gale and currents had him moving toward the eastern shore. He fought to stay on course to where he'd last noted the other boat's position but made no progress. With limited visibility, his aim was merely a guess.

He'd radioed the Coast Guard when he'd left the marina. Would they be on their way? Dangerous storms like these usually moved fast. Though it felt like an eternity already, the hard edge of the squall should blow through soon.

Jesus, calm the storm.

With the stars and moon covered by ferocious clouds, the water flowed murky and black. Nothing but undulating waves and rain.

Pete bobbed up and down. Pain in his arm throttled him, and his legs weighed a thousand pounds. How long could he keep this up? If he'd been thinking more clearly, he'd have put on his life vest.

After what seemed like a lifetime, but likely was only half an hour, the wind died down some, and he strained to see through the downpour.

Maybe ten feet ahead of him, he spotted something moving. Or were his eyes playing tricks on him? It could just be a buoy or crab trap. Or it could be that wretched man.

But if there was any chance… "Skye!" He yelled again and again.

Please let it be her.

Though whitecaps crashed over the object, it appeared to be closing the distance between them. Then a head crested above the waves. *Skye!* Water streamed down her face. *Thank you, God!* Now to just get them out of this mess.

Her mouth moved, but he couldn't make out the words. She swam quicker, her arms fighting the surf.

"Pete?" She swiped her eyes as she came nearer.

He kicked as hard as he could manage until he reached her. "Are you hurt?"

She touched his face with shaky fingers. "Is it really you?"

"Real, and here to save you." His voice broke. Seemed like he'd failed his mission. "I love you. I never should've let you go. I might have stopped him."

"I love you too." A swell lifted them up, and her eyes rounded. "Where's your life vest?"

Salty liquid rushed into his throat, and he choked. Black water covered his face as he sank.

A fist grabbed his arm and yanked him up. Skye held on tight, towing him. "We've got to find something to hang onto."

She must have had the same idea about the bridge, because she struggled to swim that way, though the currents barred much progress.

"Don't wear yourself out," Pete sputtered.

He tried to kick through the radiating pain and fatigue, but he felt as if he were sinking into a cold bottomless pit.

"Don't you give up on me." Her jaw tense, she swam harder.

Pete tried to blink away the fogginess in his brain and keep his mouth above the waves.

"God has His eye on us," Skye called over her shoulder. "He knows exactly where we are. And I asked Him to send help."

Though he knew it was possible for God to save them, he also knew from experience that prayers weren't always answered in the way humans would expect.

Still, he breathed another request skyward.

Help us, God.

They continued on that way, chill and exhaustion working against them. Skye had to be tiring.

Then, into the blackness, a light shone. Skye went dead still. "What's that?"

"Answer to our prayers. If we can hang on… And they don't run over us."

As the lights from the boat drew closer, Skye waved with one arm while still gripping Pete with the other. She was so strong.

They saw them, didn't they?

Finally, a spotlight shone their way. A Coast Guard vessel neared, but so slowly. Two men and a woman in uniforms and bright red life vests made their way to stand in a well along their boat's side. They called directions that Pete couldn't make out.

In the waves, both Skye and the boat undulated, but somehow, she got them to a rope with a flotation device and held on tight.

~~~

In the waiting area of the Mobile hospital emergency room, Skye rubbed up and down her arms, still warding off the chill of being in the water for so long.

What was going on with Pete? The doctors had finished with her an hour before, but there was still no word on him.

"They're taking care of him," Caleb assured her for the tenth time. He'd perched in a chair next to her and had yet to move. In his quiet way, Caleb offered comfort. And security.
~~~

Because there had been no news about the Coast Guard finding Denny.

Though she wore the dry set of clothes Hope had brought, a chill charged through Skye at the thought of the man who'd taken her. Around her shoulders she pulled a small blanket that someone had given her along the way to the hospital.

Heels clacked on the hard floors, and she looked up to find Hope sashaying down the hall with two white cups. The pretty woman had dropped everything to be here.

"Here's a coffee. That'll warm you inside." Hope handed one to Skye.

"I appreciate it." And she meant it. Skye took the offering and sipped the hot brew.

"This one's for you." She held the other cup in front of Caleb.

He shook his head, that shyness covering him like it always did in Hope's presence. "You keep it. I'm fine."

"No, sir. You've been up for hours, and I've had plenty of caffeine already."

Glimpsing up at her, he finally accepted, then Hope sat on the other side of Skye and patted her leg. "Are you sure you're okay? No dizziness or nausea?"

"I'm fine."

This scene was beginning to remind her of the first night she'd come to the island. Except now Pete had the worrisome injuries. She'd been bruised and had a mild concussion, but Pete had taken in so much water. He'd been beaten up by the storm. "Pete shouldn't have come after me. I hate this. He's hurt. And the boat—"

"The boat's insured, Skye." Caleb held up his palm. "I just wish I could have been there to help. Shoot. To remind him to put on his life jacket."

Another hour passed before double doors opened and Pete walked out, his father behind him. A cast covered Pete's lower arm, and a sling held his shoulder in place. Though his skin blanched pale, his blue eyes lit up when he spotted Skye, and he smiled that sweet smile that melted her heart.

She rushed to his side. "You broke your arm? What else?"

He cupped her face with his free hand. "What about you?"

"Pete, tell me." There had to be more, he'd been back there so long.

"Broken ribs. Bruised sternum. But I'll be fine." Then he brushed a kiss to her lips, and her entire being warmed.

"Sorry about your boat." He had to be devastated losing something so steeped in family history.

"I was thinking about a career change anyway." His gaze searched hers. "Maybe in a new town. I heard Florida's nice."

Her heart pounded at the implication. Did he mean with her and Sparrow? Would Pete actually consider going with them? Though Denny hadn't been found, who knew if the man might turn up? And there was still the issue of his parents.

"I might know a place." Skye could barely speak above a whisper.

"You *might?*" He nuzzled her nose.

"I do. About five hours down the coast." She managed a small smile. "They have fish there." What a dumb thing to say.

"Who needs fish?" His thumb traced her lips. "I just need you and Sparrow in our lives."

"I'd like that." More than anything.

He gave her a serious look. "If you hadn't rescued me, I would have drowned."

"God rescued us. He rescued my soul too." Tears gathered on her lashes. For the first time in her life, she finally felt whole. "You rescued my heart."

Epilogue

One month later.

"I still can't believe you're here." Skye stared at her sister, standing in front of her. Though it had been almost a week since Star had shown up in Florida, the joy of it still hadn't worn off. And Star was as beautiful and spunky as ever.

Smirking, Star laughed. "It's a miracle either of us is here and not locked up somewhere." Her expression sobered. "But your Miss Lydia sure sounded special. She had to be to get that letter to me in Kenya."

Another shocker. Star and her husband served as missionaries in Africa. Who could have imagined? Already, Sparrow was asking to visit there. And it would be amazing to see the beautiful country Star described.

"I wish Miss Lydia were still here. You two would love each other." Just the fact that the sweet woman had searched for Star from her hospital bed—while she was so sick—floored Skye. Miss Lydia hadn't wanted Skye and Sparrow to be left alone without family.

Skye's eyes burned, and she reached up to swipe at the moisture.

"Don't even think about it." Hope caught her hand. "You'll smear the mascara." She dabbed Skye's skin with a tissue. "Hold still one more second." Now Hope fiddled with her hair for the millionth time that day.

Snickering, Star rolled her eyes. "Girl, Skye doesn't care about all that. Never has."

"It's her wedding day." Hope huffed. "Everyone should be a princess once." A tremor of sadness flickered across Hope's face. This had to be hard, but she'd insisted on being a part of her best friend's wedding. The best friend being Pete, of course.

Her wedding day.

Skye touched her necklace that Pete had salvaged and had repaired. A bit of nerves skittered through Skye's midsection. Only Pete's parents, his brother, Caleb, and Hope were there, besides Star and the girls, and the ceremony would be on the beach. So she shouldn't be nervous. Though Denny had never been found, she and Pete would be making their home in Florida for the next few years. Far enough away to avoid Denny's parents. Pete had taken a position as a youth minister at a local church. Their fresh start—together.

Yet, her old fears tried to nudge their way in. She prayed God would help her be a good wife and mother. Pete, Olivia, and Sparrow deserved that, and there was no way a woman with her background could accomplish such an important feat without His help. The last few months had taught her so much, including the fact that she could love, and love deeply. She could trust herself to some people.

Though her life growing up had been ugly and hard, somewhere, in the midst of it all, God had been there.

In the darkest times, He'd shown her the marvels of His creation. He'd whispered His beauty in a cool breeze, in the sparkle of the sun on cresting waves, and in the flutter of the wings of birds. Though evil sought to destroy her, He'd held her up until she reached this place of healing balm.

"Perfect." Hope stepped back and surveyed her work. "You'll make Pete so happy." Tears shone in Hope's eyes.

Skye stood, and Star took her arm.

"You ready to do this?" Star asked.

"Ready." So very ready to start this new life that emotion choked her.

"I'll give you away then." Star giggled.

Grinning at her sister, Skye nodded. They'd had a running joke about doing this since her arrival. Too bad Star's husband hadn't been able to come. Maybe they'd meet someday.

"I'll go outside and start the music." Hope ran ahead of them to the porch of the beach house they'd rented for the weekend. The woman was organized.

Star peeked out the window. "You know, that Caleb guy reminds me of someone. What's his last name?"

"Hope's signaling for us to come out," Skye whispered as her heart flipped. "This is it." Star and Skye waltzed through the door together.

Tail wagging and tongue hanging out of his mouth, Frodo ran over and gave them both an appreciative nuzzle while steady Sam stood at his post beside Olivia and Sparrow—her flower girls. Her daughters.

Two butterflies swirled in a dance nearby. Shore birds glided over the Gulf. Waves glistened and rolled in the distance. A perfect day for so many reasons.

Thank you, God.

Stepping forward, Skye's gaze met Pete's and she wondered how she'd ever considered telling him good-bye. She could barely focus on his father's words as he led them through their vows, the love shining from Pete's face captured her so.

Later that night, the sounds of the sea outside the window lulled her to sleep as she lay encircled in the arms of the man who loved her. No fear, no shame, only healing and a deep sense of peace.

The End

Don't miss the next book by Janet W. Ferguson Holding Onto Hope

Would you like to be the first to know about new books by Janet W. Ferguson? Sign up for my newsletter at https://www.janetfergusonauthor.com/

Have you read other Coastal Hearts stories by Janet W. Ferguson?

Magnolia Storms, Falling for Grace, The Art of Rivers, Star Rising, For the Love of Joy

Have you read the Southern Hearts Series by Janet W. Ferguson?
Leaving Oxford, Going Up South, Tackling the Fields, and Blown Together

Did you enjoy this book? I hope so!
Would you take a quick minute to leave a review online?
It doesn't have to be long. Just a sentence or two telling what you liked about the book.

I love to hear from readers! You can connect with me on Facebook, Twitter, Pinterest, the contact page on my website, or subscribe to my newsletter "Under the Southern Sun" for exclusive book news and giveaways.

https://www.facebook.com/Janet.Ferguson.author
http://www.janetfergusonauthor.com/under-the-southern-sun
https://www.pinterest.com/janetwferguson/
https://twitter.com/JanetwFerguson

About the Author

Faith, Humor, Romance
Southern Style

Janet W. Ferguson is a Christy Award finalist and the FHL Readers Choice Award-winning author of realistic inspirational fiction. An avid reader, she loved books so much she found a job as a librarian so she could be around them all day. Then she turned that love of story into writing faith-filled novels with characters who feel like best friends. You'll laugh and cry as the quirky heroes and heroines chase their happily ever after.

Janet and her husband live in Mississippi where they say y'all a lot, and she forces him to visit the beach as often as possible. They have two grown children, one really smart dog, and a cat that allows them to share the space.